GOLDEN ACORNS

Flight from Iran

By

Michael Plunkett

W & B Publishers
USA

W & B Publishers

For information:
W & B Publishers
Post Office Box 193
Colfax, NC 27235
www.a-argusbooks.com

ISBN: 978-0-6922942-9-1
ISBN: 0-6922942-9-5

Book Cover designed by Dubya
Printed in the United States of America

Introduction

Our hero, Ismael—based on a real person—was a former Nuclear Physicist working for the Iran Regime. As a trusted member of the Iran nuclear research community, he learned many details and projections that the nation had under consideration. This information and the knowledge of Iran's state of accomplishment and readiness to exploit nuclear capability made Ismael a valuable source of information, if he could be persuaded to defect to the Western powers.

Included in the data to which he had access was the details of a possible attack on the United States of America utilizing an Electronic Pulse Projection (EMP) by detonating a nuclear device high in the atmosphere above the unsuspecting Americans, or by the use of a Coronal Mass Ejecton (CME) both salient to a primary threat to the existence of the free world as we know it today.

Becoming a valued informant and having repudiated the diabolical scheme of the Iranian government, Ishmael made an impassioned plea before members of Congress, the State Department and scientific experts in support of the much neglected status of the U.S.'s electric grid and the lack of effort to strengthen the vital resource. The public should be hearing about this almost every day in the news, however opposition by commercial interests—as it may impact profits—and their paid cronies throughout the government. Ishmael's plea was for the support of a popular movement by the citizenry to immediately rectify this omission as a nation defense issue is featured in the conclusion and a major point of his exhortation. Among his suggestions was convincing the public of the seriousness of this threat through media and mobilizing Mad Mothers into the popular effort, to enhance effect and marketing appeal.

While Plunkett's *Golden Acorns* is a work of fiction, the threat to the very existence of the United States and the probability of an attack by the I.S.I.S. and other radicals is real.

....Jonathan Penroc
Author: War of the Gods

Prologue

Before the Shah of Iran, Reza Pahlavi, was spirited away by U.S. interests, and knowing he was ill, perhaps fatally, he bequeathed two series of gold-backed bearer bonds to his two trusted nephews. Now more than sixty years later, they are worth hundreds of millions as art objects, from J.P. Morgan bank and the increase in the value of gold. On the free market, that is. The trick is to retrieve them from Iran.

In "Gold Bonds, Billions and Yellow Cake," by the same author (W & B Publishers), the surviving first cousin and an American partner flee Iran with one of the series and thereby create an International incident involving several Security agencies, a jet chase across air space borders and a rescue by the Israelis, before they could get these Bonds back to a Swiss Banker, who could block them as securities.

The escape of the second family would not be able to duplicate the first. Iran national security was on high alert. Anyway, only a fool would try a second time; a fool or someone that can't resist a challenge.

***

An American Aircraft carrier, The George W. Bush and two missile cruisers began entering the Persian Gulf in an effort to quell an uprising by the militant factions of

I.S.I.S. The militants have managed to bring Iraq to its knees, now that the Americans have pulled out. Actually, I.S.I.S. was asked to leave by the Taliban, the group was so radical. These rebels have taken over five cities with be-headings and mass executions and are hell bound for Bagdad. The Iraqi's are screaming for U.S. air support!

It seems that every minute counts. American President Obama refuses to get into another expensive land war and will not put troops on the ground until and unless the Iraqi's muster up and show some gumption. And for good reason. The Americans spent Billions and lost four to five thousand soldiers over ten years. People all over the world are sick of these Middle Eastern barbaric ventures. The sentiment is quickly becoming; let them kill themselves. Actually four billion dollars has gone missing.

Is it any wonder that Ishmael and wife Ruth want to get out? Their inheritance will make them very rich, but not in Iran. They have two children to think about.

Little do they know that the region is about to catch on fire! If they can escape, it just might be they could enjoy fabulous luxury and world class wealth. If not, imprisonment, torture and death.

The Shah most fervent desire would be that both of his favorite nephews escape the tyranny that now rules Iran with their families and the enormous fortunes left to them by himself.

Obama's Arab Spring was about to turn into a Red Hot Summer!

Chapter One

So many Details:

The call came late on a Friday night. There was hesitation on the other end of the line.

"Hello, Hello," Bobby King said.

Then the hesitation gave way to a thick Farsi accent. "Hello," the other voice said.

Bobby recognized the accent but not the voice, yet.

There had been many calls from the Area code he was looking at on his caller I. D., since the dramatic retrieval of his inheritance and the attending publicity. He and his partner, Michael Charles, had been basking in the sun on a very private island hideaway in the Pacific, to recover from their ordeal. They had been incommunicado for a month with strict orders not to take phone calls. Their security team had insisted. This voice was oddly familiar, something from the distant past

"Is this Mr. King – the former Buruse Bakka? "This is Ishmael, your cousin," he quickly added. "We used to play together as boys. Do you remember me? College?"

Bobby hesitated waiting for the memories to congeal.

"Oh yes, of course, soccer, Cambridge!" They had been college buddies twenty some years earlier. "Ishmael, how are you?

"Well, I am stuck here in Iran. I learned of your 'escapade'. You retrieved Great Uncle's German gold bonds.

What news, Buruse! What a narrow escape Buruse! I read the whole account"

"Please call me Bobby," Bobby corrected him immediately. "Ismael, I must tell you, before you say anything else, that our conversation is being monitored. This call will put you in danger. If there is one thing I've learned throughout this ordeal, believe me, they are listening" Bobby assumed officials had not put Ismael up to the call. But he was aware of that possibility.

"OK, Bobby, but I must talk to you, somehow. I dare not say more but that we have much in common, my friend."

"OK, Ishmael, I've got your number on my caller ID. I will have someone else get in touch with you. Probably my attorney or a Security team rep. OK? Good. Hope you are doing well, Ishmael. Goodbye."

Ishmael hesitated. He heard an additional 'click' before he hung up and it sent a shiver down his back. He reflected that he had a wife and six children. Even though trained in Physics and was valuable to the Regime, he had witnessed their brutality, when one was on their wrong side. He shuddered at the thought.

***

Even at that moment—two miles in the air—a surveillance drone was being tasked to reconnoiter Ishmael's property with photos and GPS parameters, ingress and egress. Technology purchased by the Iranian government from Russia several years earlier. The "Prop Jockey" at headquarters was enjoying this. Ishmael would not be able to move about easily, now.

Bobby mused...., "Much in common", what did he mean. Then it hit him! *Ishmael must also have an inheritance left by Grand Uncle! Oh No.*

Grand Uncle Reza had put both of them through Western schools. Only the two of them out of all of the relatives, There had existed a bond, a loyalty between Uncle Reza—the Shah—and these two nephews. *Of course, it is a possibility! Now, how to contact him? I will call Michael, He'll know.* They had obtained secure phones from the security team, at considerable cost. *Let's see where is Michael now? Doesn't matter where he is, really, he will get this call.*

***

"He said we had a great deal in common but I refused to talk about it on an unsecured line."

"That's good"

"I told him you or security would call him back. Just hear him out. He is a friend and family member. He may also have an inheritance package."

"Dude! Do you remember just about getting killed a few weeks ago? Now we are rich and shouldn't be taking these risks! The international, Big Boys are in the game! Did you notice? We made some people very angry."

"Michael, I am very close to him, or was—we went to school together. I have a hunch he also has an 'inheritance' he needs to remove from Iran."

"Yeah," Michael said. "That's what I am afraid of. Those jet engines haven't even cooled down yet!" His mind spun, contemplating how they could pull anything off over there again.

"Ok, for you, I will call him. Are you prepared to meet with him at Dr. Bern's in Switzerland, if necessary? Can he travel?"

"I don't know but isn't that getting too far ahead?"

"No, we can't discuss anything while he is in Iran. Let me feel him out."

"OK, call me back after you have spoken to him," Bobby closed.

"I'll be in touch," Michael said. He hung up.

***

"Is this the secure line, Dr. Bern?"

"Oh, yes, Hello, Michael How was your rest?"

Dr. Bern was very cordial and accommodating, as usual. The two men had a nice talk.

"Yes, of course you are welcome to come to the Chalet to conference with Ishmael. There are two, lead-lined, walls for security reasons and all the usual accoutrements. Velcome, Velcom, Michael," was his response.

"The Bonds are doing very well. The publicity your plight generated internationally has made them even more attractive!"

"Dr. Bern, we may have more bonds or securities. Could you handle them for us in the same manner?"

"Oh, marvelous, Michael, of course we can. What is their origin?"

"Well, let's just say, it's all in the family."

"Oh?" Dr. Bern hesitated.

"Yes, Bobby got a call from a close cousin. The two were Reza's favorites. He sent them both to college in England. They were his confidents, to a degree. Ishmael is his name. He indicated, after seeing our news coverage, that he too had a similar 'situation'. We did not speak in detail because it was an unsecured line. I don't know the details, and I am being very careful. Perhaps you could attend our meeting, Dr. Bern"?

"I would be happy too, Michael. Just let me know when."

"OK, thanks, Doctor, I am still in the preliminary fact finding stage at this time.

"I understand, Michael. Be very careful. Secured telephones only."

"Yes Sir, I'll be in touch."

"Ok, and be well, Michael. Stevern will be excited for your stay. He likes you two, very much."

"Yes Sir, that is mutual. Oh! And can you alert our security team of our potential needs so they have a heads-up to make some arrangements? We will fly commercial to Geneva but would like to use your jet, with its 'extras', if we go further on to Iran."

"Certainly," was the reply. "But I wouldn't go back into Iran for a long while, Michael. I am still getting threats. You would never come back! So narrow an escape the last time. If it weren't for the Israeli Air Force they would have shot you down, Michael. "

"Yes sir, I know. Have to have a different plan, this time. A full consult with you and security. That's why I would love to have you ALL present at the meeting."

"Gut! Take care, now.

"Yes, Doctor, you also." Michael hung up.

***

Michael sat back and took a deep, reflective breath, of contemplation. *Ok, step one!* He rubbed his hands together, wondering what he may have embarked upon. *Next stepm a call to Ishmael. Let's see... no last names*

He hit the speed dial button for Colonel Reeder. "Hello, Colonel, Mike Charles here."

"Hey Mike, What's up, son?"

"Can you arrange a secure call that will show Geneva as its source if I make it from here in the USA?"

"Sure, I could disguise its origin point for about ten minutes. Where you calling?"

"Iran, Sir", Mike replied.

"Oh boy! Yeah, it can be done but you can't talk beyond ten minutes or they could trace its origin. Although on the secured phones, they wouldn't be able to hear its content."

"Yes sir, I know, but any call from the US would jeopardize the client. Oh, and if necessary, could you meet with myself, Bobby and Dr. Bern at the Chalet, say, in two weeks' time?"

"Sure," Colonel Redder said. "Any problem?"

"Certainly not with your team, we may have another set of bonds from the Shaw, left to Bobble's cousin. Just fact finding right now, but I can't talk in Iran. Too much heat." Mike said.

"Well, son, you got that right. All kinds of chatter in the air from last time. You guys are real celebrities over there! Smart to disguise the call", Reeder said. "I'll have the capability ready for your call by tomorrow. Just let me know beforehand," he added.

"Yes sir, will do. Gotta' go now. Later"

***

Ishmael walked outside for a little air. He heard the wine of air over a wing in sharp descent, then low engine noise. His eyes followed the noise and he thought he detected something moving through the air, against the cloud cover. There it was! A drone aircraft heading right for his house! "Oh my God" he exclaimed out loud. "What is to happen? My family!" Panic ensued and he instinctively ran away from the house, thinking it would be bombed with a rocket!

The drone flew over and away. It made an immediate, sharp angle climb and banked right away from the house. What a relief. His heart was pounding.

***

At control center, prop jockey was chagrinned. Embarrassed that he and his drone had been discovered. He saw the panic over the immediate feed camera mounted in the drone. *Poor guy,* he thought for a moment, *it's only a camera! Film surveillance.* Of course he did not know why the drone had been tasked in this way. Couldn't ask, either. Well, there must be some reason.

***

Streco Tower building in New York City. The nine top floors and tower are leased by NSA and provide a super server for transmissions all over the world. 90 floors and with the building antenna, another 100 feet. This was the master surveillance facility for most government agencies attached to the USA's mission, in the world. Stereo Tower was not in play here at the time, although they witnessed it on the record. This was an Iranian operation, which raised some curiosity in the West.

***

Ishmael attempted to calm down. His adrenalin was pumping! Heart beat still pounding! He breathed slowly in an attempt to recover his composure and walked back towards his home. His one thought—*I must move my wife and children tomorrow. No, not grandma... let's see..., uncle Brahmin. Yes, he will not be suspected. I haven't listed him on any forms. He owes me a big favor anyway. That ordeal with his daughter a couple of years ago. He will be the one.*

His cousin Bobby was right about warning him of danger. *They already have me on their radar after that one call.*

He went to the kitchen and poured himself a drink, and then he went to the bedroom and retrieved his pistol, and underarm holster. He would carry it now. Before his training in Physics, he was with 'Special Combat Forces' in the regime army. He had high marks and therefore was a candidate for advanced school. That was how he became a Physicist. He did not agree with the way this knowledge was being employed, however. He had no objection to progress through the development of alternate energy sources to enhance infrastructure for his nation's improvement. He deeply resented this knowledge being hi-jacked for weapon development and military uses. What was the point? It seemed that nobody had thought through to the end scenario. How absurd. A radical agenda of sociopaths. For what? Wake the sleeping lion again? What was there to gain? The 13th Caliphate? Nonsense! There would not be anything left to rule. They could use some Chess game lessons but they are blind! They all needed baby pacifiers. He often thought of sending 10 cases of them to the council. He was getting angry now.

***

The Patriarch Abram fathered 3 great world religions. The Ishmaelite's or later, Islam was one. The Hebrew another and from that Christianity. The tenants of peace and love to fellow men and were the underpinnings of all three. Many years later, the leader Mohammed advanced Islam further into the Muslim religion. He did not claim to be a deity. Only Jesus Christ did that, of the three religions. Ishmael was not a Christian but lived his life in peace with everyone.

***

"Uncle Brahmin," Ishmael spoke into the phone, "how are you, these days, sir?"

"Doing fine, Ishmael, just fine. I recognize your voice."

"Sir, I have a personal family problem," he went on, "and I would like to talk with you about it face to face

Mr. Brahmin was taken aback for a moment at this prospect but said, "Well, of course, Ishmael, I'd be happy to help you, if I can."

"Do you remember that diner on Route No. 65 in Kazool where we met for coffee years ago? Said Ishmael.

"Why, yes," came the reply.

"This is Sunday, could you meet me there at say 11:00 AM on Tuesday?"

" Yes, I will, Ishmael."

"OK, I will see you then. And thank you," Ishmael closed the conversation.

He heard the bustle and noises out in the garage. Ruth and the kids must be back. He wasn't looking forward to what was ahead. Ruth was a refined and intelligent person. They had met in college. She held an advanced degree in psychology, which was rare for a woman in Iran. She was from a good family. Three generations of merchants, they wanted their only child to go to college. Uncle Reza had seen to it, sending her to Oxford. She would be reasonable, especially when it came to the safety of her children. Being from a merchant family, Ruth had also absorbed a certain street sense. A trading mentality and logic. An understanding of the way things were in the real world. She could wheel and deal with the best of them. Barter was a way of life. She thoroughly understood self-ish motives of others.

Still, this will be awkward. I don't want to scare them. He thought he had put them in harm's way already, but decided he would wait until he met with Uncle Brahmin and to hear back from Bobby. The move would so disrupt the family routine. Yes, he would wait until after Tuesday and stay off the telephone in the meantime.

***

TUESDAY, 7:00 AM:

Ishmael needed two and one-half hours' drive time to get to the diner where he would meet with Uncle Brahmin. He had called in for a sick day, but didn't really want that on the record. Nevertheless, he threw on some sweat's and headed out. He took notice that there was no one behind him. The drive was quite until traffic started building. He checked his gas gauge before he got out of his area. He didn't want a record of a refill or any stop a couple hours out. Besides, there was some desert between the two locations where one wouldn't want to run out of gas. He pulled into a Petrol station at the edge of town, before the main highway. It could also have been on the way to work, if he were going to his job site. *Good job, Ishmael,* he thought to himself, proud that he had thought of these strategies.

The drone had been re-tasked temporarily. It needed fuel itself, or they (Headquarters) would have seen him leave and tracked him. A little luck.

Full of fuel, enough to get there and back Ishmael proceeded to the highway. *No tickets,* he reminded himself. *Do the speed limit. Don't be anxious,* he was thinking.

***

Without interim stops, he arrived at the old diner at 10:30 AM. He parked, careful to stay out of any security cameras outside the entrance. He tipped his hat down and went inside. Uncle Brahman hadn't arrived yet. He sat at the rear and ordered a coffee. A couple of police agents came in, eyes scanning customers. Then they sat down for coffee and donuts. Ishmael decided this was just coincidental. They were probably just ending their shift at this hour.

Here he is now, coming through the doorway. He looked a little older. White hair now. He was a well-educated man. A professor at the community college. Sociology was his field.

Ishmael caught his eye and with a broad smile of recognition.

Uncle Brahmin made his way to the back where Ismael sat. Ismael stood with his arms stretched out for an embrace.

"Uncle! How are you? You look very healthy sir. It is so good to see you. It's been years," as he hugged him earnestly.

Finally they sat down and ordered iced tea.

There was small talk about the old days and then Uncle Brahmin paused. He looked Ishmael directly in the eyes, with compassion, and said, "Now what on Earth brings you all the way out here, Ishmael?"

" Well Uncle, do you still have that large farm with the big house?"

"Yes, I do," he said.

He paused. "Uncle, I think my family is in danger and I would like to hide them away for a while.'

"Why, of course, Ishmael but what is going on?" Uncle was very concerned.

Do you remember recently when Nephew Buruse retrieved his inheritance from your brother Uncle Reza and all the commotion it caused in the world press?"

"Oh yes, Do I ever!. Our leaders were not happy. They came to interview me, Ishmael!"

"Well, I have a similar situation."

Uncle Brahmin raised his eyebrows, "Oh, you do?"

"Yes, uncle and I am going to retrieve my inheritance in a clandestine way. I cannot talk over a non-secure telephone line. I did once, with no details revealed, mind you, and a day later, while I was in the yard, a drone swooped down through the cloud cover over my farm. I think surveillance, just pictures but, you see, I can't subject Ruth and the kids to the brutality of the regime."

"Oh, no, of course not," urged Uncle Braham. "I have many rooms and hiding places out at my farm. They would be safe, I am sure," he added.

Ishmael spoke quickly, "I would secure my family before I made a move on the securities. At least, I think they are securities. Bonds, like Buruse had. We were in college at Cambridge when Uncle Reza made accounts for us. I think there are diamonds, as well.

"I would probably seek asylum in Switzerland or in the USA afterward. You know, the Regime considers these to be their assets and will nationalize them when they are uncovered. Burse's bonds were bearer securities so all they have to do is get hold of them. This is why Uncle Reza kept them so liquid.

"I don't like what direction the regime is going. They want to prepare for war, not improved the infrastructure our people desperately need. I want out. They want to spin more uranium into weapons grade material.

"I just need to impose upon you for a short time while I plan. All communications will be over secured line, I am sure. I am waiting for a call now."

"Whew!" Uncle Brahmin exclaimed, trying to take it all in. He was in agreement with Ishmael, as were most of the intellectual community in his country, but this was a very risky undertaking. Still, the rewards... Those bonds had gained so much value. Buruse was rich beyond all reason, he reflected according to financial publications.

"I will send for you, Uncle, if you like."

"Oh, I don't know..." he trailed off.

"When do you want them to come, Ishmael?"

"I'm not sure, but soon, sir." Ishmael responded.

"Ok. Well, just call me." Uncle Brahmin nodded his head, up and down. He reached for Ishmael's hand

To convey a sincere emphasis. "Peace, my son. May Allah be with you and may He be praised."

They both stood up and made their way to the parking lot.

"Don't stop for gas or anything where a cameras might be if you don't have to, Uncle."

It was a mild, sunny day. They went to their vehicles and waved good bye.

:Oh boy! Uncle thought to himself. The regime had threatened him for information when Buruse escaped.

What now? He didn't want Ishmael to know. Yes, he did know about surveillance cameras!

He was Grand Uncle now. He let his mind wander back to the days of his brother Reza, The Shah's rein and the revolution. *Oh yes, this will be dicey!*

\

***

The Pahlavi family of Shahs dated back to his Grandfather

Mohammad Reza Pahlavi came to power during World War II after an Anglo-Soviet invasion forced the abdication of his father Reza Shah. During Mohammad Reza's reign, the Iranian oil industry was briefly nationalized under the democratically-elected Prime Minister Mohammad Mosaddegh before a US-backed coup d'état deposed Mosaddegh and brought back foreign oil firms, and Iran marked the anniversary of 2,500 years of continuous monarchy since the founding of the Persian Empire by Cyrus the Great. As ruler, he introduced the White Revolution, a series of economic, social and political reforms with the proclaimed intention of transforming Iran into a global power and modernizing the nation by nationalizing certain industries and granting women suffrage.

***

The drive back home was given over to serious contemplation and planning. Ishmael knew this move was life threatening for his family and that he must be very circumspect and take the upmost caution at every step. He was impatient for a call back from the U.S. to plan forward. He didn't have to wait long. As he was pulling into his driveway, his cell phone rang.

"Ishmael?" "Yes"? There was nothing on his caller I.D. "This is a secure line, routed thru from Geneva, Switzerland. I am in the U.S. and I only have 8 minutes before it could be traced as to country of origin. This could put in danger, if we go long."

"Yes, I've already had a drone fly over my property." He said nervously.

"OK, understood, hence forward. This in Michael Charles, Burse's partner. I will be brief, sir. First, you must send your family to a safe place."

"I have already made such arrangements," was Ishmael's immediate response

"Oh, excellent, Ishmael, I see we are on the same page. We want to meet with you in Geneva. Can you fly there"?

"Yes," said Ishmael

"Security will pick you up at the airport in Geneva. Do not leave a paper trail. Pay cash if you can. We will meet with our banking connection at his private Chalet in the Alps. You, myself, Buruse, security and Dr. Bern. Travel light. Plan on at least two days."

"Yes, ok," replied Ishmael.

"Now, one important thing."

"Yes?"

"Before you leave, go to your securities location and look inside its container. Survey what is there. Do not remove it! Just make a brief inventory. Do not take a briefcase and dress simply so that you could not conceal anything. Be very circumspect. Go preferably in the afternoon when the depository is likely to be busy. Can you do these things, sir?"

"Yes, sir."

"Now here is a secure number to contact us when you are ready."

"Ok," and he took it down.

Well, here we go, he thought, *no turning back now.*

***

He backed out of the driveway and went directly to the bank. No sense wasting a day off. He went to the safety deposit area and introduced himself to the teller. "I need to see my box for a moment, Mame"

"Of course, sir, may I see your number and ID"?

Ishmael provided it.

She noted the last name. He was dressed in shorts and a soccer shirt. "Come this way, please"

Through stainless steel gates and into the safe, they went. "Do you have your key, Mr. Pahlavi?"

Ishmael produced it.

They did the double key routine and she said," I will leave you alone, Mr. Pahlavi.

I'll just be a minute, Ishmael told her.

Well, he certainly looked innocuous enough, but she had been instructed to call a number upon any attempt to open this box.

Ishmael worked fast. He knew he could have triggered something already. He looked inside. There were several stacks of these bonds, wrapped in black paper. They were Gold bonds! And then there was a velvet bag with a draw string. He wasn't going to be bothered but decided to look inside. He had opened up a bag full of rather large diamonds. ! There must have been a hundred of them and 1 very large Ruby at the bottom. Wow!

Better get out of here, now!

He closed the lid of the box. He slid it back into its space and was gratified to hear the "Click" when it was secure again.

He left, making it a point to tell the teller he was finished, making certain she could see he had taken nothing with him. "Thank you and goodbye," he waived.

That was quick, she thought, feeling guilty for having called. She punched the number for re-dial.

"Hello, headquarters".

"I just called in regarding the Pahlavi security box."

"Just a minute, mame."

Another voice came on abruptly.

"Hello?".

She recognized the voice. "Yes, I just called you about the Pahlavi security box, as instructed."

"Yes?"

"He has left now. Was in there only 5 minutes......" No, he took nothing with him... Because he had on shorts and a soccer shirt. I would have seen anything he had."

"OK, mame, thank you for the call. Please call if he returns."

***

Ishmael was thinking.... he should rent a vehicle for his wife and children to travel to Uncle Braham's. Schools would have to be given an explanation to avoid inquires. He would have her leave in her car and drive to his friend's garage. In the front door in her car and out the back end in the rental car. Actually, Jocosey's will have one. *Yes, that will work,* he relished.

He went directly home.

Now for a conversation with Ruth.

The kids were off and Ruth was cleaning up the kitchen from breakfast preparations. Ishmael walked in.

"You were gone early, dear, now back so early? His wife had thought he was at work today."

"No, I took a sick day."

She glanced over at him with surprise, raised eyebrows. "But, Ishmael, you are never sick and you look alright to me. Does a sick man leave home at 5:30 AM and return at 10:00 AM?"

"I can explain. I need to talk to you when you are finished here in the kitchen."

"Oh?" with question in her voice. "Just two minutes."

"Good, I will see you in the living room then"

"OK, momentarily," she reiterated.

Ishmael left the kitchen and headed for the living room He would simply tell her about his trip and why.

Ruth walked in with two cups of tea on a tray. "Oh, the ever thoughtful wife. Thank you, dear."

"You are welcome and now, what has my husband been up to this morning?"

"I went to see Uncle Brahmin, this morning. I needed a favor."

Ruth was alert and all ears, patiently.

"It concerns you and the children," he added,

Now Ruth moved to the edge of her seat, "Really?" she declared.

"Let me start from the beginning," as he stretched his hand out palm down to indicate calmness.

"A few weeks ago, I was approached at work by high placed superiors inquiring about Buruse, his inheritance and that whole episode a month ago."

"I was waiting for that," she replied.

"Of course, I told them I hadn't had any contact with him for years. Since college, actually. They went on about national treasure, duty and the Regime and then they asked if I too might have an inheritance. I saw where they were going with this. Next thing, they might want a list of my bank depositories. Of course, you have assets from your family that they would question." She nodded her head in agreement.

"The news said there were billions involved with the increase over these intervening years. They are wanting that kind of money for their *Scientific* agenda. HA!" He laughed. "I can tell, they feel it is my duty to turn any assets acquired from the Shah after the revolution over to them as a repatriation of assets. They maintain that they were stolen from the regimen by Uncle Reza. I know them. They will eventually seek control over all of our funds! Perhaps, including yours!'" He could see Ruth was getting nervous and angry. He stretched out his hand again indicating there was more to tell.

"I made a call to Buruse the other day. We discussed no details. He told me I and my family would be in danger because of the call and that he would continue only on a secure line. It was very brief. Even so, Ruth, I walked outside for fresh air an hour later and I saw a drone through a momentary break in the cloud cover. It dove right over our house and then swooped back up. Probably taking pictures and getting coordinates. Scared me to the bone. I know what the regime is capable of. Burse's partner, Michael Charles called me from Geneva, a few days later, declaring this is a secure line. He said he had 8 minutes before it could be traced back to the US. He routed it round the world, terminating in Geneva. They didn't want the country of origin to be the U.S. for our safety."

Ruth gulped her tea.

"Next, he said for me to move my family immediately and come to Geneva for two days to discuss my inheritance with the principals, Buruse, himself and their Swiss banker, along with their security team. AND, if we moved the assets, you and the children would have to defect to the US or Switzerland or your lives would forever be in danger."

Ruth shuddered. She knew he was right.

"So, I went to Uncle Brahmin this morning, asking for the favor of putting you and the children up for a few days while I go flesh this operation out. I do not want you at home. They are watching it already.

"We will switch cars to a rental at Jocosey's garage. In the front – out the back in a rental."

"I can tell you've given this a lot of thought already Ishmael." His wife said. "I appreciate your concern and planning. I trust you with our lives. I want you to know that. I will go and empty my secure box this afternoon."

Ishmael was gratified to hear her comments, and thanked her for her comments.

"We may have to completely up-end our lives but I think we will be very rich and in good hands. Now, go prepare to travel. Pack lightly. You are off to Uncle's farm. The children love it out there as you know. For their safety, tell them nothing."

Ruth shook her head from side to side.

"Aan early school vacation."

"OK", she agreed.

Ishmael was pleased that that went so well. Now, he thought, *what next?*

He called Swissair to see when the next flight might be available. Friday, Flight Number 1292, departing at 10

AM would fit. He booked it. He remembered he should get the cash— $1,200.00—for the ticket, and take a pair of skis along for cover. Tehran International was 20 miles away. *Better get to the bank this afternoon for a withdrawal and drive to the airport to purchase my ticket, this evening.*

Next, he called Uncle Brahmin to confirm the next day or Thursday as an arrival time for Ruth and the children. *A long weekend at the farm, that'll fly,* he thought. Now, how will he remove them from there to another country? *Don't know yet.*

***

Ishmael went up to the bedroom to tell Ruth of his plans for tonight and the results of his call to Uncle Brahmin. "Let me know as soon as you are ready," he told her. "I need to leave for the bank right away or they'll be closed for the day. I am going to go directly to get my ticket with cash. I will bring you some money for your needs while at Uncle's farm."

"Oh, good", she said, as he left the room.

"Oh, and if you see my skis please bring them out of hiding. I will need to travel with them. Ski trip to the Alp's, you know," he winked.

Ruth understood.

"OH! Another thing, do you have two old Burqa's in storage?"

" Ha!" Ruth laughed out loud. "Why?"

"I may need a disguise at the airport."

"Good idea, I knew those would come in handy someday. I think I'll have everything ready by tonight", Ruth commented, surveying the mess in front of her. "Also, I must go to my bank." She said, looking at her watch. Now!

"OK, good, we may leave in the morning." Ishmael declared. He made a mental list. *Still have to call Jocosey's garage, he will have a rental car. And Mr. Charles and give him an ETA.*

***

Ruth ran out the door and got into the car. Her bank deposit box was only six blocks away. She got to the bank with fifteen minutes to spare.

She presented her key and went back with the teller. She pulled her box and waited for the teller to leave. She had brought a large straw beach bag as a side carry. She quickly emptied all the contents of the box into the beach carrier, put the box back and prepared to leave the bank.

"Oh, are you ready already, Mrs. Pahlavi?"

It startled her. "Oh, yes, just a small item," she replied. *Ok, that is done now*, she sighed and headed back home. *Have to prepare dinner for the rascals.* Ishmael was watching them while she was gone. At ages 6 and 71/2 years old, they were always a handful. Endless questions.

***

Ishmael had a little farther to travel to his bank but he also arrived in time, leaving after Ruth had returned. He made an eight-thousand dollar withdrawal which raised a few eye brows. "Buying a new car," he said out loud to the teller for cover. "Allah knows, I need one." He smiled and left the bank.

Now for the airport and Swissair. He had his ID and passport. He wasn't sure how this worked.

What a busy place, this airport! He parked what seemed like a soccer field away from the Swissair sign. Finally inside, he walked slowly and purposefully to the ticket counter, like he did this all the time.

"Hello, I would like to purchase my ticket in advance, to expedite my departure. Reservation number 271305." He said and placed his documents on the counter for the attendant to view.

"Oh, yes, Mr. Pasha."

That was the name he had given. *Hope he won't have to look at my passport.*

"Swissair direct to Geneva, departing Thursday at 6 AM sir. Is that right?"

"Yes sir," Ishmael replied.

"Ok that will be $1,252 dollars. How will you pay?"

"Cash, sir," and he began to count the money out. There was a stare from the agent. "I won a wager," Ishmael offered with a smile.

"Oh, yes," and a laugh from the attendant. "And now you are going on holiday?"

"Yes, skiing in the Alps.'

"Ah! We are here to help. Would you like an upgrade?"

"No, that won't be necessary. Is the plane crowded?" He asked.

"No, light, really," The attendant said. "You are confirmed on flight No. 271, nonstop, arriving at 6 PM in Geneva," and handed over his ticket and Boarding pass. "You may go directly to gate No. 11 on Thursday."

Ishmael took the ticket in hand.

"Here is your boarding pass, sir.:

Ishmael took it. He turned and left with a sigh of relief. "Yeah"! He almost shouted. His heart was racing. He checked his phone for Mr. Charles number. The secure line.

"Hello, Mr. Charles? Ishmael here. Swissair, flight no. 271 Arriving 6PM in Geneva. I may have a Burqa on."

Mr. Charles said, "You will recognize Buruse. A red shirt." He added. "Good, see you then."

"Oh, Gold Bonds and Diamonds, Mr. Charles." *Now,* he thought, *done, done, and done!* Very proud of himself.

***

Hello, Dr. Bern? We need your jet and security team to travel from Dulles International, general aviation facility, to Geneva by 5 PM on Thursday. We will all proceed by the Hilo to the Chalet for the evening and next two days. There are gold bonds and diamonds."

"Yes, Michael, I will arrange it. See you then."

***

Michael called Bobby. "We're going to see your cousin in Geneva on Thursday. It's all arranged. Dress light, bring your skis, that's a must and be at Dulles by 6 AM. Look for me at the general aviation lounge. Yes, there are Gold bonds and diamonds."

"Oh?" was Bobby's reply. "Ok,good."

***

Bobby's (Buruse) dad was a Prince in the royal family. Unfortunately, he was killed in the Iranian revolution when Bobby King, (His Americanized name) was young at the time. His uncle was the Shah, after his Grandfather. He was sheltered most of his life and shipped out to America and England for schooling. His dad was dashing and so Bobby was also a very handsome Middle Eastern man. Black curly hair and a jovial personality he possessed a million dollar smile. He had pure white teeth and could make a person happy just looking at his broad expression of it.

Mike Charles had met him in Florida when Bobby came to work for a large marketing company. He had worked under the, then vice president, Mike Charles. They had become friends. Bobby was interesting, intelligent and easy going. Also, he was now very rich, as was Michael Charles as a result of their recent retrieval of an inheritance of German Gold Backed Bearer Bonds left to him by the Shaw, his uncle. These items, now art objects, along with their gold value increase were worth billions.

Now his close cousin Ishmael wants to liquidate his inheritance also.

The Government (Regime) however has other ideas. They believe these funds to be assets were stolen from their country when the US extracted the Shaw after the revolution. These monies would help with their current plans to expand their uranium enrichment programs. They wanted these funds repatriated. Bobby and Mr. Charles had spirited them off, somewhat clandestinely, to a Swiss Bank where they were held in trust. The regime was livid. They scrambled two F-16s and were it not for the intervention of the Israelis (Mossad) with opposing and armed F-18s They may have been shot down. Then the regime staged an armed assault by a terrorist group on the Swiss bank where the assets were held and on the streets of Geneva but both attempts were put down. What they might do this time was unpredictable! They were still working thru diplomatic channels to recover the first batch of bonds. There had been international participation of many national security agencies up to and including the U.S. State department in enabling the safe return of the players. Military assets were used, exacerbating the rage.

Chapter Two

What would they be prepared to do this time?

Because he and Bobby had a previous business relationship with Dr. Bern, on similar German Gold Bonds before, they knew precisely how to "Block" the bonds into a credit facility.

The two of them could die this time at the hands of a fanatical regime who would risk all to stop this transfer of assets: However, in any man's court today, they belonged to Bobby's cousin, Ishmael Pahlavi.

To return to Iranian air space would be a big mistake. *Oh, will they ever be ready for us! We cannot start a war with a sovereign nation!*

***

Ruth got up early and roused the children. It was the day they would drive to Grand Uncle's farm. Ishmael had gone early to Jocosey's garage. His friend was very willing to help. He had a used mini-van that he wouldn't miss for a few days. He understood and was sympatric to Ishmael's plight. Yes, that would be fine. Roll in one end and out the other in a different vehicle. He knew Ruth and the kids and was glad to aid in their safety, Many people were not sympathetic to the current Regime. Ishmael returned just in time to see Ruth and the children off.

Ruth took a long look at the inside of their home. It had been seven eventful years since they had moved here. Now, so much uncertainty. Just a few days ago..... *Well, better not to look back.* In her heart she suspected she would never see this place again.

"Jocosey's is all ready for you. I will follow you down there in my car. We do not want too much activity, this morning though. Remember, there are eyes in the sky."

Ruth nodded understanding. *When will we see each other again?*

Ishmael sensed her nervousness and embraced her, saying, "Oh, Ruth, this will pass. You and the children will be alright. This is mostly precautionary."

The two of them were not unfamiliar with these tactics since they both had lived through those revolutionary days past.

"Now, off you go. I will be right behind you by a slightly different route."

"Be careful, Ishmael," Ruth gave him a squeeze.

"Yes, I will, Ruth," came the answer.

Ruth stepped out the kitchen door, two steps down to the garage. The children were already in the back seat, fussing with each other. Of course, they had no idea what was really going on or how their lives might change. This was a holiday to Grand Uncle's farm. A place they loved to spend time. *What an adventure.*

"I am going to ride the donkey this time," young Joseph was heard to say. "Bye, dad," and "bye, dad."

"Hey, I am coming to see you off," Ishmael said.

Ruth left first. A few minutes later, Ishmael walked out in the yard to see if he could detect any movement in the shy. He listened very carefully and scanned for lights. There were none.

He got in his car and headed for Jocosey's by another, circuitous, route. When he arrived, Ruth and Jocosey were still exchanging greetings. He parked outside and went in. There at the rear, inside the garage, was a minivan and a large exit door, still closed down. Ruth was beginning to transfer car seats and suitcases. The children were eager to help her.

"Wow, this van is neat," Joseph said, as they got familiar with it.

"Feel free to use Ruth's car in any way you need, Jocosey, until we return."

"Ok, I will, thanks. I will use this one," he tapped the fender of the car, "for clients while their car is under repair".

"Good, feel free," Ishmael waved it off with his arm. Ruth had started the minivan and Jocosey went to open the exit door.

Ishmael opened the van door for one last goodbye. "Have fun children. Listen to your mother, now."

"We will, Daddy!". Came the replies, simultaneously.

I'm going to ride the donkey," Joseph said again, asserting his intention to overcome his fear of the beast.

"Is your GPS set, Ruth?" he asked

"Yes, Ishmael. But remember, that goes both ways, they can track me also."

He had missed that.

"You're right. Don't use it then", he said.

"I know the way." she said.

"Ok, I will call you but can't talk long. I'll be back home in a few days. Stay at Grand Uncle's until you hear from me Oh!" He almost forgot, "Here is a few thousand in paper money in case you need anything while I am gone." He handed her the envelope, thankful he remembered. "Do not use your Wizard card," he cautioned.

Ruth leaned to give him a final kiss. Ismael responded and closed the door. "Allah be with you", he said as he closed the door.

Ruth drove out to the main road. No one was behind her.

A sigh of relief and Ishmael turned again to thank Jocosey. A warm handshake. "I am not sure, Jocosey, what is next, but, I promise you will be made whole again, if needed, from this venture."

"I know, friend, just be safe. Go with God."

"I am very grateful, old friend." They had served together in some bad times.

"I will see you," and Ishmael departed.

***

The drive back home was full of reflection and anxiety for the upcoming week. They couldn't be too careful. Now he had to prepare for his own trip.

He decided he would show up at the gate with his snow skis. He would check the skis through. When he got aboard, he would go to the airplane restroom and change into the loose-fitting Burqa. This, he hoped would give him anonymity. No one would speak to him as long as he was wearing it, thinking he was a woman. His face would be mostly covered all the way to Geneva. There were security cameras everywhere He would keep the Burqa on until he was onboard Dr. Bern's Hilo. Then, on to the

Chalet, without it. If any recovery surveillance was done, it wasn't likely they would pick him out. Women were not noticed generally. He thought he could bring the bonds along but had been told not to try that without the security team in place. *Yes, I should hear 'the deal' first. It would be good to get away from this rock, desert, dust and adobe.* He once attended a Physics seminar in California. The U.S. was magical! *The children would love that "Disney" place.*

He snapped out of the reverie and concentrated on necessities. OK, he most needed to pack his small luggage for the trip. Tomorrow was Wednesday and he was leaving Thursday. Should he drive to a motel in the airport area and stay overnight? The early morning flight almost made it necessary. "Of course," he said to himself. "Call work. Death in the family must take time off and travel south to Kashan for all arrangements." *That's my cover. Then call the Imam Khomeini International Airport official hotel and try to book a room for tonight.*

He pulled back into his garage and went inside. It felt lonely all of a sudden. No family and probably not ever again in this place. He punched in coordinates for Khomeini Airport. There was Hotel advertising. He called.

"Hello, Khomeini, Airport Hotel, can I help you?"

"Yes, I need a room for tonight. It doesn't have to be fancy. Just one person. I have a flight in the early morning.'"

"Ok, let me check," came the reply. "We are pretty full, but there is one small room, no view, down by the boiler room."

"I'll take it," was the immediate reply!

"I will need your card number to hold it. Do you have one?"

"I do," said Ishmael. "It's a Wizard account. Here is the number." He read it off.

"OK," came the reply, "and you can check in any time after 4:30 PM. Here is your reservation number."

"I will pay cash when I arrive. Please don't process that card.

"OK, understood."

He would pay cash when he got there and retrieve the Wizard card paperwork. He had done it before

That is done, now to pack. There were papers he was working on in his briefcase concerning research he had painstakingly done over the past three months. He wanted to take that. *Check.* And the skis, they had a cover sack.

Maybe some pictures and two changes of casual clothes. *Those new sneakers.*

He would buy the rest in Geneva if he needed any-thing. "OK! I am ready," he said to himself, feeling exited and, at the same time relieved.

***

Ishmael took a short nap and got ready to leave for Tehran. It was 20 miles but 40 minutes at rush hour. He took a sweeping look around his house. So many good memories with the kids. He tried not to dwell upon it. He was not one to live in the past too much. "OK, let's go," he said out loud to nobody, unless the house was bugged. "Oh shit!" he hadn't thought of that. He looked franticly under lamps and inside the telephone cover. Up high be-hind artificial plants. "Are you listening?" he shouted out in desperation. "I am going on vacation. Going skiing in the Swiss Alps. HA! Send your little drone, I saw it you know!" He was getting angry now. This was his inher-itance! *Screw those guy's, anyway.* He was growing weary of walking on eggshells. In another life he was para-trooper trained and wanted to rumble!

He hoped they were listening.

They were!

Superiors were notified.

An agent was called in the Tehran office and a surveillance plan was set to follow Ishmael on his trip. Especially to Geneva!

***

Ismael got in his car and headed to the airport hotel. He drove a little fast. Risky. *So what*? he thought. *Enough of this crap. I am Ishmael Pahlavi, descended from the Royal Family. We have thousands of years of history, standing for our country and our people. And now, you Marxist punks want your way.*

Bring it on! He remembered his War Turban. The Burqa deception he would employ for tactical not practical, purposes. He would beat their game. *Bring it on!*

Before he had gotten into the car, he had walked outside and scanned the horizon. He looked up in time to see the drone way up high. At least 10,000 feet. He chuckled to himself and waived wildly at it. Then he gave it the middle finger, wondering if the lens was good enough to catch it. *OK, fight mode now.* He felt ready.

Ishmael got into his car and backed out of the driveway. He was careful not to speed too fast, a little was okay. He didn't want to play into their hands with a traffic citation or worse.

He drove to the airport hotel. He took the garage parking ramp and noticed a black sedan fall in behind him. His skis were attached to the roof rack. He would take them to the room, lest they be taken. The first three floors were solid with no openings. He went to the fourth floor and there were several places open. He took the first one and the black sedan pulled in across the way and two spaces up. He ignored the driver. He got out and reached for his small bag. Then he moved to unlock his skis.

"Need any help with those?" Came the comment from the other driver. "It is unusual to see skis in this climate. I used to ski myself." Obviously he wanted to make small talk.

Ishmael looked him hard for a moment and said, "Yes, the Alps are great this time of the year. Taking a small holiday, to work them out."

"Sounds like fun," the stranger said, and with a wave of the hand, he moved toward the elevator at the corner of the building. "I too am going to the Alps region, on business. Perhaps I should work in a visit to the slopes. I may see you there." The agent wanted to warm-up to him. The elevator would take them directly to the motel lobby.

There weren't that many flights to Geneva, daily. *Certainly, he will be on my flight. So much for the Burqa disguise. Pointless now, anyway.* Ok, Ishmael would play along. He was sure the man was an agent. This seemed to be a new strategy. Get close and friendly.

As the elevator doors closed on them, he decided to take the lead.

"Hello, I am Ishmael Pahlavi, grandnephew of the former King.

"Yes, I remember the Shah. I am Absalom Dufay. Hey, your cousin sure pulled a 'coup, last month. I saw it on the news."

"Yes, he did." Ishmael replied. He added. "I haven't seen him in 30, years."

They shook hands.

Now in the lobby, they both went to the front desk. They got different agents behind the desk. Ishmael checked his reservation.

"Yes sir, room 314," the agent said and handed him his key card. Ishmael thanked him and headed for the elevator. He pressed 3 and the doors closed behind him. Up he went and to his room. He heard another elevator door open. He knew it would be Mr. Dufay, also on his floor. He waited a minute and then peeked out his door. Sure enough, several doors down Mr. Dufay was slipping his key card into the slot. *Well, here we go.*

He freshened his face up and decided to go to the lounge/bar for a drink. He usually did not drink but he wasn't a fanatic. He needed a respite. It would help him relax and plan ahead. 4:30 AM came early and it would be a long day. His head was spinning a little.

Well, of course, he thought! In walked Mr. Dufay. He was kind of a squatty, sloppy, fellow. There was a noticeable bulge under his sport coat. Ismael raised his hand in a wave of recognition. Dufay moved toward his table.

Ishmael straightened up and putting on his best John Wayne voice said, "Watcha' packing under there, Pilgrim?"

Dufay instinctively pulled at his coat in an effort to smooth the bulge.

"Ya know, you better not forget and take that on the plane. Lock it in you're the trunk of your car if you ever want to see it again, unless, of course you are an air marshal."

"No, and that's good advice. I completely forgot I had it."

"I subscribe to Sky Active Defender, myself," Ishmael went on. He couldn't resist.

"Oh, what is that sir?"

"Well, it's a laser in the sky. When I push this button," he held up his car key fob, "Sky Active Defender does a quick focus and then Zap! , the threat is neutralized instantly." He swung his arm for emphasis!

Mr. Dufay was wide eyed, eyebrows raised. "Really? Can this be?"

"No," Ishmael laughed and added, "No, I saw it on a cartoon my son was watching! I am a physicists and I was wondering how that could be made to work."

They both had a hearty laugh.

"I work in security part time," said Dufay. "I am always forgetting I have my weapon on." It was the best explanation he could think of.

Ishmael was rather enjoying the sparing. He ordered a refill and invited Mr. Dufay to join him. Ishmael was developing a rosy glow already. He grew amused at these puerile efforts and the Regime's antics.

He was toying with the agent. His old warrior self was manifesting. He could deal with these jerks. They couldn't be more obvious if they had a sign around their neck.

He said, "Well, my flight is early. I going to retire, Mr. Dufay. Have a good evening, sir," as he rose and went to the bar to pay his check.

"And you as well,sir"

Mr. Dufay thought; *this guy is smart and is on to me already. 'Sky Active Defender', he had me going,* laughing to himself for being drawn in. *Hey, I like that. Maybe next year.*

***

Ishmael sauntered down the hallway. His stride, long and proud. A smirk on his face and disdain for the regime's investigation strangely, though he liked Mr. Dufay. He seemed harmless enough. *No doubt, a "short notice" spy.* He laughed to himself. *What a well-meaning bumbler.*

First thing, Ishmael ditched the Burqa. It would surely work against him now. He knew Defray would be on the flight. He had made strong eye contact with him and it would exacerbate suspicion, now. He was a guy on holiday.

***

The call came early. An automatic message to rise up and remember to say your prayers. He threw some cold water on his face. There were tea and coffee packs in the room. He chose coffee. Strong. He wanted to get down to the breakfast buffet before he boarded the plane. He put on his robe and went to Agent Dufay's door, three doors down. He knocked and said in a loud voice,

"Rise and shine, I am leaving for the breakfast buffet now. Let's not have egg on our faces! See you in 10, my friend." And he went back to dress.

Dufay heard it barely and thought, *OH! Shit, this was going to be a trip for the books. Wait until my fellow agent's see this report!*

***

Ishmael put on his soccer best with $200.00 sneakers and went down to the lobby buffet. Sure looked good. He was sure exited. This adventure would change him and his family's lives forever. Nothing was going to get in the way.

He had faced the enemy and he had different color socks on! So to speak, of course. He had lived under repression for too long. His cousin's bold move had motivated him. *Oh yeah!* He went back for steak and more eggs.

Dufay walked in. He scanned the room until he saw Ishmael. He walked over and said, "I am going to get fired, you know! "

"Nonsense," Ismael replied. "I'll play along. Listen, none of this will matter or be important a year from now. Relax and enjoy. Nothing can stop me anyway. Don't you know you are working for a bunch of first class JERKS! I am a physicist and I know what's going on. I am fed up and looking for the Oasis!

"You speak the truth, sir," Dufay said with his head lowered.

"Soooo, Dufay, if you think your heart can take it, come fly with me! The breakfast steak is very good!" He left the table and went to the front desk check out.

"Room 314, he said, "checkout," as he slid his room keycard under the glass over the counter. "And I would prefer to pay in cash if you will please return my Wizard card paperwork given to hold the room."

It meant extra work for the clerk. She said "Why? I can just process your card."

He assumed it was just laziness, and leaned closer

"Because, I was screwing the sheep that I snuck in last night and I don't want to be traced, later!" He told her as if trading a confidence. "I hate it when that happens, especially when the little sheep BHA! So loudly, you know. Now would it be too much trouble to fetch it?"

"Oh, of course," she said, red faced, "I'll get it for you." *Wow! What a weird character he is!* She thought, as she went to get the old receipt.

He counted out the amount with a flat, deadpan look right into her eyes as if to say, "Wann'a argue some more, you prissy little......," and then he thought of his own daughter and relented. He knew he was reacting to the Regime's heavy hand. This would be over soon. He had an image of Frisco Bay, sailboats and true freedom. He had been in the desert too long!

He settled the account and went down the long hallway to the airport concourse. He had his skis and went directly to the gate area where his plane was departing. He was a little early.

No sign of Dufay yet, but he was behind him, finishing breakfast. *Maybe he is conscientious enough to call in and replace himself, since he has been so compromised.* He asked about early boarding and was told that he could board now if he liked.

Ishmael preferred the aisle seats for a quick exit and easy path to the lavatory. His had not been assigned, so he picked one halfway down the aisle, over the wing. He knew the wing spar underneath was the strongest point of the airframe. He sat down and got comfortable. The airline had supplied a long cardboard ski container box. He had checked them in baggage.

He told the ticket agent, "These are good skis. I am reluctant to check them into baggage, but please make a note, sir, they do not have little feet, nor do they have wings. I expect to pick them up at my destination."

"Oh, yes sir, they will be there, I am sure."

"Please tape the box tightly at top and bottom."

"Yes sir," and reached for his heavy, secure, string, tape. Adding a comment," This is how I do mine, sir."

"Good and thank you, young man."

***

Well, what do you know! Down the aisle in a line of people, here is Mr. Dufay.

He stopped at Ishmael's seat.

Ishmael looked up and said "Well hello, Mr. Dufay, fancy meeting you here."

Dufay looked at him and said," Oh, sure,: with a grin. "Could I have that seat next to you? I would like to talk with you without shouting all over the plane. I've been thinking."

"Certainly! Absalom, it is Absalom, isn't it?"

There was a nod.

"It's my pleasure. It's a long flight."

"Oh, thank you," as he squirmed past Ismahel to the middle seat.

"Ishmael,,, may I call you Ishmael?

"Certainly, as long as you remember to genuflect," and they laughed out loud. :Now let's order a drink, that oil of conversation, and you can tell me what's on your mind. OK?"

"OK."

***

The airplane taxied out and turned onto the runway. Next, full throttles were applied and the thrust was significant. Once they were airborne and had climbed out to their first flight level clearance a tone sounded and out came the flight attendant's to take any drink orders. Ishmael preferred Jack Daniels, sour mash, himself. Dufay ordered a scotch.

Ishmael looked around Dufay and down at Tehran. He was remembering the glory days when his family ruled. Was on top of any and all developments in the country. *Heady days,* he thought. And now, as he watched the mosques grow small. The parapets get small, the city reduced to snapshot size, there was a pain of the heart. It was his life, his heritage disappearing before his eyes. Somehow, he knew he would never live there again. He would return, briefly to escort his family out.

This was a poignant moment. He paused and took a deep draught of his drink. Mr. Dufay caught a glimpse of Ismael's expression and surmised he would not return.

"Not coming back, I see"

"Oh, is it that obvious"? Ishmael said, somberly. "I do have a wife and children, Dufay"

"Yes, sir. and I hope you have made arrangements for them, away from your residence. Not asking, mind you, but, I was reading you file last night and I know you saw the drone, that day.

"They are relentless and a few, at the top, are really incensed, that any export of assets, if there are any, not be happen again. I've never seen them so visceral. Ya know, you have to draw the line somewhere. I am drawing mine. They would have your family in a gulag, just for spite.

"Believe what you will Sir, but this is not a trick to gain your confidence but when my surveillance takes me to Geneva. I will ask for asylum. I am done"

Chapter Three

Double Agency

"Sir, you don't remember me, but I served under you, years ago. In the 4th regiment. I was a grunt in the Emperor's, your uncle, Reza's service. You, sir, made a change in our operational plan one day and it surely saved my life. The remnant left behind was wiped out with overwhelming and devastating consequences. You were mush younger at the time.

"After the war, I had no choice but to join in the service of the Regime. I had to eat. I joined the service of the police and advanced to where I am now.

"My boss, a real hard ass, was home sick when the call came in to monitor you. I was second choice and the only one available in the office. But, really, I am not unsympathic to your plight. What is yours is yours. I'll offer no resistance." He raised his glass and tapped it to Ishmael's. It is an honor, sir."

"The 4th regiment was heroic." Ishmael said as he met Dufay's glass. "This much, I remember."

Ishmael was silent for a minute. He was trying to remember the incident that Dufay was citing. There were so many spontaneous decisions when in the field of battle.

"Wow!" said Ishmael. "Happy Day, in a deep baritone voice."

If this were true and Dufay would have to prove it out, Dufay may be helpful at the bank. Showing credentials to the manager. But he would have to be sure. Otherwise it would be like putting the wolf in the chicken coup. *We'll wait and see.*

"I appreciate your sentiments and your loyalty, Defray." He put his seat back to stretch out a little. He raised his glass to the attendant indicating that he would have another drink. She came by and he said "Could we have another drink, please? A Jack and a Scotch."

Dufay heartily joined him.

***

Dufay, was feeling like a tremendous weight had been lifted from his shoulders. He had been thinking of this action for a long time now. *See how Allah works...? I am with the prince and we are both defecting.* He felt confident of Ishmael's direction. Even safe!

They each sat silent for a while, just the hum of the jet engines. These were momentous decisions being made.

Finally, Ishmael asked, "Do you have family back home, Absalom?"

"No sir," he said. "They were killed in the square during the revolution. They were on your side. They were gassed."

Ishmael winced, regretting his question. "I remember that day, I was in the Palace I am very sorry, Absalom."

"It's been a long time ago now. We were young then and full of spirit, sir. I never re-married," Absalom added.

Ishmael dared to glance at him to gauge his sincerity. His eyes were moist. "I think you are an honorable man,

Absalom," he said, raising his glass in Absalom's direction.

"Thank you, sir," Absalom nodded recognition of the compliment.

They sped on in silence. Absalom was looking aimlessly out the window as they proceeded gradually to 35,000 feet. Cabin pressure changes were impacting their hearing just now. That day in the square so long ago was crystal clear in his memory. He usually tried to shut it out but let it play out this time. *Oh what could have been*, he thought. *We were young idealist back then. In over our heads. We were crushed by the revolutionaries. I want to sail a pleasure boat and lay on the beach a little.* He had seen some travel advertisements for St. Petersburg Beach, Florida, Florida in the USA. Even U-tube videos. Sure looked inviting. He had saved money for this dream. He decided that the best revenge was to live well. Life was short. What fate had placed him in this crazy part of the world? No, he would not be loyal to it. What ideology were they fighting for, anyway? It was too obscure for him. Often just someone else's ego. He could still work. He knew security. Maybe in the hospitality industry, he speculated. Actually, he was sure that Ishmael would be able to help him with this long dreamed of goal.

A panoply of European cities were visible below as they headed West by North West, each man deep in his private thoughts. Famous structures, monuments and historic places, lakes and rivers were pointed out by the co-pilot as they proceeded on their route. Each man was aware that he was being carried far away from home. A slightly queasy feeling, their new and irrevocable destiny.

***

Bobby King and Michael Charles arrived at the same time at the Dulles International Airport. They proceeded to the General aviation facility. It was very early. They each parked. There were very few others at this hour.

They could see Dr. Bern's jet off across the tarmac. It was being inspected and re-fueled.

"Hello, partner," said Michael and embraced Bobby heartily.

"Ah! Michael," Bobby returned.

They were both very suntanned from their stay in the Pacific.

"You are looking great, Mike."

"Hey, you too. Bobby." Mike said.

Looking off toward the plane, Michael added, "Haven't we been here before?" He meant the situation and not the place of departure.

"Ya, man, thanks for helping out with my cousin. We will soon see what he has."

"Sounds like more gold bonds and some jewels. Diamonds. Sounds like a few hundred carats altogether," Michael confirmed.

"Ya, Ishmael was older and I think Reza liked him more," as if to explain away why no diamonds had been left to him.

"No matter really, what we must concentrate on is how to get them to Geneva after what we went through. so recently. That will be the trick", Mike said.

"I believe he has sent his family away to our uncle Brahaim's farm for a few days."

"Yeah, he described a surveillance drone over his house already." Mike said.

"We... I think we are all agreed that we can't send the plane back in there at this time," Mike added. "I was looking at a map. Why can't he make a night trip by car over to Kuwait and we could extract him and his family from there. They are friendly to us and I think we could get accommodated there."

"That's a good idea. Let's explore it with Colonel Reeder and our security team," Bobby said after a moment of contemplation. They were coming up to the plane now. Just then Colonel Reeder opened the plane door and dropped the stairs on the special Lear 75.

"Gentleman!" Colonel Reeder exclaimed. "How are you?" Reeder offered his outstretched hand.

Each man pumped it enthusiastically. They had shared much danger together on their last trip to Iran.

"Good to see you both so healthy looking." He was their chief of security and had supervised, in cover, their recent 'get-away' trip to the island. "We will have a lot to talk about at the Chalet. This could be a little dicey, so soon. They ain't goanna let this jet in their air space again."

"We know, Colonel, tell ya what we were thinking."

He was all ears.

They briefly recited the idea of a clandestine road trip to Kuwait and an extraction from there.

Interesting idea, Colonel Reeder thought. *They have no horse in the race. They are friendly and with a little grease, they will likely give us some military escort coverage.*

'I like it," he said. "Let's discuss it with everyone when we get to the meeting."

They boarded the plane and greeted the rest of their security team and made themselves comfortable for the long trip.

The engines wound up and they began to taxi.

***

"Tower, this is Nancy 91710, leaving staging area, General Aviation. Requesting taxi way for flight plan N91710, this morning."

"This is the tower, N91710. Proceed to taxi way No. 6, to runway 36. We have a right departure. Wind from the west at 12 miles per hour."

"Roger that, Tower. Taxi way 6 to runway 36, N91710, over."

And so it went. They were on their way.

Bobby was really very anxious to see his cousin after many years.

"Tower to N91710, Visual on runway 36. You are cleared for takeoff and to Flight level 12. Heading 260o. We will turn you over to regional control."

"Roger that tower, N91710

The takeoff roll began. Swift and powerful was their takeoff roll and assent to FL12. Pressed into their seats until they reached their first 'level off' altitude. They adjusted to the heading and awaited contact with regional control.

"This is Herndon, Virginia Regional control center calling N91710"

"N91710, Control."

"Squawk 8989 and proceed to FL 35" Stay on heading of 260o

"Squawk 8989 and proceed on 260o to FL 35, Roger that. N91710 out."

They awaited Vector instructions when they reached FL 35. They did not need the 'burners' this time. There was no need to waste fuel and it would draw attention to the sassy Lear.

They leveled off and the attendant asked if anyone wanted Juice, toast, muffin, Bagel or sausage and eggs. Everyone was hungry and wanted to fill-up and nap for a while.

The trip to Geneva was a long one. Since the Learjet 75 had a range of 2,000 NM, even though modified with larger fuel tanks, they would still have to stop in Reykjavik, Iceland to refuel.

Bobby, taking more control this time, was animated, gesturing to Colonel Reeder about his plan for cousin Ismael and family to escape through Kuwait. The Colonel had contacts there. His company had several Sheiks as clients.

"On the face of it, Bobby, I like it. I have contacts there. We should give this plan serious consideration. I think we could disguise a small caravan cover. Perhaps put a small travel trailer on a flatbed truck. Put them in the trailer. We could follow close behind in what looks like a safety control vehicle. And a lead vehicle, of course. Heavily armed personnel, front and back. Radar on the RV roof would look normal.

Bobby was rubbing his hands together in anticipation, tapping his feet"

Michael could tell Bobby was pushing his plan with Colonel Reeder. That was just fine. It was his cousin and he should play a significant role in helping him. Besides, he had good ideas and knew the territory.

After a while, Michael gave Bobby a sign to move to a more private area on the plane.

They sat down further back. Bobby said," Yeah, man, what's up?"

"You had a great idea back there about Kuwait," Michael said .

"Yeah, Reeder likes it. He's thinking about a camper trailer on a flat bed, with heavily armed escorts front and rear, like a wide load transfer. Ishmael and family inside. He has connections in Kuwait. Clients, who for a fee will insure we get across the border without incident."

"That sounds like a plan, Bobby! Nice going. "So, can Reeder leave from Kuwait on a road trip to retrieve them?"

"Don't know"

"Better, no flights into country. Big tip off if they detect him."

"Yeah," Bobby said.

"Now, this is a little delicate but I'd like to get it out of the way"

"Yeah," Bobby responded

"What is our split going to be." Need to be able to negotiate with Dr. Bern?"

"Hey, Michael, Just like before." He held his hands out with open palms. "We will expect one half for our facilitation and you and I will split that. Don't know what he actually has yet, but I am happy with that arrangement, Michael."

"Ok, me too. Just wanted to check."

"I understand completely."

"Operational expenses, security, facilitation for Dr. Bern, etc. will be paid first. All proceeds will be net of that," Michael said for final clarification.

"Yes sir, I agree with that," Bobby confirmed.'

"OK, we're off to see the Wizard," as he slapped Bobby on the leg and returned to his former seat.

Bobby did the same.

It was nap time. They flew at 540 mph and at least 500 feet above airline traffic. A higher service ceiling. After last month, when this bird was up, people would be watching. Various agencies in the US and Western Europe had had time to be alerted by now. *You can bet we were pinging somebody's radar!* Mike reflected as he fell off to sleep.

The pressure changes stirred him up as they began a decent from 40,000 feet. This was a long ride down.

He assumed they were heading into Reykjavik. Midrange for fuel. There was some bantering and war stories reverie among the security team. A great crew. When you come near death and escape it together, there is a strong bond formed. Especially with these guys, in this profession.

***

"They're descending into Reykjavik, sir," the C.I.A. radar tech yelled across the room. He had been assigned the watch for N91710 for the afternoon. Standard profile for the Lear 75 en route to Geneva. He attached the file to the NSA control center in New York. From there it was relayed to the Pentagon. It didn't raise any eyebrows. But, they were watching.

No more international incidents, in sensitive political areas! The order had come from the White House.

"Let me know if they go past Geneva." The radar room Chief said.

"Yes sir", the tech answered "So far, everything is matching the flight plan filed, and no deviation detected sir."

"Roger that, agent. Keep me posted if there is a change."

"Sir, yes Sir."

***

They touched down and taxied to the re-fueling depot. All planes with superior range had to stop in Reykjavík to take on fuel before heading on to the Continent.

Everybody in the plane got off and stretched their legs. Colonel Reeder went aside with his secure phone and made a call to a certain Sheik client he knew in Kuwait. A few days head's- up notice was needed to set things in motion.

He explained his mission, briefly and was given assurances that "This could be done." The price would be $60,000 for guaranteed safe passage, convoy and all, with Kuwaiti Nationals. I.D.'s, papers and passports; etc. would be supplied. Colonel Reeder thought that was a little high and said so, but this Sheik was top grade. A perfectionist and experienced in such matters as clandestine border operations. On second thought, it was worth it, he decided. He agreed to call as soon as he had a more definite time frame. He would bring up this arrangement at their meeting.

He returned to the plane with new confidence that he had a solution to 'Problem'. A desert fox run. Now for munitions, he wanted a supply of grenade launchers just in case. Open desert presented many dangers.

***

They strapped in for takeoff. Reykjavik had very high capacity fuel pumps to facilitate demand. There were acres of underground tanks and almost daily re-supply activities. Tanker planes could always be seen in the distance. They had separate runways.

***

Meanwhile, 3,500 miles away, an infra-red drone flew low and detected no life form in the residence of Ishmael Pahlavi at a time when there should have been someone there.

This was interpreted and reported as "They've run!" A military ground team was dispatched, forthwith, to take a closer look. Once inside the home a radio call was made.

"No one here, sir, but nothing has been removed."

The security Guru in charge considered the possibility that they were visiting somewhere else. A relative? He would find out. After that recent call to Buruse, his cousin, it would be his ass if they ran and he lost them.

"Get me all relatives' addresses", he barked and sent underlings scurrying! No one wanted to cross this martinet.

It wasn't long before the name of Great Uncle Brahmin cane up, mostly because of the significant land holdings he had. It was worth checking out.

***

Ishmael and Agent Dufay were beginning to descend into the Geneva TCA (Terminal Control Area) area. Dufay suggested that he should call in to re-assure headquarters that he had Ishmael under surveillance and there was nothing unusual. "They will be wondering. Best to keep them informed. You may listen in, sir."

"Ok, good idea." Soon, they would be too low for phones to be allowed.

He made the call. "Yes sir, Dufay here."

"Yes, he is two rows up from me."

"Yes, alone."

"Oh? Do you know where they are, sir?"

Ismael sat straight up in utter panic! That could only mean one thing!

'Infra-red," Defray said, shifting his eyes to look at Ismael. Yes sir, checking the uncle;s land holdings." He nodded at Ishmael.

Ishmael was white with fear. His family would be in danger. He grabbed for his secure phone and made a call to Ruth.

"Hello, Ishmael," she could see his I. D.

"Do not ask questions. You must leave immediately. Go to the nearest Holiday Inn. Check-in with the cash I gave you under the name of Wilson. I will find you. Once there, don't go outside. Tell them your husband is parking the car. Now Go"!

Dufay was finishing up, "Yes sir. When I get off the airplane I will be able to stay in touch, Sir."

He looked at his would-be captive with eyes wide!

"Tell me!" Demanded Ishmael.

"Their infra-red drone detected no life forms at your house. It lead them to speculate. They are conducting routine search for your wife's whereabouts. A sister, a friend. They have targeted your uncle's as a possibility." He could tell by Ishmael's moving larynx that that was the place.

"My experience tells me that this is where they are. You have told them to leave, I assume. No need to confirm," he added with a wave of his forearm, palm down. "That is good. They would hold your family under their new screwy laws."

"I need the closest Holiday Inn to uncle's address. Here it is." He trusted Dufay now.

"There are two that I can think of. I will use my credentials to check them out."

"They will be under the name Wilson"

"O.K., I got it,", said Dufay. "Soon as we land I will go to work on it sir."

Ismael said, "We may have to leave a day early. I must get to them!"

"He would call Bobby or Michael and explain the urgency for stepping up the schedule. He did not know what the plans were.

They landed in Geneva. There was a man in fatigues with a sign that read Pahlavi. Ismael walked up and identified himself and his colleague, Mr. Dufay.

"Welcome, sir, please follow me to the Hilo pad. It's out back, this way sir."

Dr. Bern was inside. "Velcome sir. And you are Bobby's cousin." That is how ve know him.

"Yes, sir. Ishmael Pahlavi. I am honored to meet you, sir."

"Ah! Soon ve vill all be at the Chalet. Food and refreshments are prepared. ve vill be there soon."

"Sir, this is Agent Defray of the national police of Iran. He is defecting with me. He is an honorable man who once served under me in the Revolution. His wife was killed before his eyes. I trust him with my life."

"I too am ex-military. I understand, sir. I have the connections to help you both with that, in Switzerland."

Ishmael couldn't contain himself. "Sir, there have been some developments that may impact our schedule"

"Yes, Mr. Pahlavi?" Dr. Bern inquired.

"I have reason to believe the Regime is closing in on my wife and children as we speak. Mr. Dufay has confirmed that for me."

"Ve have the very best security team. They will know just what to do. Let's get to the Chalet and discuss this vith Colonel Reeder."

"Yes sir, thank you, sir. I am beside myself right now."

The Bell Ranger lifted off at Dr. Bern's nod to the pilot. It turned north and came to speed quickly. Dr. Bern put in a call to Colonel Reeder.

"Yes sir?" Reeder responded

"A problem has developed with our client, Ishmael Pahlavi."

"Oh?"

"Yes. It seems that the authorities over there are closing in on Mr. Pahlavi's family. He took the precaution of moving them, but the enemy seem to be motivated," Dr. Bern said

"I have already taken steps with my contacts in Kuwait to insure his family's safe passage into that country without our having to make any presence with the aircraft in Iran."

"It seems they are safe for now. I just wanted to give you some advance notice on the situation. Ve are en-route to the Chalet now in the Hilo. ETA 20 min. I vill send the Hilo back to the airport for you all. Vie will talk at the meeting. Vhat is your ETA?"

"About 45 minutes, Sir." Reeder Replied.

"Gut, vie vill see you then."

***

Reeder hung up and turned to Bobby and Michael.

"We have a development." The authorities are closing in on Mr. Pahlavi's family. They are suspicious and you know they will hold them as insurance. I have made arrangements with contacts in Kuwait for their extraction, but not yet." Right now, they are safe."

Bobby was aghast and wide eyed!

"We should all be in the Chalet within an hour. They are en-route now."

"Oh good, I see you have it in your hands, sir. We trust you. Please don't let anything happen to them!"

"Roger that, Bobby."

***

He called the Sheik. "Everything is a go, my friend. Please prepare the equipment necessary for immediate extraction. I personally guarantee payment."

"This is good enough for me. My men will initiate and commence, Sir. Right away!" We will have the truck, the camper and personal ready and in country. My brother is a dealer there. He has agreed to lease me a RV travel trailer. Your people will be inside. It will look like a normal delivery. Taped and covered with plastic. There will be papers for delivery to a Kuwaiti RV dealer. We'll wait for further instructions from you, sir"

"Excellent. My friend." Get close to Tehran and park the vehicle. We will assist in the extraction." Said Reeder.

He felt comfortable with arrangements so far.

"Oh, I almost forgot, Colonel.

"Yes," said Reeder

"This is another and unrelated matter, Colonel, but I don't get to talk to you very often."

"Anytime, you are my client, honorable Sheik Hamoud. How can I help you, sir?

"It has come to my attention that the Americans are discontinuing to produce the airplane, A 10- Warthog.

"So I have heard," Reeder said.

"A great low level attack airplane, I think. And very well armed. Ah! With that nose cannon! So maneuverable, too."

"Yes sir, this is all true," Reeder admitted, wondering where he was going with this.

"Well, I'll get to point," the Sheik said. "I have been offered a chance to purchase one of the surplus planes. It is in good working order. Rarely used. The price is very good. I have an airfield here on my compound property. I have grandson who trained in this model airplane as pilot. He is coming home."

"Pretty high maintenance, Sir. Whatever would you use it for?" Reeder commented.

"Oh, you do not know but sometimes we encounter Bedouin tribes on our transport routes from other countries. Many are thieves and would attack and pillage. This is why that flatbed we are using for you has a steel seat in front and rear for a .50 caliber mounted assault rifle. The A-10 flies fast and low, avoiding detection from foreign nationals. The mere appearance of an A-10 will discourage any attacking thieves. We have sustained big losses of merchandise last year. One volley across the bow, so to speak, will send them fleeing. If my grandson doesn't come, do you have any connection for a trained pilot? A soldier of fortune. I would pay very well for this protection."

"Let me think about it for a few days and make some calls." Reeder said. His brow wrinkled at this new revelation that there were hostile parties along the open desert. He did not want to place Bobby's cousin Ishmael and his family in any danger. He made a mental note to re-inventory his armaments for the trip. Rocket-propelled grenade launchers would have to be added to the inventory.

An A-10, Warthog, wow! He thought. *Yeah, that plane could kick some ass! And in style.* Yeah, he knew some X Jockey's that might be interested. He mentally put it on the shelf, in favor of the business at hand.

Chapter Four

The meeting

The Bell Ranger touched down lightly onto the landing pad at the rear of the Chalet. Stevern opened the door, greeting everyone. He helped Dr. Bern out. Dr. Bern gave instructions for the immediate return to the airport to pick up the others.

They walked down a few stairs and into the rear of the middle floor of the Chalet, through double—what looked like brushed gold—French doors.

Impressive, Ishmael thought.

The artwork on the walls. The Swiss lead crystal chandlers and wall sconces were breathtaking. They bespoke of Royalty. Really this was a very impressive piece of real estate. It reminded Ishmael of the days at Oxford. This was the genre of this massive construction. It was at least four stories high. About one hundred feet square, and made of grey field stone with very heavy wood trim. There were four chimneys with copper downspouts and flashing. Two circular driveways led up to the front portico and then around to the Hilo pad. Coming in he could see the slate roof. It was quite large. There was statuary all around and concrete columns buttressing both front and rear elevations. Exquisite landscaping, you could tell there were several acres. This appeared to be built for two-hundred years of use. Very solid. A fortress. There was a cupola on the roof. He could make out a defensive gun emplacement inside the cupola. It must have cost millions to build. It was a lot to take in all at once. No wonder it was referred to as "The Chalet" by those who had been there. Well, he thought, Dr. Bern was a world-wide mover and shaker, from what he had been told. This was an outstanding, world class, structure.

Mr. Dufay was feeling a bit uncomfortable. He was mentally preparing a speech to quit himself that would be convincing to the others. He knew he would have to 'clear' himself right away. He had some ideas about how he might be most useful in helping Ismael.

They walked into a luncheon banquet with shrimp, lobster, roast beef in the form of a steam ship, round casseroles and deserts of various kinds. Stevern had prepared a feast fit for kings.

This was lunch, Dr. Bern style. The others were used to it but this was new to Ishmael.

"Gentleman, please be comfortable until the others arrive vithin the hour. Refresh yourselves. Stevern here," — Stevern nodded to them – vill assist you vith anything you may need. There are restrooms on this level of the Chalet. I assume you will be staying, at least tonight. Stevern can show you to your accommodations upstairs, if you vould like to get that out of the vay. I see there is very little luggage. Excuse me, I vile be back momentarily. Ishmael, may I see you privately for a moment?"

"Yes sir," Ishmael responded and they walked into the anti-room where there was assume privacy. Ismael looked at Dr. Bern with a questioning look.

"First of all, I vant you to know that our primary concern, right now, is the safety of you family. I have already spoken to our security chief, the very capable Colonel

Reeder. He has already made arrangements to secure your family's safety. He vill explain further when they arrive. Now secondly, I must call my bank and set in motion my underwriters, research, blocking and advance marketing initiatives. Can you give me some idea of what you saw in your box at the bank?"

"Yes sir, gladly," he went on. "There were several packages, or I should say blocks, like bricks, of waxed, black wrapped paper. I peeled one top back and saw he words 'Gold Bond'. I had very little time. I didn't want to linger. It was then that I saw a velvet bag. I didn't think it too significant but I looked in anyway. There were at least 50 or so large, bright, loose diamonds. Then wrapped separately at the bottom was a very large Ruby, or so it appeared. I am, no jeweler, but under the circumstances, I'd bet on it."

"OK, Dr. Bern said. Ve vill proceed on that information. Bobby's bonds vere vrapped in the same manner. I am going to assume, for now, that they are from the same issue as his. I think you vill do very vell, Sir."

"Excuse me and Dr. Bern went into his office and picked up his direct line to the bank. "Top floor, underwriting, please, Helga."

"Yes sir, she snapped to recognizing his voice.

Dr. Bern was a gentle man, but he did insist on efficiency.

"Peter Voles here, yes sir"

"Ah, gut Peter, I am glad you answered." Peter was highly placed and didn't usually answer the phone.

"I may have another batch of those Gold Bonds, in the same series as Mr. Charles and Mr. Papal had. In fact, a cousin. Also left to him by the Shah. Also there are some large diamonds and a ruby. They are not in my possession as yet. I would like for you to vork this transaction personally, along the same lines. Same facilitation, same group of investors, if you know what I mean. Feel them out. I need to know their marketability. I vill be at the Chalet until I return to the bank"

"I believe I know exactly what you want, Sir. I will report back, hopefully by tomorrow, sir"

***

Back in the main room, Mr. Dufay pulled Ishmael aside.

"I would like to address the group right up front to explain myself. As long as the Regime thinks I am following their orders, I can be of tremendous help to you. For instance, along with your security team, I can interpose my agency and credentials at your bank for their unquestioned compliance and silence. Otherwise, I am sure they have a number to call when you arrive. It is a long way out. They are sure to apprehend you"

Ishmael thought a minute. He had been nervous about how he might go back to the bank and extract the goodies without being apprehended. This could be a real blessing" *Praise Allah!*

***

"The group will hear you out, I promise."

Ishmael and Dufay ambled around the food table and sampled a few items. They would wait for the others but everything look so inviting, and they were hungry.

Before long there came an ever increasing rumble, engine noise and the unmistakable air chop of the blades of the Hilo. The others had arrived.

Ishmael was excited to see his cousin for the first time in at least 25 years. They had taken such different paths since their college days

Ishmael walked back through the hall to the French doors to meet his cousin. They were settling the last 3 feet onto the pad and he could hear the engine throttle being cut. Now, Dr. Bern was at his side. Stevern was already out on the pad and heading for the passenger door. A fatigue clad, military-looking gentleman was the first to emerge from the chopper. He instinctively scanned the area. Ismael figured this was Colonel Reeder. Dr. Bern confirmed when he said "There is the best man in security. Colonel Reeder. You may come to appreciate him, Ishmael."

Next an athletic guy in casual, sport, clothing. Dr. Bern said "And Michael Charles."

Then, unmistakably, there was Buruse, his cousin.

"Ah!" Ishmael exclaimed. "He looks good!" Ishmael pushed on the heavy door to greet his cousin.

"Ismael, my brother!" Buruse exclaimed in a loud, exited, voice. He rushed up to embrace him. They embraced in a long, tight, squeeze. They were sincerely warmed of heart.

"This is Michael Charles, my partner and then here is Colonel Reeder, our knight in shining armor," he introduced them as they passed into the corridor beyond the French doors.

"Now Colonel Reeder has a lot to tell you, right away. About your family."

"Oh,' said Ishmael, I am very anxious to hear anything!

He turned to the Colonel, who had heard the exchange.

"Yes, Ishmael, I am very pleased to meet you. I have been working on a plan to remove your family, safely, I hope, please come inside and sit with me."

"In speaking with Bobby and Michael, we have decided that we dare not fly back into your country. We are certain we would not be permitted to leave."

Ishmael nodded in agreement.

"We would have to file a flight plan; etc." We have developed a plan, overland, to and through Kuwait. It is about a four hour drive but here is what we propose.

I have a client who is an influential Sheik in Kuwait. He is very familiar with the incoming trade routes. His brother owns an RV dealership located in the outskirts of Tehran. He will assemble a team to transport and make what will appear a delivery of an RV vehicle, wrapped in plastic and mounted on a flat-bed delivery truck/vehicle. The truck will depart from his warehouse with all pertinent papers for conveyance through to Kuwait. Duties paid, tolls and associated fee's border clearance arranged. It will appear sealed in Visqueen, a plastic wrap. Your family and you will be inside the trailer for the delivery trip. It will not be questioned. He is influential and knows the procedures expected and required. You will arrive across the border in Kuwait where we will have our airplane ready and waiting. From there, we will return to this Chalet, where you can stay and make your future plans. Meanwhile, Dr. Bern will be working on your portfolio and you will have ample funds, advanced, to proceed. He will also liaison with the immigration authorities. Asylum acceptance folks. With your "Deposit" you will have instant approval. We will follow with armed personnel in the front and rear as though we are part of the shipping crew for a "Wide load" vehicle. How does this sound to you and where is your family at this time? Bobby thinks, your Great Uncle's?

"No, I had to move them. I received intelligence that authorities were closing in fast. Infra-red surveillance indicated that they were not in our house when they should have been. A proactive and motivated agent initiated a kind of dragnet to find them. The regime is not above holding them until they are satisfied that I have no intentions of removing assets.

Reeder was listening and nodding.

"They are in an unknown minivan. I, upon learning of this pursuit, removed them from Uncle's farm with just minutes to spare and sent them to a Holiday Inn nearby. They checked in under the name of 'Wilson'. They paid cash, I don't know which Inn yet. They have strict orders not to leave the room for ANY reason. I will have to find them."

"I can do that through H.I. headquarters with highly placed personnel. I should know of Wilson's on their roster in a few minutes.

"Good! This sounds like a well thought out plan, already." Ishmael said. "I am gratified."

"We have been working on it. It will cost about $60,000, I should tell you.

"Ah, well worth it for a safe trip back for my family," he said.

"We still have to get the bonds, etc. out of the bank. Incidentally, who is your companion? Please tell me about him."

"He is an agent of the Regime, I should say former agent, but they don't know that yet. He has made me privy to their telephone communications or the Regime would have my family already.

"He used to serve under me in the military. He has earned my trust. He wants to defect with me, but I get ahead of myself. He can be very useful to us but I promised him that he could address all of you himself, up front. You decide, sir. It will be up to you."

"Fair enough," said Reeder, with a somewhat skeptical expression.

***

The food table became the hub of, introduction, conversation and camaraderie for the next fifteen minutes. Mimosas were served. A little oil of conversation.

Inquiries of Mr. Dufay only brought the response, "I am an enemy agent", followed quickly by, "I will explain, before we begin."

Raised eyebrows and laughter usually followed. They weren't too sure how to take him, but Ishmael was laughing along with them so they allowed forbearance.

"Gentlemen," Dr. Bern raised his glass. "Shall ve all adjourn to the conference area in the next room? Does anyone need the rest room? Ve vill start in a few minutes." He led the way.

***

The conference area had a long table and a more informal grouping of leather chairs and a TV monitor for digital presentations. They all choose this less formal venue.

"And now, it is my understanding that Mr. Dufay vill address us," said Dr. Bern. He held his hand out towards Dufay.

Dufay rose and moved to the center of the floor. "Thank you, gentlemen, for the opportunity to address you, before we begin discussing and divulging your plans."

Before he could go on, Ishmael rose. "

I want you to know, I have very good reason to trust Mr. Dufay implicitly. He served under my command during our Revolution and he has already saved my wife Ruth and my children from the imminent grip of our secret police. Please hear him out, objectively." And Ishmael sat down.

"Thank you, Ishmael," Dufay said.

"Yes, it is true. As fate would have it, my unscrupulous boss and senior agent was ill, leaving me available for this assignment. To monitor Ishmael as a result of intelligence gained through certain aerial and telephone interception surveillance. Still, I approached this assignment without much enthusiasm. You see, years ago, Ishmael had saved my life, although he did not remember it, when I first began to tail him. Nevertheless, I have personally been unhappy and not symphathic, as many of my countrymen have not, with our current government. Frankly, I wanted out some time ago.

"Ishmael has provided me an avenue towards that goal. In other words, I am just too old for this crap."

They all laughed.

"For now, as a double agent, I can offer my services and have done so already, to help Ishmael." He paced the floor, using hands and arms gesticulating for emphasis.

"I have gleaned, through our discussions that a particularly critical time for this 'recovery' will be when moving Ishmael's 'material' from his bank. Headquarters was already informed when he was their last. I could provide credentials to that teller as though all is compatible with Government policy as he removes items. Therefore, they will not feel the need to notify anyone. I will direct her not to. Colonel Reeder, you will accompany as an aide and an enforcement officer. Please dress the part. You may shoot me immediately if I am lying.

"Then we can leave in my official vehicle to whatever location you have prepared. You may scan myself and my vehicle for any tracking devices. I will not be offended. I hope to leave Iran in your company. This should provide you the time you need, undetected, to prosecute your exit plans.

"Please give this careful consideration. My boss will be relentless in pursuing Ishmael and family if he is convinced there may be some expatriotriation of these assets. His head will roll and he knows it. Without my cover, he will certainly be notified.

"In any case I will not return to live in Iran. I consider myself a free man. Please consider this carefully.

"Bravo!" The applause began spontaneously from everyone!

Ishmael took him aside and said, "I will take care of you, Absalom. I know you are giving up a hard earned pension. You will not want for anything."

"Oh no, sir. That is not why I am doing this," he protested"

"Nevertheless, Dufay, I will owe you a tremendous debt, sir .You are correct, this is the most sensitive part of the whole operation."

He grabbed Dufay's shoulder.

**

"I must call in and report everything is normal for a ski holiday. Colonel Reeder, you are welcome to listen in.

God forbid, they have found the family. He will up-date me also. Please join me, sir, in a quiet room.

Dufay did not know of the plan already in place.

Colonel Reeder agreed and rose to go lead him to an anti-room.

Once situated, Dufay pressed an auto dial.

"Hello sir, Dufay here. Sir, my arms are full for the moment, may I put you on speaker phone.

"Anything sensitive?" came the terse reply.

"No Sir."

"Ok, Dufay, go ahead."

He did so.

"What's going on there, Dufay?"

"Really nothing, sir. Normal for a ski holiday, I think he will be returning tomorrow/ according to the flight reservations. How about there, sir? Last we talked, you were checking on the uncle's farm. Did you find the wife, Sir?"

"No, no one there but the uncle."

He glanced over at Colonel Reeder.""Perhaps a relative or friend. She may be on a holiday herself, sir."

"Yeah, maybe," was the reply.

Ishmael had tip- toed into the room and heard the last part. *Thank Allah,* he thought. *They got out in time.*

"I will see you soon sir."

"OK, don't let him out of your sight, Dufay. I still have a bad feeling about this chicanery."

"No sir, not out of my sight."

Dufay hung up.

They each breathed an audible sigh of relief.

"You're good with me, Dufay." Colonel Reeder said and slapped him on the shoulder.

"Now, let's find that Holiday Inn." Said Ishmael.

"On it," said Reeder.

***

"Hey Whiplash, how is the hospitality business?" Colonel Reeder fenced with his former college. He referred to an old Humvee incident when they were a mission together.

"Hey, Colonel! How the heck are ya?" He recognized his old friend's voice.

"Oh, mak'in passes and kick'en asses," he replied

Whiplash laughed and said, "What I can do for you today?"He knew the Colonel Wouldn't be calling unless he needed some help.

"You have a couple of franchises around Tehran, don't you?"

"Yeah, do you need a room?"

"No, I just need to know the address of the one who has a 'Wilson' registered. And the phone number. You can call me back on the following number: He gave him the secure line.

"Ok, Colonel, but you didn't get it from me."

""Roger that," said the Colonel "This is for a friendly, though."

"Give me 20 minutes, sir."

"Roger that." He hung up.

Ishmael was pacing. Elated that they were all right and anxious at the same time. He wanted to speak to Ruth. They made small talk among themselves. Bobby came into the room to see his cousin.

He said, "You can trust these guys, Ishmael. Ruth and the kids are in good, safe hands." He attempted to console his cousin. "It sounds like he has a good plan worked out. I am impressed.

"I will fly back with Dufay in tow, that way there will be no tail on me. We will go to the Inn where Ruth and the kids are. I assume once we know their location for sure, the truck and trailer will be in the warehouse somewhere nearby. We've only to arrive and get in before it is sealed up."

"Sounds like a plan. How long a drive will it be?" Bobby inquired

"I make it about 450 miles. On those roads and at delivery speed, I imagine about 12 hours. Into Kuwait. Mr. Dufay will provide a mis-direction cover story for the duration. Maybe a shopping mall and direr trip," Ishmael offered.

Colonel Reeder's phone rang.

"Yes sir", the Colonel Said. He bent over with pen in hand to write on the napkin on the table.

"Three locations, Wilson", he was repeating for Ishmaels benefit. "The phone number" And the Room number is? 124," He wrote both numbers down.

"Got it. I owe ya! Big time. Thanks. Keep it quiet. I will see you."

He handed the number over to Ishmael

"You are the man." He immediately excused himself to the next room to call his wife.

***

"Good Afternoon, Olliday Inn on de square."

"Room, 124, please."

"I will connect you sir"

The phone had been silent for nearly 2 days. It startled Ruth but she knew Ishmael must make contact.

"Hello," she said, with trepidation.

"Ah, Ruth," the familiar, baritone, full-bodied voice of her husband was heard."

"Oh, Ishmael, She gasped, "How are you, where are you," she exclaimed in one breath, she was so excited to hear from him. The children came running to her side. They had been so quiet for these days. Not wanting to draw any attention.

"I am never so glad to hear your voice," he uttered. "How are you and the children?"

"Good, so far. We moved so fast from Uncle's." She said with a question in her voice.

"Yes, Ruth, they were closing in on you all. I will tell you later how I found this out. And, it was just in time."

He paused momentarily.

"We have a good plan in place for your rescue. I am flying back in the morning. Arriving in the afternoon. We will come to your location, immediately. I will explain then. This is a secure line- re-routed, as before, but I don't want to be on it very long. How are the children holding up?"

"Good, good, Ishmael."

"Tell them we will go to Disney World, if they remain well behaved," said Ishmael.

"I will tell them. They will be happy to hear that!" said Ruth

"I will call you when I arrive, Ruth," Ishmael promised

"All right, Ismael. We will be anxious for you to arrive." The children were shaking their heads, up and down enthusiastically. They knew they could not yell.

"I must go now, Ruth. Love to you all!" and he hung up, feeling very relieved, now.

He walked back to the others. She is very well, thank you for that facilitation, Colonel Reeder nodded.

Chapter Five

The Plan

"Shall we?" Reeder indicated with his outstretched arm back to and through the dinning to the conference lounge. He waited for everyone to be seated but he remained standing. He was obviously going to address everyone.

"Gentleman, it is time to get to the business at hand. We are here to decide how we might help our new colleague, Ishmael Pahlavi, recover and transport his lawfully owned assets from his country, Iran to the bank here in Geneva. Dr. Bern will take charge of them, in trust, from there.

"You all know of similar efforts last month on behalf of his cousin. It is an understatement to say it caused quite a stir around the world. Therefore, we must try a much different approach, this time. Low profile. No screaming jet air planes firing in hot pursuit, this time.

"The Iranian security forces are extremely sensitized to this potential operation. Recent intelligence confirms this. And—to say the least—they are motivated to keep these assets from leaving their country.

"We have developed a plan within the past two day, leading up to this meeting. As your security team, our goal is a covert and safe operation for rescues. This time we must also factor in a wife and children, along for a dangerous ride. Our fee, by the way, will be approximately the same as the last time. $300,000. This includes the $60,000 I've have already committed, on my word, to the operation. The following is already underway as we speak. It is as follows: I have engaged a certain Sheik, and his company assets, He is in Import/Export. He has many 'connections' and many years of experience along the trade routes. His company is well known among the authorities. They will not be bothered, or detained. He is a Kuwaiti national and a client of mine.

"We propose sending a flatbed truck to his brother's RV dealership, near Tehran. A 26 ft., new RV will be loaded upon it as is normal for shipment and delivery. It will be wrapped in Visqueen as packing protection from the desert sand storms. We will have loaded Ismael and his family on board, before wrapping. Also, Mr. Dufay will accompany them and a contingent of my security team. We will occupy the front and rear transport escort vehicles. We will be heavily armed. I will personally be involved, appearing as the transport company's security lesion. I will be dressed as a Kuwaiti national. We will travel the five or so hours into Kuwait, crossing the border without incident. That much is guaranteed, by my client.

"Once in Kuwait, we will depart from a local airfield where our company Lear will be waiting to return all of us to Geneva."

He was pacing as he delivered the exit scenario. He nodded towards Stevern, who was waiting to pull down a map of Iran and the border into Kuwait. Reeder produced a pointer. He pulled it out of what looked like a pen. He tracked the route along the escape path. "Thank you, Stevern," he said.

"Now, to address a critical step upon, which the rest of the operation is dependent.

"We believe there is a mole or, at lease a sympathizer at the bank whose instructions are to call their agency when Ishmael appears at the safety deposit box. This cannot be allowed to happen, for obvious reasons.

"We will depend on the good services of Mr. Dufay here. He will act as an agent of the Regime, offering credentials to the managing teller as though he were the government. Hopefully, obviating the need to report. Mr. Dufay will make a passing comment to that effect. It will appear that Ismael is cooperating with the Regime. The dialog narrative, overheard by the teller, will so indicate. Scripted and staged for the benefit of the bank official. This should assuage her, but if I detect a breach or any form of reporting from several observation points in the bank, I will intervene, severing phone lines if necessary. I will be dressed as and pose as Mr. Dufay's assistant. A gold badge goes a long way.

"We will leave by armored truck for effect. I have leased the services of one, in theater. Assets will be transferred on board the truck to innocuous-looking receptacles. This is for the inevitable review of the security cameras extant. The stop will be two blocks before the Flatbed truck warehouse. A building with a rear exit will lead to a short, covered exit by a waiting vehicle. It will proceed to the back of the loaded, flatbed garage. We will immediately enter and mount the truck and move into the RV mounted there. Workers will then begin to heat wrap the Trailer vehicle for transport.

"We will exit ASAP. And we will proceed slowly, normally, to the outbound highway. We think we have a viable procedure for a safe exit.

"Are there any questions or observations? I am open to your thoughts. That's what this meeting is about."

Each man looked at the other. Collectively, heads shook from side to side. Michael spoke up, "Sounds good to me", you are the Ace, sir.

A hum of affirmative agreement ensued.

Dr. Bern exclaimed, "Excellent! Colonel Reeder. Let us commence.

"Stevern has prepared a Chateau Briand dinner for all. Ve vile dine now. Stevern, lead the way."

The group entered the dining room and all were immediately taken back by the beautiful presentation. There was an ice carving in the center of the table, and a Steamship Round, for those who wanted something different, under the chandeliers with unique lighting all around. There were little gifts at each place setting. 14 Carat Cross pens, inscribed with the name of the person and the date to commemorate this day of meeting.

What a class act, this Dr. Bern and staff, Ishmael thought. Each man present felt that he had been treated regally. Thism as Champagne was served in crystal, for that purpose. Two large Magnums of Chateau Lafitte, A great, full bodied, Bordeaux to accompany the Chateau Briand were placed one at each end of the table.

"The skiing is perfect, tonight," Dr. Bern said, as they all sat down. "The Hilo will leave at 6 AM for the Geneva airport for your departing flights."

Dr. Bern was a very wealthy man on world account. At the same time he was well known around the world for his philanthropy. Both he and his clients returned much of their wealth to the disadvantaged.

***

Bobby and Michael were staying in the Chalet through this operation until Ishmael and family were returned back here, safely. It seemed that their lives were one long vacation, these days, punctuated by moments of panic-like experiences.

Both men had re-ordered their respective family priorities. Michael had flown to Disney World and met with his children and grandchildren. Colonel Reeder provided him with the consultancy of a former witness protection expert, now retired. Through his advice, they had relocated themselves, selling former properties and moving to an area in Ocala, FL where a 200 acre Estate Property was purchased for the construction of a compound, where all could live comfortably. A former horse ranch.

He provided an extra two weeks at The Disney World complex for all. A blanket slush fund of $100,000 was established for transition expenses.

Michael had hired an architect to design a plat map layout of their proposed compound. All were invited to contribute input into its design. Four houses and added features were already up to about five million dollars. And, of course trucks; in Ocala you have to have a truck

"Give me three of those Silverado trucks, black, red and white, please," was a special day! "Oh, does that qualify for a fleet price?"

They would not return to their former residences, which were put on the market and alternative, temporary sites were purchased as interim residences.

***

There was an exited hum of conversation at the table about the plans and the day's events.

The, gilt-edged arrangements and accommodations were an up-lift to everybody. The spectacular scenery in view through a large picture window, the snowcapped Alps, a small village, the lighted ski slopes. The ever present whoosh of the snow making equipment. Truly a wonderland. This kind of landscape was seen only in childhood fairy tale books.

There was much excitement and camaraderie around the table, as they indulged the wine, Cesar and the beef. "Compliments to the Chef," was heard, repeatedly.

"Well, Colonel, it sounds like if you can keep a lid on this operation, it will come off without a hitch".

"I hope so, said the Colonel. "We, here in this room are the only people who know of these details. I can't imagine any leaks from here, this group" he added.

***

Mike Charles, turned to Bobby and Ismael, who were seated together, and said, "How about a ski on the lighted slopes?" Adding "They are great at night."

Bobby looked at his watch saying, "Not too late yet."

Ishmael said, "I brought my skis." This may be our last chance before leaving."

"Yeah, let's do it ", they all said in unison

They briefed Colonel Reeder who said ok, he'd be watching, mostly for Bobby and Michael's sake, at this point. There was the possibility of a retaliatory strike, still.

In the hall, they saw Mr. Dufay and invited him along.

"I'd love to, as soon as I call in. Want to listen in?"

They paused a second and said, "Yeah," eager for any new news developments.

Dufay punched the buttons.

His boss answered.

"Hello, Sir."

"Agent Dufay," the stern, authoritative tone of a small-minded martinet responded. "Where are you now?"

"In Geneva, sir. Skiing, sir." Dufay knew how to placate his boss.

"The subject is on the slopes right now, sir, In my sight, sir, just as you ordered, sir."

"Have you found the wife yet, sir? You say disappeared, sir?"

He spoke with a side glance towards the others.

"Fishy, sir, yes sir."

"Well, no indication here. Yes, he has made one call, so far, sir. I would assume to his family."

"Sir, I must go now, they are getting out of sight. I'll call tomorrow, sir." And he hung up.

"Well, there you are, gentlemen," Dufay said to Ishmael and Michael. "The fact that he cannot find her now makes him suspicious. S.O.P. will have him checking hotel rosters soon, if not already"

Ishmael said, "Used fake name. Paid cash."

Dufay said, "Good." They will ask for a description."

"They have instructions not to go outside," countered Ishmael.

"Ok, for now." Said Dufay

***

There was a mid-station not many steps away from the Chalet's back porch. They suited up and skied slowly towards it. Michael was just lifting his left ski, high to make a turn, when a shot rang out. It split his up lifted, ski in two. It also deflected the projectile away from any vital areas.

"Down!" They heard a voice from behind. It was Colonel Reeder's voice. "Stay down!" Came the voice again. Now Reeder passed by with a Mac 10 mini in his hand. He knew that this assault, most probably, came from much farther away than his mini was accurate and he couldn't just spray it on the slopes. Two others on the security team soon came by. One stopped and sheltered in the snow with them. The other went by following Reeder. They were in radio contact.

Well, Reeder thought, *the cat's out of the bag." Those bastards know we are all here now.*

His number two man had already reported, "No injuries, sir. If it weren't for the ski, sir, Michael would have taken a direct hit. They are out to kill, Sir."

Colonel Reeder back-tracked to their location, followed by the third agent. They were scanning trees with infra-red night glasses.

"Nothing, sir." No. 2 said.

"Let's get them back inside." Reeder said. "Phalanx," he ordered. It was a style of rescue to surround them.

Dr. Bern was up on one chalet porch.

"Is it all right, Colonel? Do ve need medical attention"?

"No, sir; we're good, heading back inside now, sir."

Dr. Bern ran quickly to the entrance way they would be using. Stevern ran with him. In addition to his other talents, he was a Crack EMT, and MEDIC.

The house was abuzz with all occupants in a mild panic somewhat consoled to hear that no one was injured. Nevertheless, they had allowed themselves to be lulled into s sense of safety when there was still deadly danger.

Yes, they thought, *of course the Chalet would be watched. Does this mean they know we are all here? Well now, there's a 2+2!*

***

Mr. Dufay knew that he must report this development. He would consult with Colonel Reeder, as to what to report.

Reeder said, "We don't know who it was yet! My men are re-coning the wooded area for any clues. They have infra-red night vision glasses."

"Yes sir, but will it be reported?" Dufay said. "If so, I must relate it or I will be compromised for the 'bank operation'.

"OK, I see what you mean, Dufay," Reeder said as it began to sink in. *The double agency and its complications.*

Reeder said, :They don't know what Ishmael looks like. They aimed for Michael. They may be a unit from a month ago, still hanging around."

"Sometimes we contract to Hezbollah for our needs. They never give up," said Dufay.

"Yeah, I am familiar," said Reeder

"I have to create a story for how I got here. Not on the chopper. How long a drive is it and, this chalet? Is it well known?"

"Yeah, it is pretty much a show place. The drive is not far."

"Ok, sir. I will need the name of a motel close by. I'll check in. I'll maintain that I did not personally hear any shot over the over the loud whoosh of the snow making equipment. I was having dinner in the hotel dining room. I just don't know anything about it."

"They know Ishmael is here. Let them speculate who else might be here."

"I did not have time when I was assigned to the case to review the file. They know that. Very short notice. I would not know what Michael and Buruse (Bobby) looked like."

"Sounds like a plan, Dufay. Better than admitting who is actually here. Their agent's may know through their telescopic sight but you wouldn't." said Reeder.

"The fact that they targeted Mr. Charles further indicates that they may be an old team." Said Dufay.

"Yeah, since it was a miss, they might not even report it," Reeder said.

"Truc" Dufay agreed. "I will play it by ear until they mention it. Glad we had this little talk."

"I know the locals. Let me get you checked in with a back date of yesterday. Hop on my snowmobile. We'll go down there now." Reeder urged.

Dufay straddled the machine and off they went.

Man, this Reeder sure knew his way around a snow-mobile, Dufay thought as they speed through several maneuvers downhill! He thought he was certainly going to fly off his seat. When came to the rear entrance of the motel, Reeder seemed to know the man at the rear door.

"My guest, Renee. Treat him special," he said.

"Got it!" Renée fist-bumped him.

"Is your phone secure"? Reeder asked

"Yes."

"OK, call me when you get settled and make your calls. I will send for you or come myself." Reeder said.

Dufay gave a finger salute as confirmation.

Dufay was nervous. He wanted to cover all the bases. He knew the scrutiny of his boss. His paranoid boss. No gaps or unanswered questions. He needed to think.

***

Colonel Reeder sped off back up the mountain. He was thinking, *What if there was a Hezbollah unit tasked in here?* He knew that the Iranians often used Hezbollah as an enforcement arm. They would not stop. He came to a stop to call back up to the Chalet. Hello, Carter? You and Buell turn on the perimeter grid. Now.

"Already did, sir," came Carter's reply

"Good. Look for my snowmobile lights. I am coming your way now. ETA, five minutes so you can let me through."

"Roger that, sir!" Carter said.

"Listen, we may have a Hezbollah cell tasked to us. You know what that means."

"Yes, sir," said Carter.

"Vigilant on the parameter. Be ready for anything"

"Yes, sir."

"I'll be there in 200 clicks." said Reeder

"Be careful, sir."

'Roger that."

Carter went to the perimeter observation/surveillance room on the first floor. There were cameras, radar, sound devices and defense ordinance triggers. Gas powered perimeter search lights could also be illuminated, if necessary.

He saw the Colonel approach and threw the pass-thru toggle as he came through the unseen barrier. In a few moments, he was inside the chalet. "Ok, guys, full alert."

"Let's have those search lights on the perimeter."

He went to Dr. Bern.

"We should evacuate first thing in the morning. Back to the airport. Can you call in the Hilo, sir?"

"Vill do, Cornel," came his reply.

Reeder added, "We may have a Hezbollah unit stalking us still, from our first run."

"Carter, Up in the parapet observation cupola. Take the .50 Cal mount stand and ordinance from the basement storage room. Follow the search light scan." Reeder said

"Yes sir," replied Carter

Dr. Bern, nearby, nodded approval. Then he called the local police station.

"Yes, Dr. Bern, how can we help you?" It was the Chief. Dr. Bern had long been a generous contributor to their causes in the community.

"Oh, nothing really, but tell me, have you seen any unusual characters, lately? Like vith turban headdress or unusual clothing?"

"No," the chief answered. "What's up? Dr.Bern?"

"Vie sustained a sniper shot tonight." He added quickly, "No one hurt. It happened to hit an uplifted ski or there would have been.

"I have a business problem, Chief, and they may be Middle Eastern in dress. If you vould just be aware of a presence like that. Ve are vell protected here. You know Colonel Reeder and his team.

"Oh yeah, we saw de search lights from your Chalet, Dr. Bern. Vie vill keep a sharp lookout for such characters. This is a small village. They vould have to eat. I vill check out the motel, sir.

"Oh, good, Ghief. Thank you for your assistance. Ve vill be leaving in the morning for Geneva on the Hilo"

"Ve can see you off, sir. That is a big target."

"Oh yes, thank you. I had not considered that. About seven AM. The Hilo pad behind my Chalet. I vill appreciate your presence, sir," Dr. Bern said.

The security team stood guard at their posts the rest of the night. It was uneventful.

Looks like this proxy team was scared off, for now, thought Colonel Reeder.

Dr. Bern walked in. "I've been thinking, Colonel, I don't know vhat your other obligations are, but could you keep two of your men posted here in my house until all of this is over. There is only Stevern here full-time?"

"Yes sir, consider it done," replied the Colonel."I don't like the idea that the Iranians have reached out to these mercenaries, though. I am sure we have not heard the last from them. These are bad actors, Sir.' He said to Dr. Bern.

"How can I help you Colonel?" asked Dr. Bern

"Colonel Reeder scratched his head.

"Wait a minute!" it came to him. "Yes sir. Can your bank arrange for a Brinks International vault truck in Tehran? I will need one on the day after tomorrow for Ishmael's pick up for authenticity with Mr. Dufay's ruse. Then in through a warehouse. We will get out and leave the truck for retrieval by Brinks later when we give them its location. We will leave in a minivan."

He thought of Kruger. He was pacing and thinking as he went along. "From another door across the warehouse floor and onto the very large warehouse where the flatbed and RV are loaded. We will have already loaded Ishmael's family early in the morning. You have the bank connections to arrange for the Brinks."

"Ya, I can do this easily, Colonel," said Dr. Bern. "I can do this vithin an hour."

"I am leaving Buell and Carter here with the house. I will need another flight, commercial, into Tehran, soon after Ishmael's. Not the same one."

Dr. Bern excused himself to make the arrangements. "Call our travel people to make the flight arrangements. Tell them I said Top Priority", instructed Dr. Bern as he was leaving the room.

"Right away, Sir. Colonel Reeder replied.

He punched in the banks Travel Agency number.

"Hello, I have a top priority flight request directly from Dr. Bern for a non-stop from Geneva to Tehran for tomorrow afternoon."

"Yes sir, wait a minute. Ok, sir, I have one with 2 seats Departing at 1:00 PM."

"Just one seat, mame, book it please."

"Ok, one seat on Flight No. 2119 at 1:00 PM.

"Thanks"

Dr. Bern called Brinks. His bank was a big client of theirs.

"Yes, we can do that for you, Dr. Bern. We are under contract with your bank anyway."

***

The Colonel went into a deep meditation. Had he crossed the "T"'s, dotted the "I's? He went over the scenes as he imagined them unfolding. Step by step. Where were they vulnerable?

***

It was a restless night for everyone in the Chalet.

They all gathered, trickling in one by one to the coffee service anti- room at about 5:30 AM. Bobby, Ishmael, Colonel Reeder, Dufay and Dr. Bern. There was some nervous small talk.

A hard knock at the back door. The French doors. The security monitor showed the police chief standing erect.

"Ah, the chief," said Dr. Bern. No one else knew him. Dr. Bern moved to the door and pressed the un-lock and open motor lock.

"Velcome, chief!" said Dr. Bern, offering his hand.

"I have 20 men outside to secure your Hilo departure. Whenever you are ready, Dr. Bern"

"Gut, Chief, and thank you"

He turned to the rest, waiting.

"Men, ve can vait in Geneva, the Hilo lounge, until your departure. Please be ready to leave as soon as possible. Stevern vill have muffins for you to go."

Reeder was on the radio. "Carter, Buell,"

"Sir!"

"Sir!"

"Stay here at the Chalet. Watch our departure and stay until I call. At least a few days. We will return here."

"Roger that, sir", came simultaneous replies.

Dr. Bern walked to the doors and gave the Hilo pilot a wind-up sign with his finger. The rotors began to rotate, front and rear.

Colonel Reeder said, "Look sharp in the parapet, men, a shot to the rotor will bring it down," he said on the radio. And then it happened!

Chapter Six

Upping the ante

A shot rang out from the edge of the cleared area to the left. It pinged the rotor and deflected to the tail of the aircraft. Not only was this a dumb move as the Hilo had not taken off yet, but because it was still dark out, the muzzle flash could be seen from high up in the parapet. The police had taken cover. Carter laid down a hundred rounds with the .50 caliber in the direction of the muzzle flash. Nothing could survive that. Now the police were on the run to the area. There were two men in turbans. Hezbollah signature turbans. They were very dead. Hamburger rare, in fact. The mountain woke up! The .50 was very loud in the early morning, or anytime! This sounded like a war zone.

The pilot immediately shut down the chopper so he could determine the damage inflicted. The police disappeared into the woods, guns drawn. Were there more assailants out there? Who were they trying to kill?

Dufay knew he would have to call in now.

Dr. Bern was beside himself. He immediately assumed his old military posture of years past. He went out and bade the pilot to come inside the Chalet. The pilot, who felt like a sitting duck now, didn't need any more encouragement. He sprinted inside, flanked by two officers, assault rifles drawn. Dr. Bern met him at the door, pulling him inside.

"Straight back to the kitchen. You vile find coffee and some light food, Captain," Dr. Bern said. He was getting mad now. Suddenly, he had an idea. He placed a call to his crack secretary/accounts manager and personal assistant. Would she be in yet? It was 6:45 AM by now. The phone went to recorder. He quickly went to the directory in his cell phone and pulled up her cell phone.

"Hello, Helga? Ah!" This is Dr. Bern. I know it's early. Are you near the office yet?"

"Hello, Doctor, not quite there yet but close."

"Please call me on my private line when you get in."

"Yes sir, I will." She knew it was urgent. Dr. Bern would not be calling at this hour. She stepped on the gas.

Twenty minutes later the call came to his cell.

"Yes, Helga, do you have access to the accounts computer?"

"Yes sir."

"Gut. I need for you to check, don't vie have a major account from that group which we believe to be Hezbollah? It is a large one."

'Let me check, let's see, accounts over 100 million, scanning, sir," she was mumbling, "here it is! Yes I see it here."

"Gut, I need the number of our contact. The account manager, right away, please."

"Looks like that would a Majir Hershel, account manager."

"Ok, an account number and a phone contact." He took the numbers down.

"Thank you, Helga." He hung up

He made the call,

Reeder walked in.

"Hello, I need to speak with a Major Hershel, please," he said. "This is Dr. Bern. President and CEO of the Swiss National Bank." He said with authority. There was a momentary pause.

"Yes sir, please hold, sir.

Dr. Bern looked over at Colonel Reeder. "Vhat is the time zone in Palestine, vhat time is it now?"

Colonel Reeder consulted his world watch. "An hour earlier, sir, I think." Said Reeder.

A male voice soon came on the line. "This is Major Hershel. How may I help you and who am I speaking to, please?"

"This is Dr. Wilhelm Bern. I am the president and C.E.O. of the Swiss National Bank. And, formally, Majoer General Retired of the Swiss national army. I believe you use our bank as your depository, Sir. Something a little over 300 million, sir."

"Yes, I am in charge of that account, Sir," he hesitated.

"Ok, sir. I am sure this does not concern you personally but my house, my multimillion dollar Chalet is now under attack from one of your terrorist teams. They have attempted to shoot down my personal Hilo this morning. They are now dead, sir. We believe this to be a proxy unit of Iran. They are trying to enforce a civil matter. I need for you to contact whoever is charge or knowledgeable about this before I find some reason to freeze your account, sir!"

Reeder was laughing at Dr. Bern's savvy response to the problem. He was nodding his head.

The line went silent. Then, "Oh, ah, are you sure, sir?"

"I have two dead bodies in your uniforms in my driveway. You may verify this through Chief of police Gerhardt Schelling in the ski village of Bask, Switzerland. He has over 20 officers surrounding my house right now. I am trying to keep this from hitting the news and becoming an international incident.

"Please have whoever is responsible for this deployment call me ASAP, Sir." The military training and respect for the Rank of General took over.

"Yes Sir, right away, Sir!" Came the "snap-to" reply

"Here is my private number," and he gave it to the major.

He looked at Colonel Reeder and said, "Let's see if that stirs up the pot a little."

"Good call, Sir," Reeder said.

**

Ishmael and Dufay stood packed and ready to board the Hilo. They would have to make their flight in Geneva to Iran. Dufay motioned to Ishmael and Reeder to follow him back to the anti-room.

"Gentleman, I will have to call this in or it will blow my cover and place the retrieval at the bank in jeopardy. I want you to hear my call"

He punched the buttons. "Yes sir, Dufay here." Sir, I have heard a heavy caliber machine gun fire coming from the Chalet where my charge is. I am in the motel down the mountain and there seems to be a large police presence scurrying around, sir. We are scheduled to return to Tehran this morning, sir. Do you know anything about that, sir?"

"No, Dufay. We had a team pursuing the last group, last month but not now."

"Yes sir, this will surely alert my charge of danger. This is not good, sir."

"Damn renegade group! That's the problem with hiring these mercenaries'. They don't know when to withdraw."

"Yes sir, so far this has just been a ski holiday from what I've seen, sir. Have you located the family yet?"

"No, not yet.".

Ismael was visibly relieved.

"I hope this doesn't cause our subject to alter his flight plans, Sir"

"OK, Dufay, stay with him." Irritated with this development. He hung up.

"I think we are clear now. It's the only explanation that makes sense." Colonel Reeder said. "They are a holdover. They want something to get paid for."

***

Finally, the call came through.

"Hello, this is captain kick ass, Hezbollah for sale!" Dr. Bern said.

"Is this Dr. Bern, major general Ret.? Of the Swiss national forces?"

"More to the point, sir, the CEO of your bank" said Dr. Bern. "Where should I send the two sacks of hamburger I have on my lawn?"

"I do not know what you are talking about!" said Captain Kick Ass.

"Of course not, Capt. And when you find out and call off the unit, I vile un-freeze the 300 million your organization has on deposit here! I'll give you a clue. You are a proxy for Iran officials in a civil matter. This is over a month old. They have no claim on the assets held in my bank. Sir, he went on, you are about to meet some of your superiors and they will be kicking your ass, Captain. Am I clear, Captain? I'll let you go now, sir. You have a lot to do. You may confirm this action to me through Major Hershel, your account manager, sir," and Dr. Bern hung up.

"I think I have them by the balls! He chuckled. I don't believe vie vill have any more trouble. He looked around at the entire group, all of whom were listening.

***

The Hilo pilot had carefully checked for damage to the Hilo. There was a small hole in the fuselage of the tail extension. No real problem affecting the aerodynamics of the craft, but there was a small chip to the edge of one rotor blade mounted on the tail. He looked at it closely. Feeling with his fingers, he didn't judge it to be significant enough to shut down the flight back to Geneva, where he could find a replacement.

"Gentleman, we are a go," he announced. In a few minutes all were on the move. They all went and boarded the chopper with an escort of Reeder and the local police, just in case. There were no additional incidents. The engines began to whine. The rotors were engaged when the proper rpm was reached. After a suitable warm –up, manifold pressure was reached, they began a slow lift off. They turned slowly using the rear rotor. No problem. They came to a heading and departed over the town, waiving to the police gathered below.

Once on their way, the pilot made a call to Vector Aerospace in search of a new rear rotor blade. He could sense a slight vibration caused by the imbalance of the rotor, no doubt.

It was his duty to keep the Bank's Hilo in top condition.

***

The rest of the flight was uneventful. The helicopter hovered over the top floor of the Bank and set down on the Hilo pad on the roof. Dr. Bern led the way inside. The hallway ended at the door to his office suite, on the top floor. The nerve center of the bank. *This is where Real Power radiates from,* Ishmael thought.

Dufay was also suitably impressed.

Reeder called to him.

"Yes?" Colonel Dufay said.

"Where can I get a standard issue police uniform to back you up? Is there a store or an issuing facility?"

Dufay thought for a minute. "Write down your measurements, sir. Inseam, chest, waist is all we will need. I will requisition a new uniform. I will tell them I am sending someone to pick it up. After all these years, the tailor knows me and my voice. We are, roughly the same size. Of course, you are in much better shape. Tell him you are my valet. He will have it ready by the time you arrive."

"Good thinking, sir. Dr. Bern has arranged for a Brinks truck to enhance the ruse we are perpetrating. We will need a garage or warehouse where we can switch vehicles and all travel to the second warehouse where the flatbed is located. A quick switch. I am renting a small minivan to pick them up and make the transfer. It's your city. Know of any place fairly close to the bank and the larger, second warehouse?

"Ah, let me think," Dufay said. He held his head to shut out all other stimuli. He mentally scanned the applicable geography, street by street, from the bank to a route for possible dumping and transfer. *Where? Where?* he struggled. Then in a flash it hit him! "Wait, there is an old large abandoned steel fabrication factory on route, only several blocks away from where Ishmael told me the Sheik's trading business depot is located. It is open at both ends and deep. The Brinks will not look out of place there for a short while. That's the place," he reaffirmed to Reeder.

"Sounds good. I will have Ishmael's family waiting for us."

He called another member of his team. Really just 20 floors down to the lobby.

"Yeah, Kruger, you're going with me to Iran this afternoon. We have a mission."

"Yes sir," said Kruger.

"Come to the top floor offices now."

Roger, sir"

He called the travel office."Up that reservation to two for my flight this afternoon, right away, Jenifer," he said. "Confirm it back to me."

He called the Lear pilot and said, "This is Reeder, make ready for a flight to Kuwait. There is a corporate airfield belonging to Sheik Hamoud. See if you can find it on your charts. It's his company's headquarters. They are in import/ export. Here is his number."

" Will do sir."

"Let me know if you can't find it. Wait on the tarmac. You may spot an A-10 Warthog, he bought at surplus."

"Really," said the pilot. "I have a lot of time in one of those. Another lifetime, sir," he said

Reeder walked in and said, "Gentleman, time to go to the airport. I'll will be on the next flight with another of my agents. We will locate your wife and children, some uniforms and rent a large van. We will be in phone contact. Secure phones only, gentleman. If all goes well, your wife and children will see you when we dump the Brinks. One of my very best men will bring them. I will be on the Brinks with Ismael and Dufay. You will get into the van without noise, when I direct. Lay down on the seats. The drive will only last a few blocks, and then you will be able to cut loose a little. We will all board the camper/trailers on the flatbed and they will wrap the camper/trailer in Visqueen for the trip. Even so, try to stay away from the windows until we are well into the desert." Any questions?"

"I think we have it, Colonel. Good luck, sir." Ishmael said.

"Good, be alert at all times, watch for anything unusual. We must be swift and certain with the ruse at the bank. Can't have any outgoing calls to the wrong people. I'd cut their phone lines but there may be a reverse alarm or Wi/Fi for that. It is a bank. We should be rolling out of town and into the desert before any word leaks out." They shook hands all around saying, "Good Luck"

They went back to the main room in the office.

Dr. Bern was there. "Men, you are in good hands." as he nodded toward. Colonel Reeder. "I think I have the bad guys in check now. Not the Iranians, the Hezbollah mercenaries, I mean. Ve vill see you safely back here by late tomorrow. The Lear vill be vaiting in Kuwait, on the runway, ready to go! No danger once you get there."

They could hear the wine of the Hilo engines, winding up outside. They each looked at the other. There were fist-bumps and they walked outside and went, heads down, quickly to the Hilo. They got in and belted up. Lift off was normal and they were away to the airport.

***

They were just away from the pad when Dr. Bern's phone rang. "Hello"

"This is General Jackal, with the former P.L.O., now the Free Fighters of Hezbollah." He said with pride and authority. "It is quite dangerous, what you are doing, sir!"

"I too am a General, sir. And I can assure you it is quite illegal and against International Law. It violates all turpitude clauses in your banking agreement. Enough for me to freeze your dirty funds. Do you understand me, you coward? All I vaunt to hear from you is "All dogs are called off! My house is very well armed sir. I am returning your hamburger to you, Rare! Now do I call the Palestinian Consulate, and plead your money into an international court as trustee. You von't see it for years, maybe never. I am sure they vill re-deposit with my bank, only now I vill get the interest. Don't rattle your sabers at me. You vere still in messy diapers when I was on the front lines! Your superiors vill certainly kill you before sundown, today if I have to go to the consulate and an international court, sir, with my evidence of your transgressions in my country. Do you understand me, you, you…", he was spiting mad now. "Little Punk!" He was shouting. There was personal rage now! Their transgressions were personal. He had been forced to kill two men on his own property.

Helga jumped and ran for a glass of water, for Dr. Bern, quickly. She had never seen Dr. Bern like this before. He was always so gentle. She saw a glimpse into his, former warrior side. Others were coming into the room now because of the unusual commotion. Helga waved them off immediately and closed all the doors!

Dr. Bern, more composed now, nodded a thank you to her.

"I see your point, Dr. Bern, or.. ah.. General. Jackal was somewhat flustered now. "I will see to it immediately, Sir. One general to another. You can count on it, Sir. There will be no more interference from our group. We renounce that contract Sir. I will inform them this very hour, Sir.

"I vill take you at your vord, Sir. I vill take no further action. Your funds are hereby, released, He gestured to Helga. She knew what he meant.

"Vie have avoided much trouble here today, General," Dr. Bern said.

"Yes sir," came the reply.

Dr. Bern hung up. He went to his office and poured a Brandy. Very old and rare brandy at that. He sat and thought. He had surprised himself for a few minutes. He had not been that angry since the tragic but accidental death of his wife of 47 years, 12 years ago. That memory brought moisture to his eyes.

**

The Hilo was approaching the landing pad at the Airport. They set down and when the engines were winding down to idle, they disembarked. They had time yet. They made their way to a private waiting room, Red Door Club, as before. Not many people inside this early. Good; no one had followed them in. They all relaxed with a Bloody Mary. Colonel Reeder and his assistant, Kruger, had a much longer wait before his flight to Tehran took off. He would hook up with them at the airport hotel. The only change in plan discussed was that Agent Dufay would take this time to retrieve a new uniform. He had one dress uniform, very official looking and one ordinary officer issue for Colonel Reeder. He would have them cleaned and pressed sharply for their re-use in the morning

Colonel Reeder would have to hit the ground running to secure the Brinks truck early the next morning.

Chapter Seven

Back into Tehran. Risky business

It was time for Ishmael and Agent Dufay to board their flight. They turned and faced Colonel Reeder and recounted their individual scenarios as a kind of check-off of their duties. It eased the nervousness each man was feeling. Their lives and the lives of Ishmael's family could be at stake.

These were heady plans. They were anxious to get into action. The wait was difficult.

***

On Colonel Reeder's advice, Sheik Hamoud took delivery of the surplus A-10 Warthog. It sat in the staging area of his airfield. "I don't know if my nephew will come to work here yet. I have no one to fly it." The Sheik had offered.

"Buy it anyway," Reeder said.

There were plenty of pilots who flew that plane in Desert Shield and Desert Storm still around. It was an excellent platform to protect his import business over the desert wilderness. Thieves could act quickly and be gone. You could call it in over the radio but you needed a quick way to respond to a GPS location, with armaments. The A-10 Nose cannon was formidable. It could truly decimate an attacker. Arriving in minutes.

"Be sure and get plenty of ammunition cheap, while you can. Spare parts. Make it part of the deal. The U.S. Government will comply."

"OK, Colonel Reeder. You make sense. I will do it."

"You won't be sorry, Sheik," Reeder said. "That is a serious piece of equipment. Especially known in these parts, because of those wars, I mentioned. An opposing force will high-tail it away, just seeing it coming."

"Yes, OK, I see." Sheik Hamoud said, now convinced. He felt good now that he had placed the order.

***

They were seated now and the plane was being towed out of its gate. The engines were winding up. They began to taxi. Soon, they were facing down the runway and began a take-off roll. Minutes later they were airborne and making a low-level left, two minutes turn to a new heading. They began a climb out. Ishmael thought, *We are on our way now.* He was really missing the family. He was so looking forward to embracing them again. He would take them all to Disney World, for a respite, after this ordeal. *Private schools for the children,* he allowed his imagination to plot, create, and wander. *A new life for all of us.* He felt a rush of energy as the excitement cresendoed. His exposure to Dr. Bern's lifestyle and discussions with Bobby had projected him into a new world of adventure at near light speed, it seemed. By contrast, he was weary of the drudgery of his duties as a physicist for the Regime. Yes, they treated him and his colleagues well but he very much disagreed with their philosophy as to the best use of this advanced technology for the benefit of the people. His uncle Reza was always concerned for the people and their welfare. Their path was likely to lead to annihilation.

Power deluded and crazy men were directing the policy and future outcomes of ancient Persia. His extended family had been in control for hundreds of years. These men today had no real conception of the awesome power of splitting an atom, of what they were threatening to release. Would a wise person give a two-year-old a hand grenade? Their stated opponent has many times over their capacity to attack or retaliate with these weapons. So ridiculous and suicidal. No, his family would not endure it any longer. *This is the Abomination which causes desolation!* Then it hit him. *They are going to reduce the old 'Big Boy' down enough to place on the Temple Mount.* He was thinking of scripture. They're going to place it in the Dome of the Rock. They had access there. With a live feed video, they would be able to extort and coerce any result from the Israeli Government without firing a shot or actually triggering the device. In any thirty second period of time they could face annihilation, without ANY retaliation. Oh, this was making for a plausible scenario. *Is this what they are planning?* He speculated. *Yeah, The Dome, the other side would not think it would be placed there. It is not our most sacred place. The Hag*...His stomach flipped. That had to be it! Oh yeah, Switzerland or the U.S. would be for his family. And, plenty rich to boot. He knew much about the centrifuges. Where they were. What there spin capacity was. He could offer much counter intelligence. He would be very valuable. *Another Werner Von Braun of a former day,* he thought.

Then his mind jumped to the origination of that scripture "And when you see the abomination which causes desolation, .etc." Christ was describing to his Apostles, answering their question of when 'These Things' would happen – The end times! Yes there were many other strange occurrences these days. He, presumably, will come back here and intervene first. *Do they know of these things*, he wondered.

He remembered reading something about these same motives in a news article about his cousin's account of his odyssey retrieving his inheritance. He had scanned it and now it reinforced his theory.

"Sir, would you like a beverage?" It was the flight attendant. "You look a little pale, sir, are you all right?"

"Ah! Yes, and yes," he said, "a scotch." as he flashed out of his musings.

He was not an overly religious man but his Alma matter, Oxford was first a divinity school. Certain studies were mandatory. He had gained a rudimentary understanding of scripture to pass the course.

It kept coming back in his head, like there was a voice saying, the abomination.... His training in physics had certainly taught him that there was perfect order, balance and symmetry in the structure of the atom. Even sub atomic building blocks of matter. Not visible to the naked eye, there were a lot of things going on inside this sphere of motion. Of course, he had asked himself many times, by what chance did these multiple parts come together. His conclusion; there was no random chance. There was intelligence behind the order of things. *We just didn't understand it yet.*

We have such egos! Believing that we should be able to understand it!

He was reminded of God's statement to Job when he said "Where were you when I laid the foundations of the world? [Little man]

Then it was as clear as if it were being shouted in his head. 'That's the abomination!' The intentional destruction of this order and symmetry contained inside this atom. Not only did it release phenomenal power, which could not really be controlled, but it was an abomination in that it destroyed the Truth and Beauty and the perfect balance of His creation. All those particles which together, in balance, were the handiwork of which; the elements which we and our world, matter, were constructed of. We did not fully understand all of it but we were about to destroy it. Destroy His creation. We have a hunch that all things are energy vibrating at different frequencies. Matter is formed when the energy frequency vibration is reduced (partially, under the pressure of gravity) nevertheless the properties are intricate. Even now, we see through our radio telescopes, located high in the Andes at over 14,000 feet show galaxy's being formed with Suns, and planets revolving around a center. There are simple sugars detected with other chemicals.

Oh, the audacity of men! Like a child with a lighted match in a room full of dynamite which he does not know is there.

Whew! He took a large swallow of his scotch. These very things may be unfolding. So lucid, this picture!

If these prophetic scriptures were presented today in a digitally enhanced, melodramatic style, with command voicing, as a new discoveries found in a cave in Qumran, we might embrace these details as instructive. As it is; however, they are considered to be arcane and old religious, sometimes superstitious writings found in the sacred books, comprising the Bible. We are Jaded, Jaded! He thought.

The panoply of time, viewed from outside time, a faster vibration, would see all of this as present. I can't say – in advance, because that would involve time. Now it could be revealed, in "Time" to the subjects embroiled in this slower vibration of matter, energy and density we call time. But this was seen as though it were the end of a movie. A reality.

Einstein had theorized that one permutation of the speed of light squared was that time stood still. Length became width in a different reality.

What's in this scotch, he thought, cruising along at 38,000 feet above Europe.

He thought of the song from the 70's 'I can see clearly now, the rain is gone....' He chuckled out loud at his musings. A voice came back "Watch that now." He took another swallow of his scotch.

There is an interconnectedness. After all, we believe that Mohammad spoke to us. He spoke of peace. 'Kill the infidel, if he does not repent' language was modified to kill the infidel, period and came later from another and evil-minded source. Of course, the outworking of that instruction is kayos and acts which condemn the individual conscience. No critical thinking individual would call a Christian, a son of Abraham, a keeper of the commandments, a follower who pays homage to the Father of all (However you refer to Him) and who loves and respects his fellow man, an Infidel. The infidel is without belief.

Magic flights to Mecca, vestal virgins, Islam is already corrupted, by these petty minds who must/needs want, would need, to interpret this folklore phenomena on their own terms. Perception is 9/10's of possession.

Such nonsense! He concluded. Islam stands on its own as a great world religion, without these murderous overtones. The promise of 'Making you a Great Nation' was given to Abram and each son alike. Once again as with Eve and her attempt to upstage God' plan, now Sari had to put her mixing spoon into the broth. Change, modify the plan. I have another idea. Hey, Hagar come over here a minute! No, God would not set these two sons against each other. Each had a promise. His only regret.... "I knew I should have used two of Adam's ribs. These females keep trying to take over my deal!" Ishmael laughed at himself.

He decided he must rest. He wanted to be fresh for his family.

He turned to Dufay and asked him if he had called in recently, thinking that there is a need to keep their curiosity satisfied.

Dufay agreed and said, "Yes, I will make the call. I need to tell them that I have transportation at the airport and that after a long trip I need a day to recuperate. Also, I will tell them that I overheard you talking with your wife and you said, 'I'll see you tomorrow at the house'. They will think you are returning to your home. We can employ a little misdirection and be gone before they check on your presence again."

"Sounds good to me, you know them and how they think." Ishmael said.

"Yeah and remember, It's my ass too. I would never see the light of day, or worse, if they found me out." Said Dufay

"I hear that. I think things are going to work out fine, if we are careful." Said Ishmael.

The call in was made. "No changes," said Dufay. "The boss is looking for you all to be back at your house. I can stall him with nonsense excuses for time enough to get going well out into the desert on our way to Kuwait."

"Ya know, we ought to check and make sure we can get rooms at the airport hotel tonight," Ishmael said, wondering why he hadn't thought of that until now.

"You're right, but maybe I'll have a little pull. The Regime uses their facility often. I'll call and reserve two rooms. I even have the number."

Cell phone usage was allowed at their current altitude so Dufay punched in the number.

"This is Agent Dufay with the national security force. I am flying in now and I need two rooms for tonight. One night only. Any rooms will do.

"Just a minute, sir." Back on the line after a few minutes, "I have two but they are not located where all you agents usually stay. They are back in the South wing. Agency rooms are all booked for the symposium."

"Oh, yes, I completely forgot. Been out of town. He cringed, the place will be crawling with fellow agents. *Damn.*

Ok, I'll take the two in the south wing. I will pay privately. Yes, Isaac Al Shankar"

He got off and said to Ishmael, "Oh, man! I forgot all about that symposium. Things have been happening so fast. We are in the back and will have to keep a low profile. We will leave very early in the morning. Do you think its safe, Ishmael?" Then he added, "I wonder why the chief didn't mention the symposium to me?" *Maybe because I was talking about a rest day,* he wondered to himself.

"Ishmael replied, "Sounds a little dicey, but then again it falls into the realm of normal behavior. We will lay low. Avoid the lounge! At all costs. "We will need a good night's sleep anyway. Tomorrow is a big, big day."

"Roger that," Dufay confirmed.

***

Colonel Reeder and Kruger arrived much later and was in the hotel. He called Ishmael and made his presence known. He knew Dufay had his own agenda with the uniforms. He asked Ishmael to wait in the hotel for his call. He had to rendezvous with the Brinks people. A little later his man Kruger would pick up the family at the Holiday inn. He asked Ishmael to make his wife aware. He described Kruger and his clothing.

"She is to be ready with the children and to move quickly through the hotel to a rear entrance, where he will have a windowless van waiting. Get in quietly. There are places to lie down. Two mattresses. You will see them later."

"Okay, Sir," Ishmael said. "I will make the call. About what time will he arrive?"

"Tell them to be fed and ready by 9:30 AM. He will arrive after that. I will call you when he has them. Kruger is well trained in counter surveillance. Do not worry."

"Yes sir. No, I won't, I have every confidence in your man, Sir"

***

Dufay was going for ice at the machine one floor down. They were placed on every other floor. He was in the elevator, holding his bucket from the room. When the doors opened he was startled. There was his boss waiting to get in. With his normal confident stride he steeped in, not waiting for Dufay to get out.

Such a pig, Dufay thought. Naturally, he was accompanied by a sycophant, a yes man, ass kisser! "Ah! Dufay. You are back for the symposium tonight. Meet Agent Bly, my assistant"

They exchanged a handshake.

"Well, not really, Sir. I am still on the job, sir. The subject has returned from his ski trip and is staying overnight here, sir. I am watching closely. From overheard conversations, sir, he is planning a rendezvous with his family and then going home. I will call in as things progress, sir." Said Dufay

"I will be curious as to where he picks up his family. It belongs in his file.'

"Yes sir," said Dufay. "Not out of my sight, sir". Dufay re-confirmed. Everything seems quite normal, sir", as the doors opened for his destination floor. "Up or down sir, which floor for you?" he offered to push the button. "2" Said his boss. And Dufay departed, turning towards the ice machine with his bucket in hand. *Oh, crap*, he thought!

After the doors closed, Commandant. Azaria turned to his "puppet" agent and said. "Keep an eye on Dufay, I just sense something is awry."

"Yes sir, as you wish, Sir. I will go to the front desk and check which room he is in, sir," as he looked for approval from his boss.

"Good, Agent Bly. Also find out what room Pahlavi is in, if you can. Report back to me only."

"Yes sir, I understand," Bly replied, thrilled to be reporting directly to the Boss.

"Is there a Colonel Reeder checked in yet?" Dufay said to the motel operator.

"Yes sir, Room 119. I can put you through if you like.

"Please"

Reeder answered, "Hello."

"Colonel, this is Absalom Dufay."

"Yes Dufay", said the Colonel

"I wanted you to know that I ran into my boss, Commandant Azaria in the elevator. I was going for Ice. There is a symposium tonight at this airport Hotel convention center for my security office. I told him I was on the job and that everything seemed normal. Also, that according to my surveillance, an overhead phone call, Mr. Pahlavi was going to pick up his family and go home tomorrow.

"Yes, sounds disarming enough." Said Reeder.

"Yes sir, but he had an assistant with him, an agent Bly. He is a sycophant, a 'yes man'. The commandant is not above playing his agents against each other. Actually, he loves to. Please watch out for a tail on me."

"Will do, thanks for the call. Where can we meet for the uniform exchange?"

"I am leaving early for the tailor shop. Oh, to double check, what is your shoulder and waste size? I will return here and give it to the bell boy for immediate delivery to your room. With all these agents staying here tonight, it will look normal."

"Roger that," I am a 42 in. shoulder and a 35 in. waist. Inseam a 30 in." said Reeder. "Let's time the Brinks for after that."

"Yes, sir I will meet you with Ishmael and proceed from there."

Reeder said, "I saw a large retail mega store on this main road, about ¼ mile back. We will rendezvous there when I call you."

"Yes sir, I know the store." Said Dufay.

Reeder: "Probably about 9:00 AM."

"Yes sir," Dufay confirmed. "Good night, sir.".

***

A restless night ended as the wake–up call came from the front desk. "Your wake–up call, a service of the Airport hotel," said the pre-recorded message. It was 5:45 AM. Dufay arose and moved to the in-room coffee maker. He chose the strongest-looking package, labeled, "Sure Shot Now". And started the brew. He went to take a four minute shower, like he had to do in Gym class in school.

The uniform tailor didn't open until 8:00 am. He wanted to be outside the store at that time. They had off the shelf uniforms in several sizes, pre-made. He expected to be able to find something in stock that would suit their needs, for Colonel Reeder.

Thinking to himself, as it brewed, *I'll walk through the hotel hallway to the auto rental desk in the lower floor of the airport where I will get a car. I'll stop for breakfast at Emeril's Café, which I like so much. It is just down the street from the uniform depot. I will wait for it to open.*

He was counting on it being early enough at this time that the party goers from last night's symposium would all still be asleep.

Oooh, that coffee smells good, he thought. He poured himself a Styrofoam cup full, eschewing the china provided. He would shower later. Right now he wanted to get out of the hotel as soon as he could.

***

Agent Bly had paid the front desk a visit the night before. He flashed his badge and said, "If agent Dufay has a wake-up call, call me at the same. We will be meeting."

"Of course, Agent Bly," said the desk clerk."

He was also up and alert. He knew Dufay could ID him so he would have to be very careful, at this hour. He left his room immediately. No coffee. No shower. He wanted to place himself in a tiny alcove, within hearing range of Agent Dufay's room. He would hear the door open, shut, and wait for him to walk away with his back to the hallway. He would follow at a great distance.

Bly listened carefully until he heard the telltale click and double click of Dufay's door. He waited fifteen seconds and moved from his safe place, with excuses ready.

He saw Dufay's back and shoulders rounding the curve in the hallway. *Good, this had worked out well,* he thought to himself. *The Commandant Azaria would be proud of me.*

Dufay went right through the hotel lobby and down the ingress corridor to the airport ground level where the auto rental offices were located.

***

Colonel Reeder, also on the job at 5: AM was tailing Dufay's tail, Bly. *Oh, what have we here?* he thought He decided to call Dufay on the secure phone.

Dufay was startled to hear his secure phone ring at this hour.

"Yes?" said Dufay.

"You have a tail, this morning," said Reeder.

"Damn!" said Dufay. "I was afraid of that."

"Go ahead and arrange for your rental but don't take the vehicle out right now. Go into the coffee shop. I will call you. Let me handle this."

"Roger that." said Dufay, and moved forward.

He arrived at the rental desk and presented his credentials. Since he stopped, Bly had to duck in by the water fountain. *Wow, an early start, for Dufay,* he thought.

Dufay finished his paperwork and began to walk toward the coffee shop. As he passed the water fountain he couldn't help himself. He said, "Morning, Bly," to the man huddled over the water fountain. "I get thirsty in the morning, myself, High sugar." And he kept going.

He heard a choking sound.

*   *   *

Ishmael decided to call his wife on the secure phone before he left the hotel.

He sat down and collected his thoughts.

"Hello, my dear," when Ruth answered

"Ishmael, where are you. What is happening? Our children are very rambunctious!" She complained.

"OK, my Ruth, soon we will on our way. I am leaving the hotel in Tehran this morning. We will have a busy day. Now, listen carefully. A man named Kruger, a member of our security team will come for you this morning. Please be ready early. He is very experienced in covert actions."

"I am listening, Ishmael," Ruth said

Ishmael continued, "He will take you out through a back door to a waiting minivan. Just leave the one you have. There are no windows and it may have a magnetic sign on the doors. There will be a place for the children to lie down. Perhaps a mattress, I think. Kruger is of average height with a shock of light-colored hair. He will be dressed casually. He will call you when he gets to your motel. Go quietly with him to the van. He will take you to a large warehouse. There will be a flatbed truck and a travel trailer mounted on it. You will be loaded into the travel trailer. I will meet you a little later, this morning, after stopping at the bank we will be on our way! Just a little longer. Maximum discipline on the children during the transition. No noise." He said with gravity

"Yes, Ishmael, I understand." Ruth acknowledged. I will wait for Mr. Kruger. I can't wait to see you."

"It won't be long now. Ruth, my dear. It will all be worth it, you'll see."

"Yes, I trust your judgment, Ishmael.". Replied the good Middle Eastern wife. "I will look forward to seeing you and the children have not stopped asking "When are we going to see Daddy?"

Ishmael smiled inwardly, "Soon, soon, Ruth."

***

Kruger was up with the telephone directory in one hand and a coffee in the other. He needed to find an auto rental with a closed minivan for rent. The hotel rental facility didn't have such vehicles.

Here is one, the ad described Vans.

"Hello, can you pick me up at the airport with a minivan. Here is my card information." He reeled it off.

"We have a red one and a white one, sir." The representative said.

"The white one, please," said Kruger."

"And when would you like it, sir?"

"A's soon as possible, this morning," Kruger replied.

"Ok, how about one-half hour? "

"Great." Kruger added, "I'll be looking for you outside the lobby door. I am dressed in Army fatigues."

"Yes sir, Mr. Kruger. One-half hourm sir."

"See you then," replied Kruger

***

Dufay called Reeder; "Dufay here. When can I leave?"

"OK," Reeder said. "I want you to show your badge to the man at the inner kitchen door. Once inside, ask him to show you the rear entrance. Go out that door and circle around outside to the front of the building. There is a door leading in from the parking lot into the auto rental desk. Go in and tell them you are ready to take your car. Get the key. I will be watching. Head for your uniform shop. Call me when you're ready to meet. I won't be far behind you."

"Yes sir, got it." Dufay said. He instinctively scanned the room, a three hundred and sixty degree, as he rose from his table. His eyes found the kitchen door. He did not see Bly anywhere. He walked straight through the kitchen door, waiting to be challenged. It was so early, there was no one in authority in the kitchen. Just a couple of prep cooks. They were working at a fast pace, preparing for the morning service. They barely looked up. Dufay simply raised his badge as he headed to the exit door on the far side of the room. He received a nod or two, but no-one challenged him. Soon, he was out the door. He walked around the peripheral sidewalk in the direction of the front parking lot. Ah! There was the auto rental office, just inside to his left. He paused. He searched, carefully. No Bly. He went inside to the desk. He shoved the paperwork across the desk to the attendant.

"I'll take my car now". The attendant inspected his receipt. "Oh, of course, sir," and handed him some keys. The attendant noted Dufay's name. This was the guy he had been paid to announce to the other man. The cop.

Dufay was not oblivious to this possibility and proceeded quickly to his car. He started up and drove out quickly. He would check for a tail. And then there was Colonel Reeder who had his back and after all, he was only going to the uniform store. This shouldn't raise any eyebrows.

The attendant immediately called Bly, who was waiting 60 feet away in the lobby. He stepped out the front door just in time to see a car leave the parking lot and then turn right. He was running to his car when a man with two suitcases bumped into him, knocking him down on the ground. The man fell on top. He was apologizing profusely for his awkwardness.

"It's OK sir," Bly was shouting. "You are pinning me down and I must go. I am a policeman.

"Oh, I am so sorry, sir. Let me help you up. I feel like such a bumbler, sir. He helped Bly up, but held on to his collar, while dusting off his coat.

He continued to apologize profusely.

Bly was complaining loudly, "I must go, I must go." Reeder held on, "Are you sure sir?" I could buy you a coffee," said Reeder.

"Very kind of you, sir, but I must go now," said Bly.

Reeder had accomplished his goal and let go of the collar, dusting off his back now as he went towards the car. Reeder noted the make and model and color of the vehicle, continuing to apologize for his clumsiness.

Dufay had gotten well down the road when his secure phone rang.

"Yes, Colonel"

"You have a tail, make turns. I delayed him as long as I could. It's that Bly guy. Light green sedan."

"Ok, thanks. I am just going to the uniform store. No problem, sir. I was expecting that possibility. Had to be the attendant at the rental desk. I'll keep my eye open, and thanks, sir. I will send the uniform to your room with the bell boy."

"Roger that," said Reeder

Dufay still needed to wait for the tailor shop to open. It was too early. He took a circuitous route using up time. He didn't see a light green sedan, anywhere.

At exactly 8:00 the lights inside the shop went on. He would have to act fast if he wanted to get back to Reeder's room with his uniform and get dressed himself in his own room. Then meet up with Reeder and the brinks truck, all without encountering Bly, who was certainly lurking around.

He entered the shop and told old Oscar what he needed, describing the new size for his 'assistant' and requisitioning a new dress uniform for himself. He had only to show his ID but old Oscar knew him well anyway.

"I am in a bit of a hurry, Oscar.

"I understand, Mr. Dufay. These are stock shelf items and sizes. It will only take a minute to get them together. I will go into the back to get these for you. Have a seat," he gestured to the two seats in front of the counter.

***

Reeder, up early, decided to go to the parking lot and find the light green sedan that Bly was driving earlier. And disable it. A small electronic device attached by magnet, under the car would provide enough power to interrupt starting for about two hours. Of course he could get another vehicle from the rental counter in fifteen minutes, but this would do for Reeder's purposes.

****

"Oh, thank you Oscar! So quick. Put it on my account with headquarters. I haven't used my quota yet. I really appreciate this service."

Oscar just kept nodding his head while saying "Yes Yes."

"Oh, keep this to yourself if any asks. OK?"

"Oh, yes sir" said Oscar.

He took the hangers and a box for shirts with him under his arm. Also a small box with the standard metal insignias and approached the door. He pushed it open with his foot. He quickly went to the rear car door and hung the uniforms, placing the boxes on the rear seat.

So far, so good, he thought.

Now back to the hotel.

Wait, I will park the car back at that kitchen door and walk around to the front where I will find a bell boy. This would allow them to leave the hotel and get to the Mega store parking lot and into the Brinks vehicle, hopefully, without being seen.

He slowly pulled down the side street. He parked about forty feet from the kitchen exit.

Holding the two hangers on his finger and the shirt boxes under his arm was no problem. He headed down the sidewalk and round the corner to the front entrance. He went in and encountered a bell boy. Handing him a shirt box and the smaller insignia box he walked to the lobby couch and parted with one uniform on one hanger. Slipping the man a ten dollar bill, he said, "These must go to room 119 immediately."

The bell man said, "Yes sir, right away."

Walking down the hallway towards the lobby, Bly witnessed all of this.

Walking directly to Dufay he said, "Up and out early, Agent Dufay."

Dufay chuckled demurely and said, "Had to pick up a uniform early. Been in this one for four days. Yuck""

Bly said, "That has happened to me too," trying to warm up to Dufay.

Dufay took a chance...."You know the Commandant used to use me like he is using you right now. Spying on other agents. I've been here a long time. I've got a pension. Where does he think I am going? He gets paranoid, you know. This activity doesn't inspire much confidence in a loyal employee. You really don't have to worry about me. I know my job.

Dufay was hoping to disarm Bly a little. It wouldn't hurt to take the edge off his surveillance.

Bly said, "Yes sir, I think I understand what you mean. No offense intended, sir."

"None taken." Dufay said. "And now, back to work." He walked away feeling better for the encounter, with Bly.

***

"Reeder here".

"Uniform on its way now." said Dufay

"Roger that," said Reeder. "Meet me in the cafeteria in ten minutes."

"Yes sir," said Dufay and he scrambled to get into his new, very official uniform.

***

Kruger was at the rear door by the hotel pool. He had already reconnoitered the room number and its proximity to that exit.

He parked the minivan as close as he could to the exit door. He had stopped on the way this morning in a 24-hour superstore and purchased four large bean bag chairs. Really just large nagulhide blobs, filled with beans. They couldn't just sit on the floor, after all. He also purchased a king-size comforter to spread over the four bags.

He stepped back inside the door—he had rigged the self-closing latch when he made his first exit—and proceeded a short distance up the hallway. He looked for the number stored on his phone and pressed it.

"Hello, this is Ruth," came the answer. "

"Kruger here, mame."

Ruth, "Yes, We have been expecting you."

"Yes, I am outside your door now. I have the vehicle placed outside and am ready to transport you," he said with his thick German accent.

"We are ready, too." She replied. Her heart accelerated at the prospect of soon meeting her husband after these three days of suspense and sequester. She could not contain herself. She opened her door and peeked down in the direction of the pool. Kruger tipped his outback hat at her. She and the children filed out very quietly. Kruger turned in a motion that said, 'Follow me' and he led the foursome to the pool door exit. Without a word, he proceeded to the side door and slid it back. They knew to get in. The children were excited to see the bean bags in an otherwise austere, grey metal interior. There were no side windows. There was a little pick and choose over which color was preferential, but Ruth put the kibosh on that with a shush! She went back and picked her own bean bag. She knew instinctively that the large comforter was to be spread over all of them.

Kruger started the van and got away from the motel as quickly as possible. He had rigged the GPS on his phone and now needed an address.

McDonald's!

Yes he had heard it. And then it occurred to him that these poor kids hadn't eaten anything. Ruth was shushing them. Kruger said, "No problem. I vill do that for you but lay low, please. No noise. I vill get four egg Mac Muffins for you and small milk. No noise, now."

There was a Mac Dee's just off to the right. They were downtown, after all. Up to the drive in window and ordered four MC Muffins and four small containers of milk. No, no coffee. "I must get this back to my home. My children are like baby birds. They are chirping and crying for food." He laughed with the girl at the window.

Ruth thought, *He sounds like that actor. Arnold Swartch-something. He was just as big and muscular. He seemed like a nice guy. A good choice*, she thought and she was comfortable having Kruger watch over her family.

Kruger pulled out and over to a convenient parking place. He handed the bag back to Ruth, saying, "I must make a call now."

He sat in the front seat while the children were chomping up the muffins. Ruth said, "Thank you. That really hit the spot. They were very hungry.'"

He punched the number. "Hello, Colonel Reedah, I need an address for my GPS to deliver these flowers to, sir. OK, warehouse at," he was writing, "1709 Kapok St. at about nine o'clock, sir. Yes I've got it. The little flowers are budding, sir. I gave them water, sir"

Reeder laughed. He knew what Kruger meant. Kruger really was gentle for all his brawn.

"We will have some time to kill, Kruger announced to the back of the van. "Not too much. Best to stay moving. I vill set this address in my GPS and make a dry run, now. Ve vill have no surprise, dhat vay."

***

Colonel Reeder called Ishmael. "OK, so far, so good. Kruger has your family and is waiting for my call. I have my uniform. Dufay has his. We will exit from the cafeteria through the kitchen. We have police credentials for that. Our car is waiting there.

"When I ring you be ready to walk straight down the hall and out to the right side street. Hold your phone to your ear to discourage any conversations. We will be waiting for you. A red sedan. I will pick you up, walking behind you, when you pass through the door to make sure that Bly or nobody else is tailing you. If so, I will engage you in a conversation as a helpless traveler needing directions. This will signal all parties and we re-group after I have dispensed with him. If that happens, just hang outside like you are waiting for a cab. Do you have any questions, Ishmael?"

"No, I am excited to see my family."

"Not long now," said Reeder.

***

Dufay was spit and polish, a fully dressed agent. Brass everywhere. A red band around his black, billed cap. It was show time. *This act has to be convincing.* He mentally rehearsed his lines, as he punched Reeder's number.

"I am ready, sir. I can meet you in the cafeteria."

"Good, Five minutes." He hung up.

Dufay took one more look in the mirror to size himself up. Surveying that he had lost a few pounds on this trip.

Reeder went to Dufay's door and tapped lightly. Dufay emerged, a colorful and commanding figure. Reeder was taken aback by his visage.

Well, Sir," He spoke in perfect Farsi. "You look very good today. I will be proud to have you officiate at my son's manhood celebration today." He had just given Dufay an alibi for any encounters, Bly or otherwise. This place was still full of agents. What luck!

"I am sorry my territory is in the south country. It is far for you."

Dufay was hip now to the ruse, if needed.

Reeder locked pretty well himself. Everything fit him well. That's usually true when you are built well, as was Colonel Reeder.

Together they walked in lock step toward the dining area.

There was Agent Bly, checking out at the front desk. They had to walk past him. He was in a light dispute with the counter person. Dufay would take the offensive, since they had spoken last night.

Dufay walked up to Agent Bly and slapped him on the shoulder.

"Bly, Sir." Please meet my cousin from the south rural area. This is Agent Ezra. I am officiating at his son's manhood, son of the command of Allah, today. A great and proud day for any father! How do I look, Hey," he spread his arms like a peacock. Bly was impressed by the medals of merit he saw and somewhat chagrined that he had been assigned to follow Dufay. He thought he knew or had seen the cousin before. Probably just here at the hotel, and dismissed it.

Again, in perfect Farsi, Reeder shook his hand greeting him warmly.

"My charge is going home today anyway. I overheard his call to his family. So, I deserve the day off, after that crazy ski trip. I am too old for these things." said Dufay as he stretched his body, hand on his back in feigned pain, laughed at himself.

Well, let's go get a coffee, real quick." as he moved towards the dining room.

"Oh, I can't, sir," said Agent Bly. "I actually don't want to run into the Boss. I have to make a quick trip home. I have matters to attend to." He winked.

All the men understood. With a Ya, Ya, they parted.

Reeder said, "Well, that went well. Good move, Dufay"

"Thank you sir."

They strolled into the dining room and took a seat in a booth located near the door where they would leave from.

"Ok, he's not here yet," said Dufay. "He is the one guy I don't want to see."

It was starting to get very light outside, anyway. It was time to go.

Here we go, Dufay. This is the last I am going to see of my homeland, he thought to himself. He took out his badge and said, "Follow my lead." He stood up and went through the swinging door with his badge held up prominently, like he was inspecting the kitchen, ever moving towards the side door which led to the street.

"Is the trash out here," he yelled over the clang of pots and pans and dishwashers. He didn't wait for an answer. It was a rhetorical question.

They were outside now. Colonel Reeder went straight to the red sedan just a few feet away. He unlocked it and they both got in. Reeder, driving, immediately moved to a side street and pulled over. He sat and listened like an animal with its nose in the air. Calculating. Taking measure. Instinctively, he checked the placement of his firearm. They would be traveling 482 miles today, over the desert. He mentally checked off everything. *Let's see. At our speed, at least 10 hours. If all goes smooth.*

He needed to call Dr. Bern and advise him of their ETA and the Sheik's factory runway coordinates so he could get the pilot on it. He wanted the plane, refueled and there waiting for them when they crossed the border.

Check, check, he thought.

He called Geneva. "This is Colonel Reeder calling for Dr. Bern."

"Yes, thank you."

"Vello, Colonel how are you?"

"Everything is on schedule at this time. Bank extraction coming up within one and one-half hours. I will call you when that most delicate operation is over. Dufay has been great for us.

"I am thinking at least ten to twelve hours hard driving to cross the border into Kuwait, sir. I will need the plane to be refueled sand ready to bring us back at that time, sir.

"Ya, Ya, I can do this vith our pilot now. Give me the coordinates. If there is a question I vill have him call you."

"Sir, just be sure the pilot has the Sheik's phone number, I gave you in the coordinates. He will have exact GPS and runway information a pilot will understand. This is a private factory airfield, sir."

"Yes, I see, Colonel Ve vill not fail you. No F -16s this time, please," he said jokingly.

"We will be in touch, sir" and he hung up.

"OK, now for Ishmael," he said out loud. "Dufay, you will drive up to the door area, but not too close. Let me out and I will escort, or be behind, Ishmael all the way out the door and lead him to the car. I want to be sure Bly isn't around, now that we've met. If I am not with him or have to waive him off, you will know why. Just leave and drive to that drug store across the street. I will contact you. I'll be close by. Ishmael will know your car color. Only red one I see in the lot this morning." He pulled to the curb, a block away. "OK, switch!"

Dufay moved around to the driver's seat. Reeder walked briskly back to the hotel. He donned a white windbreaker that had been folded up in a belly pack to cover his top uniform. He didn't need any questions asked.

He walked in and directly down the left hallway to a far corner.

He dialed Ishmael's room Number.

"Hello," said Ishmael

"Are you ready"?

"Oh, yes sir," he said.

"Take your bag and head out the front door. Remember, Phone to your ear to discourage any conversations. Turn left to the southeast corner of the parking lot. You will see Dufay in a red sedan. Tell Dufay to drive to the drugstore across the street. I have your back. I will see you there."

"Got it, sir," said Ishmael. He grabbed his small bag and his skis, for effect, and went for the door.

Reeder had the benefit of a ninety degree view down the intersecting hallway. What do you know, there came the Commandant with a small entourage following him. He strode erect and proud.

Reeder thought, *all he needs is a donkey tail*. At the intersection, Reeder stood back slightly and saluted, sharply. The commandant casually, perfunctorily, returned the salute.

Ishmael was clattering down the hallway in front of them with his skis.

The commandant took notice. He knew Ishmael from the file. *Well, this fits*, he thought.

Ishmael stopped at the front desk to check out. This allowed the commandant and his group to pass him by on their way to the dining room for breakfast.

Reeder walked behind them pausing behind Ishmael. "Wait, take your time now," he murmured in a low voice. Ishmael heard him and picked up a bi-fold brochure on the counter top, asking the attendant about its contents. When he could see peripherally, that they had disappeared into the dining room, he turned and walked straight out the door looking southeast to the far corner of the lot. There was a red sedan!

Colonel Reeder walked forward around him saying in a low voice, without looking, "Good, I will see you at the drugstore across the street."

Ishmael walked, weaving between parked cars, unnoticed to the red sedan. He also took a circumspect and panoramic look around. He knew this was his parting with the country he had given so much of his life to. *To bright-er horizons,* he thought.

He opened the back door and put his skis across the back seat and sat down on top of them. "Here we go, Dufay," he said. "Reeder said to go over there to the drugstore."

"OK," and he pulled to the boulevard, across and left into the parking lot.

Colonel Reeder was already there. He walked out the door and to the front passenger side of the car and got in.

"Gentleman", he said. "So far, so good. Now proceed north to that mega store where we will meet the Brinks truck."

"Roger that," said Dufay

Reeder punched in the number he had been given.

"This is Colonel Reeder. I am calling about a truck this morning for Dr. Bern"

"Oh yes sir, where is the drop?"

"We are approaching it now. The mega store just north of the airport hotel. East side of the highway. Back of the lot and we will transfer."

"I know the place. Our ETA is about twenty minutes. One driver and two guards have been assigned, sir"

"We are three. Are there seats? Driver and one guard will be enough. We have national police, in company. We will be looking for you."

"Yes sir."

"Ok, Dufay, on to the mega store just north a mile or so. How we doing, guys?" he asked, now that they were all together.

"Good, good," were the replies. "Gather your thoughts. Time to rock!"

They could feel the change up in pace, inspired by Colonel Reeder. They had, long ago looked to him as their leader.

Ishmael shouted, "I can smell that Château Briand at the Chalet Now!" As he envisioned their final destination, dissipating some nervous energy, and hoping to instil some camaraderie in the group.

They entered the parking lot of the Mega store and pulled to the curb where they could see all traffic entering. Reeder glanced at his watch. Eight to ten minutes left. He decided to call Buell and Carter. He hadn't spoken to them in days.

"Hello, Buell. How are things going there?"

"Really quiet, boss." Buell said.

"Yeah, the old man backed 'em out pretty good. He threatened to freeze about 300 million of their common assets. I am not sure they like our bank anymore," he chuckled.

Listen, we are about to leave on our run. With any luck we will be back there in the morning. We are coming in from Kuwait. Tell Stevern we will be hungry for his special breakfast, Two children, also." It's nine altogether. I have Kruger, also. Got to go. See you soon"

It was only a few more minutes when in pulled the Brinks truck. Colonel Reeder got out and waved it over. He presented his Bank security I. D. at the driver window. The driver nodded and pulled forwards to the curb in the lot. A uniformed agent came from out of the passenger door and around the back. The rear doors opened with a loud 'Pop', released from within. They were like safe doors. He waived everyone inside. The car doors couldn't open fast enough. Ishmael, Dufay and Col Reeder were inside the truck in seconds. The attendant officer was last in and the doors swiftly closed behind him. Everyone heard the lock bars slam into place. There was a blast of cold air as the air conditioning in the rear came alive.

Reeder and Dufay went to the right passenger seat. Reeder handed the driver a piece of paper with the bank address on it. "We have it, sir." Came the reply. "GPS from Dr. Bern".

Chapter Eight

Bam-Boozel at the bank

"The gentleman to my right, Mr. Dufay, agent of the Regime, will take the lead when we get there. I will follow as his assistant. Ishmael here," he pointed. "will go inside with us. I will observe in the lobby for any unusual activity. I would like for your agent to be ready to sever the phone and cable DSL lines if his phone rings, but not until. Put him on auto dial. Only on my order. Hopefully we won't have to do that. It will only set off an alarm. Last resort only.

"We expect to be in and out in under six minutes. We will proceed directly to the warehouse. Do you have those coordinates, also? "

"No, sir"

"I will give them to you. Once inside the warehouse we will board another van with our property. You are to wait thirty minutes before driving out and resuming your schedule. Are we clear, sir?" Reeder said with authority.

"Yes sir, you are in charge. Sir."

In four minutes they rounded the street corner and pulled up to the front door of the bank so the Brinks could be clearly seen.

They disembarked with precision. The driver in uniform, Dufay in the lead.

In Iranian banks the head teller is identifiable by some kind of a special enclosure behind the teller wall. It may be special glass or elaborate wood work trim. Dufay, holding his badge up high, with the Brinks driver, in uniform, walked directly over to her location.

"May I see you, mame?" he said.

Seeing the official badge, she left her enclosure and came around the counter to face Dufay.

"I am agent Dufay. I am here to escort Mr. Pahlavi. He has decided to return his uncle gift. The Shah's) ill-gotten assets, left to him as an inheritance, back to the most excellent Regime." He continued, "I am here, with my assistant," as he pulled a willing Ishmael forward, with key in hand, "to officiate that transfer to the national depository."

"Oh," she clapped her hands together. "I will be pleased to get those assets out of this bank!" She seemed to relish cooperating. "I'll get my key." She went back behind her counter, in full view, "What was the number, again, sir?"

Ishmael shouted back 323-1. Mame."

"Yes, here it is. Please follow me, gentleman." She walked to the safety deposit room. Ishmael and Dufay followed. Reeder and the driver waited in the lobby, watching carefully.

With the two keys, they opened the box. Dufay took the opportunity to declare, "I will tell the Commandant of you corporation, Mame. What is your name?"

"I am Anna De Farsek," she replied, smiling, appreciating the recognition.

"I will suggest that he write you a letter of commendation."

"Oh, thank you," she replied, already able to picture it framed on her wall.

Dufay called for Reeder, by another name, of course. He came with his official looking leather, locking bag.

"Yes sir," he presented himself.

"We are ready. Please take charge of these contents. Secure them and walk with Mrs. De Fares'. She will see the package into the Bank truck and give us a receipt.

"Oh, yes sir," she said.

Ishmael opened the box and took the two large brick like packages, wrapped in black waxed paper. "Oh, wait a minute, there is a third one." He put them into the leather bag Reeder opened wide to accept them. Then he reached in the back of the box and pulled a good sized velvet bag carefully out of the box. You could hear that the contents were loose. He placed them in Reeder's bag.

"That is all, sir", he said to Agent Dufay

"Fine. Well done, sir," he said.

"And now, Mrs. Farsek, will you accompany and witness placing this bag into the truck. There cannot be any opportunity for a switch.

"Oh yes, sir," obviously thrilled with her role in this news worthy event.

She followed them out and saw the bag placed in a lock box in the truck.

Now if we could have a receipt for contents in Box 323-1, we will be on our way.

"Of course." She virtually sprinted inside to comply. Dufay followed her. The other men got back into the Brinks truck. Soon Dufay reappeared in the doorway. He was shaking Ms. Farsek's hand, assuring her he would endorse her to the Commandant, for recognition. "I will be at headquarters in ten minutes," he restated.

He got inside the Brinks truck and they drove off, right away.

"Ok, warehouse" Reeder said. Each man wanted to cheer out loud. "Good job, Dufay! You should have been in the movies." Reeder broke the silence.

***

"Hello, Kruger, warehouse five minutes."

"Right outside Boss," was his reply.

"Enter," said Reeder.

"Roger that, sir." There was no door. It was deep and the deeper, the darker. There were signs of homeless dwellers that had made themselves scarce.

Kruger pulled inside. The children had fallen asleep. Except for some metal containers, the place was empty.

Soon, the lights of the Brinks truck turned into the large metal building. Closer and closer it came. Ruth could hardly contain herself. The Brinks stopped about twenty feet away and Ishmael got out. They wanted to give him a few moments alone with his family before they exchanged vehicles.

When he got to the van's side door he reached for the latch and pulled it open. There, with a huge smile, was Ruth. His daughter had heard the noise and saw her Daddy. "Daddy," she exclaimed and moved to hug his neck. His son had stirred and couldn't believe his eyes. "Dad!" And he hugged his neck, also.

"Ok, kids, ok. We have a way to go now. I will need for you to cooperate a little while longer. We are taking a magical trip. I have important friends with me." He gave Ruth a long embrace. "Now at the end of all of this we are going to Disney World." He threw out the carrot.

"Yea, Mickey Mouse" the kids were thrilled.

Now Reeder and Dufay were walking toward Kru-ger's van. The Colonel had the leather bag in hand. As he approached, Ishmael turned to his wife, saying, "I need for you to meet these two men. They have been a God-send for us."

Ruth came to his side and he presented Colonel Reeder and Absalom Dufay to her. She was a little taken back by their uniforms and held out her wrists saying, "I give up. Do you want to handcuff me now?" They all laughed.

The Colonel said "We are very pleased to finally meet you. And where are the little rascals," as he walked closer and peered into the Van. "Hi, there" he said to them.

Kruger waived to the Colonel And said, "Hi, Boss."

"Good job, Kruger."

"Now, Dufay and I have to ride a few blocks down with you in your van, where we all will transfer to a travel trailer, mounted on a flatbed truck."

The children were wide-eyed with excitement as he bent down and delivered this message directly to them.

"Ishmael and Dufay, you can share a bean bag, I will take the passenger seat. I want you to out of sight. Just be quiet and move swiftly as I direct you. OK?"

\Everybody nodded.

"Wait until you ride Space Mountain!" He added looking at the children. Their feet and knees jumped errat-ically, hands wringing with anticipation.

He pried his bag apart and showed Ishmael that the contents were intact and just what he had put in there. It was sheer habit. Protocol and procedure. Ishmael waved it off as if to convey, "I trust you sir".

"Ok Kruger, take us out the back and out to the street."

"Roger that, sir," said Kruger and he looked back to see that everyone was seated, not standing. Two left turns later and he was perpendicular to the main street.

Colonel Reeder said, "Make a right turn. Go down to Komani Boulevard. Make another right and back three blocks to the factory warehouse." Kruger proceeded to follow the instructions. After the final turn, he had the warehouse in sight. He pulled in the large entrance and then 100 feet back alongside the flatbed. The camper/trailer was already mounted on the flatbed. He noticed two turrets mounted fore and aft of the trailer. There were no guns but they did have a shield with a slot at each chair. "Expecting trouble, Sir?" he turned to Reeder.

"No. S.O.P. for these over desert deliveries. Bedouin tribes. Thieves. The sheik supplies guns and personnel for the trip. Only way to get the package insured."

Kruger nodded.

Now the employees were sliding a wooden staircase, it looked to be five or six steps up to the flatbed surface. Reeder understood they would mount there and opened his door and then the sliding side door. He motioned for everyone to exit. Ismael rose first and Reeder said, "Go up those stairs, help your family up."

Dufay brought up the rear behind Ruth who was corralling the children. Once on the bed surface, another employee led them to the camper door. They filed in to find a late model, fairly luxurious camper. The children were exploring every room, nook and cranny. The fridge had food and cold drink. Cabinets were filled with snacks. "This is really cool," they were heard to say with each new discovery.

The attendant said, "We will wrap now. Air condition vents will be open and power will come from the truck generator. Sheik Hamoud said to make you all very comfortable. Do you need anything else?"

"No, it looks very complete," said Ruth"

"When will we be there?" cried out one of the children.

"About 10 hours, if all goes well. We will follow in escort–'wide load' trucks, in front and back. The law requires it anyway. I will be your host. I will be on the front truck. If you need anything, contact me, please. I am known as Jabari. We hope for a safe trip, but in the event of gunfire, you must drop to the floor. There can be robbers out in the desert. We have armaments in front and back, he pointed at the locations. You will be safe. And now we will get started."

Three man had been wrapping the travel trailer with Visqueen and a heat shrink devise, usually used to protect the products surface from damage. There was advertising for the RV Company on the side, placed over the Visqueen. This was done to make it appear as a normal delivery of the RV product.

***

They were rolling, slowly, now. There were yellow caution lights blinking in the wide-load trucks as they moved to the main street. They turned left and headed for the long route 37 that extended all the way to the border of Kuwait. It was two miles further down from the warehouse to that entrance right of way.

Inside, each person had quickly picked a comfortable site. There were two queen-size beds and a sleeper sofa. The children would use one of the beds, if they wanted a nap. Ruth busied herself offering items from the refrigerator. There were prepared trays of shrimp and vegetables. Bottled drinks. And she started a ten-cup urn of coffee brewing. They were on their way to a new and very different life. Still, there was anxiety. Best to stay busy, she told herself.

They moved slowly and with caution toward the junction where they could enter Rt. 37. Once there, they made a slow turn and rolled gradually to a speed of 55 mph. They were rolling. Each person was busy with a puzzle, a book, a phone game or magazine. The hum of the diesel truck engine and the sing of the heavy tires was mesmerizing.

Chapter Nine

Good police work

Commandant Azaria walked into the cubical where Bly worked. "Glad you could make it back, Bly," he said sarcastically.

"Sorry, sir, I had to get a fresh uniform"

"Of course," Azaria said. "Anyway, I have a file I want you to review thoroughly. It is the file on the last removal of assets we endured by the criminals in Switzerland from the Pahlavi account. You are to familiarize yourself with everyone involved. Study it thoroughly.

"Yes sir, right away sir."

He opened the file and looked through the pages. There were photographs of Michael Charles and Buruse, the nephew, now called Bobby, he read their descriptions and what was known about them. Next came surveillance photos of the extraction team. Then the security team. He flipped a page and drew a sharp breath! He grabbed his own head with both hands. His heart raced, beating instantly out of his chest! He gasped for air. There was a picture of Defray's so-called cousin. The one he had spoken with in the hotel! Who had invited him to join them for breakfast. Only, this caption said, Colonel Reeder, head of security! He had been duped! He desperately tried to take it all in. And Dufay! What could he be doing? Was he fooled? No, he introduced this Reeder as his own cousin. He had gone to the other side! His head was spinning. The commandant must be told! Now! He didn't want to face that, but time was critical. He gathered all his courage. He grabbed the file and pushed the intercom button for the commandant. He got his secretary.

"I must speak to the Commandant right away. Emergency. This is agent Bly."

"Hold on, please."

"Sir, it's Agent Bly. He says he has an emergency."

He punched the button, "yes Bly."

"Sir, I must see you right away. It's the file, sir, may I come down to your office?"

"Come ahead, Bly."

"Two minutes, sir,' and hung up

He knocked and went inn when he got there. He was ashen white. The commandant arose with some compassion at Bly's visage. Bly had the folder in his hand shaking.

"I wish I had seen this two days ago, sir!"

"What is it, Bly?"

Bly put the folder on his desk and opened it to the picture of Reeder, pointing. "He's here! I've seen him! He was with Dufay this morning. Dufay introduced him as his cousin. He was in one of our uniforms!'"

Commandant Azaria slapped his hand down on the desk. "I knew it," he shouted!

"Yes sir, you passed right behind them at the front desk."

"Actually, he saluted me in the hallway, that son of a bitch."

Dufay must have gone to their side. They are all going to defect! That's why the trip to Geneva. His mind raced. "Oh shit, the inheritance!" Pictures flashed the possibilities across his mind at what seemed like light speed. Dufay in dress uniform make an impression…

"The Bank! We can catch them at the bank!" They ran down the hall and out to the black sedan that was the commandant's.

"Bly, grab two men and let's go to the bank."

In the car he called for two more units over the radio and a call to the Air Force authorities. "Full Alert: watch out for any flight plan which includes a flight from Geneva, Switzerland to our country. Any airport. Particular attention to a Lear Jet Nancy 97617. Watch all radars for in-coming flights.

Sirens wining, they sped towards the Bank.

"I have a teller there reporting anything strange to me," said the Commandant.

Tires squealing, sirens blasting, they all arrived at the same time.

The Commandant burst through the door, followed closely by Agent Bly.

Ms. Farsek was thinking, *Well, here is the Commandant now with my commendation. Such fanfare!*

Azaria walked rapidly to the head teller's window enclosure and opened the file in his hand to a picture of Ishmael.

"We have reason to believe this individual, the one you were to call me about, is going to attempt to expatriate the contents of his safety deposit box and defect to a foreign country. He is also a Physicists working for our government."

"Yes sir, I did everything as instructed. Your agent was here with his assistant about an hour ago. It was quite official. They had a Brinks truck for conveyance. With Mr. Pahlavi's full cooperation, the contents were transferred to the national depository. There is a copy of the signed receipt I gave your Agent Dufay." She had it in her hand now and was reading Dufay's signature.

"And did he have this man with him?" He opened to Colonel Reader's photo?

"Yes, his assistant, they were all dressed rather smartly in their uniforms.

"Traitors!" He shouted. "I will need to take these files and your surveillance films inside the lobby and outside the building.

"How long ago did you say?"

"About an hour sir, is something wrong?"

"They tricked you! We will catch them! "He shouted hysterically.

"You are not under arrest but would you come down to my office to give a statement for the record? Here is my card. Just call ahead, please.

Ms. Farsek said nervously. "Yes, of course, sir. I must sit down, I am going to faint."

The commandant ran around the counter and quickly got a chair for her.

***

'Oh, now don't worry yourself. You couldn't have known. These are professionals. Experts at mis-direction and ruses. This is not your fault.

She was in apoplexy. Breathing heavy, red faced.

"I too was duped," he said in an attempt to assuage her self-recriminations.

"Call the staff to my conference room in fifteen minutes." He said as they exited the bank.

***

Assembled in the room was the entire staff. The Commandant briefed them all.

He put the file on a power point overhead screen.

"I want full alert. That means airport arrivals and departures. They must still be in the country. I have communicated with General Aviation and all Radars, and flight plans for that Lear Jet that pulled their team out last time. They won't get away. These assets belong to the people of Iran!

"Check all the street surveillance film on the streets beginning with the bank. Follow where that Brinks truck went. They left heading north from the bank. Confiscate all the film footage." They are not invisible. We will find them. They think they can fool the old commandant! No, No! And, if you see Agent Dufay, shoot him on sight! He is a traitor and a defector. That Ishmael Pahlavi, I want back here! Regroup here in 5 hours with results! This will be Command center for this investigation. Call in anytime you have something. Drop all other lesser investigations. This is what dey call de 'Full Court Press'." He paced back and forth as he disseminated his orders. His adrenalin was flowing. Just speaking these things gave him a sense of command and control of the eventual capture of these villains.

There was a nagging feeling in his gut that if he didn't, he would suffer a demotion. A family disgrace.

***

The street cameras tacked the Brinks to two blocks north and then a right turn. There were no cameras on that street and would require some shoe leather to inspect and scope out any information from that area.

Bly rounded the corner on foot, wide-eyed, looking for anything unusual. The commandant had said he had an appointment to interview the Dispatch station at Brinks. He wanted to know the route taken. Who were the drivers? Who purchased the services?

The dispatcher demurred; "You gotta go upstairs for that information Commandant."

"Who were the drivers?" He demanded!

"Not my pay grade Sir, upstairs," he pointed to the staircase to administration.

Chagrined, the commandant stormed up the stairs as if this were his own office. In his brightly colored uniform and bill hat he pushed through the door with his chest forward and demanded, "Who is in charge here!"

There was some scrambling until a man of about 40 years, came out of an office down the hall.

"I am Carson Billings the chief of Brinks, Tehran Region. You certainly look colorful, sir. Who in the hell are you?" He didn't take any crap.

"I am Commandant Azaria of the National Police And I need some information about a pick-up/delivery yesterday. We believe your company was used in the commission of a robbery!"

Carson replied; "Ya know, Commandant, I hate it when that happens." He laughed and said, "Perhaps we can talk in my office."

Azeri was bright red as he followed Mr. Billings down the hall to his office. The Brinks office was like unto an Embassy. This was really American soil, (with appropriate immunities. Billings resented this man's approach. He felt he needed to put Azaria in his place.

"I am the national government here on this piece of land. Now, let me hear about this robbery. We will be glad to corporate. Who is the suspected perpetrator, sir?"

"Whoever rented your services yesterday morning for a withdrawal at Second National Bank on Third Street?"

Carson reached for a flip file on his desk labeled Dispatch. He leafed through until he found the stop mentioned. After studying it for a few minutes, he burst out laughing. "Sir, this one of our oldest and most respected customers, worldwide! And two of our best drivers were called for. What was stolen?"

Azaria fumbled, fumed and mumbled, "The contents of a safety deposit box."

"And exactly, what were those contents, sir," Billings said.

"We don't exactly know"

"Let me refer back to the report." He scanned it. "It says here that they secured and transported the contents of Box 103 belonging to one Ishmael Pahlavi, I think you know that name. The teller was present and receipted the transaction. She even commented that she was glad to have these contents out of her bank. The man who leased out services is an international banker and multi-billionaire who, frankly, could buy your country. The owner of the bank was present. Three security men and one Agent Dufay, of your National police.""

Azaria was getting bright red as he could see where this was going.

'That man Dufay is a traitor!" Azaria shouted, pounding his fist on the desk.

"This is very serious, too serious an accusation for my company or myself to be involved in, without council. I will have to consult with my Embassy here in town."

A look of horror mixed with rage crossed Azaria's face. His wide eyelids and protruding eyeballs were otherworldly.

"Of course I will have to notify our client of these accusations right away, sir. There may be legal preparations necessary."

Azaria was begriming to think he had walked into a beehive. All these permutations! He felt that he would be in very hot water in a short time. He had gone a bridge too far! He didn't want international involvement. This was spinning out of control.

"Look, Mr. Billings, can I just talk to the drivers before this goes any farther?" Azaria said in a much softer, conciliatory tone. "We feel that we have a claim to what we believe was in Mr. Pahlavi's box and I am just trying to track where it went."

"Ya know, I read where the last time you tracked a similar withdrawal you did it with fighter jets. F-16's I believe it was," said Carson Billings.

"Your government has no authority to command disclosure of our records, but I tell you what, working relationships are important. I'll call those two guys in and you can talk to them. Our in-house attorney present. Agreed?"

The Commandant could only tap his feet, nervously. He had been the one that ordered the F-16's to be scrambled, in pursuit the cousin, Bobby, when he had made his withdrawal, last month.

"OK sir, I would appreciate that."

He pressed the intercom and asked if the team was available in the employee waiting lounge.

"Ok, please ask them to come to my office. Next, the in-house Barrister, Mr. Harold Hillary."

The attorney got there first. He was introduced to Commandant Azaria.

Mr. Billings, "The Commandant here would like to question two of our drivers about a delivery. I presume its destination," he looked in Azaria's direction.

He handed the file to Mr. Hillary. Hillary began to peruse the file. "Hmm," was the response as he flipped the pages and notes attached. "This is one of our Charter customers, over a hundred years ago. I suggest you get permission from them before allowing disclosure of any information. Call this man here. He pointed to the name of Dr. Wilhelm J. Bern on the letterhead of the contracting party. A' We have an obligation to our client."

"Of course," Billings said, "I will call now." He pressed the number in Geneva.

"Hello, National Bank," came the voice. "How may I direct your call,, please?"

"This is Brinks security in Tehran, Iran. I need to speak with Dr. Bern."

"Oh, the boss, I'll put through to his secretary." There was a click and then;

"Dr. Bern's office," came the reply.

Billings repeated the Who's and why's for his call.

"Just one moment, we have a time difference. I believe he is still here."

"Vello, this is Dr. Bern"

"Yes, Dr. Bern, sir. This your Brinks contractor in Tehran. "

"Yes," came the reply. "How can I help you?"

"Sir, we have one Commandant Azaria of the national police here in our office. He has inquired about the route taken by the hire this morning, our time, by your bank. Our Barrister is present in my office and he advised me to call you. He would like to interview our drivers. I am not certain what his questions are. We try to keep good relations with the police. We realize our relationship with the country of Iran is like a Sovran embassy. Would you like to speak directly to the Commandant?"

There was silence on the other end of the phone while Dr. Bern gathered his thoughts.

"Can vie do this on speaker phone?" and then added, "I vile get my in-house counsel in my office."

He raised his eyes to both Azaria and Hillary to gauge their reaction. Both nodded their approval.

Azaria already perceived that he was going to run into a wall but wanted this on the record, if his head was going to roll.

"Yes sir, all are agreed. We will record for the record."

"Of course" said Dr. Bern. Billings pushed the record button on his phone set.

"Yes, Commandant, how may I be of service to you?" Dr. Bern announced.

"Sir, we have reason to believe that the Brinks truck you provided to Mr. Ishmael Pahlavi was used to remove disputed assets from his safety deposit box here at the 5th street bank in Tehran."

Dr. Bern's barrister injected, "Have you seen or can you identify these so-called disputed assets, sir?

"Well no, not exactly." Commandant Azaria realized how ridiculous this sounded.

"Ok, let's proceed," said Dr. Bern." He wanted to know what they knew.

"We have surveillance from street camera's and storefronts that show your truck at the bank. We know your Colonel Reeder and our Agent Dufay a traitor, were present, along with Mr. Pahlavi and he removed the entire contents of his safety deposit box."

"Yes?" said Dr. Bern.

"We believe he is in the process of removing these contents from our country. We dispute his ownership of same. We believe they belong to the people of Iran."

"Yes and how is that, sir?" Dr. Bern inquired.

"The contents, of considerable value, were left to him by the former Shah, Reza Pahlavi, his uncle, whom the Americans extracted and gave asylum to back in the 70's.

A cousin got away with removing similar assets, last month, from his bank and they are believed to be on deposit in your institution at this time."

"I cannot confirm that now. Ve have tens of thousands of accounts."

"We are playing footsie. I want to talk with drivers to determine where they left the contents of the box Will you cooperate sir.'

Both barristers, the one in Brinks office and the one in Dr. Bern's office gave a resounding, "NO! simultaneously. "We have an obligation to our client. We believe that these articles or 'assets' as you refer to them, are the property of Mr. Pahlavi, who is now a citizen of the sovereign country of Switzerland. And, for your information, so is Mr. Dufay." Dr. Bern's barrister added, "I caution you to do them no harm. They are no longer your subjects."

This was alarming news to Azaria. He struggled to understand the scope of its meaning. *What ramifications now in pursuing them? They are foreign citizens.* His anger was building. "We have a responsibility to our countrymen," he finally said. A little less sure of himself. The specter of an international incident loomed in his mind. Something to be avoided, if possible.

Dr. Bern sensed a weakening in Azaria's resolve and said,

"In the interest of cooperation, you may ask the drivers where they left the items in question." Of course he already knew it was a dead end for Azaria. He received daily a progress report from Colonel Reeder.

"Alright, thank you, sir", said the Commandant.

Not knowing what Dr. Bern knew, the Brinks barrister, Hillary, still objected, as a matter of course.

The drivers had entered the room. Their loyalty was to Mr. Billings. He was their boss.

Billings turned to the drivers and said, "Gentlemen, The commandant here would like to ask you a few questions about your stop at the Fifth Street Bank this morning." He stretched his hand and arm in a sweeping motion indicating to Azaria to proceed with his questioning.

"I really have only one or two questions. Is it normal to have clients on board in your truck for a pick-up? What role did our Agent Dufay play? And finally, where did you drop your clients off?"

The tall driver took the lead.

"They hired us, sir. We try to accommodate our client's request. Agent Dufay, if that was the one in the Iranian uniform, he led the way, displaying his credentials to the head teller. He accompanied the package back to our truck, under guard, of course. The teller witnessed the carriage of the package to the truck. We do not know what, specifically was in the package. The client directed us to an old steel mill warehouse in a nearby area, 13th Street South, I believe it was. We pulled in as directed. A rendezvous vehicle soon appeared and they all exited our truck and entered this vehicle. Our duties terminated at this point.

"And what kind of vehicle was that, sir?" Azaria said. Looking to Billings for as nod, he said," A mini-van, I think. That's about all we know, sir."

Billings waived them out of the room and they went back to the drivers lounge.

"Well, gentlemen, I thank you for your cooperation. I will take all of this information into account. Good bye, Dr. Bern." He said into the desk phone. "Oh, you are cautioned not to try to enter our air space in that special Lear Jet of yours."

Dr. Bern returned, "After the last time, I wouldn't think of it, sir. Then added, "We have a whole fleet of aircraft, Commandant." He didn't want to give too much away.

Azaria took his leave and was like a hound on the scent. He called Bly.

"Re-check all cameras for a minivan leaving an abandoned steel factory warehouse on 13th Street. I want to know where it went."

"Yes sir, said Bly. "Right away sir." Bly reviewed all of their surveillance tapes, one by one, in the tape review room. Slowly, he began to track and see where the van had gone on from 13th Street. It appeared to be a few blocks down in the same industrial area. There was an active business and another large warehouse. As far as he could tell, the minivan never emerged from there. He checked the street address against a listing of businesses at the property tax office. It was an RV dealer. New and used. Time for some shoe leather, again.

He drove slowly around the premises of the building to ascertain its purpose.

Finally, he parked the government car a block away and decided to approach on foot. He rustled his hair and put a jacket over his uniform shirt. He was looking for the minivan. He saw one off in the distance on a back lot. *Does that mean it never left here? What did? Or are they still here?*

He walked back to his car. He removed his jacket, revealing his police agent uniform. The next stage in his plan involved a show of authority. It was getting close to closing time so he had to work quickly. He walked up to the simple wooden desk at the entrance to the warehouse. There was a worker standing close by. He held up his badge and asked if he could see the manager.

"Yes sir," and he went to find him.

Moments later an older man appeared. He looked like he had some authority. "Hello, I am Scofieo, sir, I am the manager on duty. How can I help you?"

Bly said, "We are following up on a robbery report. I noticed that minivan parked out beyond that fence. He pointed out to the minivan. It was tracked by surveillance cameras to this street. It looks like the one we are concerned about. Can you tell me where the people that were in that minivan are now, sir?"

Scofieo looked back in the direction of the minivan.

"No sir, it must have been on the earlier shift. Those workers are gone for the day. I don't know where they are."

"What do you do here," said Bly

"We sell Campers, Travel trailers. This is the final prep warehouse. Perhaps someone took delivery of a unit."

"Can you check your roaster for this morning?" asked Bly.

"Sure" as he walked to the desk and retrieved a clip-board. No nothing local, sir."

Bly could tell he wasn't getting anywhere, this late but he felt he was on to something.

"Ok, thank you sir." Must be mistaken. I will come by in the morning and talk to the morning crew."

Scofieo had been with the company for 12 years. He had heard rumors about this morning's delivery. It had taken the night before to load the trailer on to the flatbed. They were told to watch out for possible questions regarding this delivery to Kuwait.

"Yes sir, Agent. I am sorry I couldn't be of more help to you."

Bly raised his arm slightly and tipped his finger. "That's ok." and he turned to walk away. He knew what he would do next. The minivan vehicle had driven in there and was still there. He now needed to study the street surveillance cameras in the area to see what left. Back to the film lab at the office. He had isolated the last known location of his perpetrators. He was ebullient with expectation as he pushed through the lab doors.

"I need to see those films again. I will need to look at a later time than this morning."

"Yes, Agent Bly," the young tech said. I'll get the next series of cassettes. Right away sir."

After hours of research and painstaking matching of traffic coming out of the street where the warehouse was located. There was no direct camera focused on the ware-house, only an angular view from a drugstore parking lot camera from an intersecting ninety degrees half a block away. Agent Bly, weary eyed, finally noticed only a large flatbed truck, leaving the street. There were two wide load caution vehicles, front and rear. The pay load was wrapped in Visqueen for delivery and there was a company advertising banner wrapped around the payload. It appeared to be a travel trailer underneath, tied down with heavy canvas straps for cross wind protection. It really wasn't what he was looking for. For all intent and purpose, it appeared to be a delivery of the type of product the company sold.

When he matched the times on the film, it fit the general time frame.

But this Dr. Bern fellow told the Commandant their bank owned a fleet of aircraft. Certainly that would be the quickest and most efficient method of extraction. I need to check the highways that lead to any airfield, he thought. *The more obscure, the better. What vehicles went to these locations?* Time was becoming very important now. *What if they had already escaped our airspace,* he asked himself.

Bly rubbed his temples and decided that things were becoming a blur to him through fatigue and he would take a fresh look in the morning.

Just at that time, Commandant Azaria came through the front door of the building. Bly could hear his booming voice. *Ah!* He thought. A chance to show the boss how diligently he had been working. He poked his head out the film room door seeking to be noticed. It worked.

"Well, Bly, I see you're working late tonight. Turn up anything?"

"Well, sir, I am checking all roads for traffic to obscure General Aviation airports where they could get a plane in. Even a smaller one than that Lear.

"I have poured over the footage from the network of streets. I expended some shoe leather, went to the warehouse and found the minivan we tracked still in a back lot.

They drove it in but they did not leave in it. Only a large flatbed truck left with a trailer delivery, all wrapped up in Visqueen and advertising banners. There were two wide load escort trucks front and rear but I could see that there were only company workers inside the escorts. They had the required caution blinking lights. They could have left in practically any vehicle from that back lot where there no cameras."

"Does the company have a security camera on that back lot? "Said Azaria

"They didn't say so, sir." I spoke with the afternoon/evening manager, Scofieo."

"Seems like they would," said Azaria. "Let me see what you've got, Bly,"He quickly added.

Bly was thrilled for the attention he had garnered.

Azaria studied the films intently.

Suddenly he jumped up, ran into his office and retrieved a phone number from his rolodex. He didn't often use this numbers, so it wasn't stored in his phone. Bly was running along behind with curiosity. What had Azaria seen that he hadn't and what would it cost him? Azaria pulled the little card out and held it up. It reads Air Space and Drone Agency. He had to speak with a General in the air force. He paused for a moment to gather his thoughts and to mentally explore the ramifications in light of what he had recently learned. These were foreign nationals now. He didn't want to step too deeply in the camel dung. The news was still fresh from the last episode with Ishmael's cousin. *Damn news people. Didn't they have anything else to write about?*

Then, "Hello, General Seeger, this is Commandant Azaria with national police. I am a little surprised you are still at it today. It is getting late. You are a dedicated man*." A little flattery never hurts.*

"Yes Commandant, I remember you very well, I am still reading about your license with my F-16's. And enduring the constant snickers about how the Israelis turned us back because we were not even armed.

"There are still plenty of jokes on late night comedy, round the world. You know how those damn Britt's have a dry sense of humor, Oh! And that David Letterman guy, he tore us a new afterburner. Kid's cartoon shows on Saturday are taking it up now. Tell me, have you seen any of these? Every fighter pilot I know would like to "ping" you. Now what fool's errand are you calling me about?"

The commandant knew immediately that he had a mistake. His last adventure had made fools of them and their agency.

He stuttered before blurting. "I am requesting drone surveillance, sir. I believe a similar situation is now developing with an attempted escape, over land with another, so called, inheritance, which rightfully belongs to the people of Iran. I am just doing my job, sir." He stated emphatically, pleading for understanding. It was evident in his tone.

Bly stepped out of the room, temporarily. He didn't want to witness his boss's humiliation. That was the kiss of death. He had learned in Psych 101 that it was easier for a man to get over his own mistake than to forgive another for having witnessed it.

The General, feeling a little guilty for being so critical, replied, Aren't we all, Commandant. What are the particulars? I'll see what I can for you. You know we don't have many of those yet."

The commandant was emboldened slightly and continued, seeking to enlist the Generals empathetic cooperation. "Well, sir, the closest contiguous country to ours is Kuwait. Friendly to the Swiss banking machine, they would be the most likely place. We believe the parties have boarded a flatbed truck bound for the delivery of a camper/travel trailer across the desert on a road route which will eventually cross their border, sir. I need to get eyes in the sky to find them. If I find them, I will follow-up with police Humvees and possibly a Hilo team drop to apprehend them. It is a big desert sir. I need the eyes."

There was silence for a minute.

General Seeger, "Let me see where they are and if I can re-task one of them to that area. Do you have coordinates?"

"Nothing specific sir. Just south west from Tehran to Kuwait, sir. Any road route. A flatbed is a big signature."

"How do you know it is a flatbed, again?" said Seeger.

"We observed with street cameras and the owner of the distributorship has a brother who is a sheik in the import/ export business in Kuwait."

Seeger, "Ok, I need this information for probable cause for my colleagues. I'll try, I call you back."

Bly had overheard the part about the sheik and the import/export business. He hadn't gained that information from his interview with Scofieo. He asked Commandant Azaria how he knew this.

Azaria, reading his mind, the mind of a good cop, answered, "You couldn't have known, Bly. I play golf occasionally with the owner of that distributorship. Cards at the club, etc. I have heard many stories about his brother, the sheik. He is formidable. It may be nothing. The sheik imports many products from that warehouse. They do a lot of business together. I will call my friend, but not yet. I don't want to alert them at this time. I hope I can get this drone up. There is a chance they are in that camper on the truck. Now, listen to this. Both subjects have renounced their Iranian citizenship. They are foreign nationals. We have to be careful how we proceed. This could blow up in our faces with the resources behind that Dr. Bern guy." There are treaties, I imagine. We will call our State Department Liaison and run it by him, before we are up to our gun turrets in Camel dung." They both laughed.

Bly noted that Commandant had a softer, humbler side to him when one was working in concert with him. He actually had a sense of humor.

Bly was thrilled to be taken into Azaria's confidence. He felt like a player, now.

"Bly, call ahead to our barracks depot in Markazi," ordered Azaria "The base is in Arak, close by there. I want them to put a couple of military- grade Humvees on reserve if we need them. They need to be able and ready. No sense in trying to catch them from here."

Bly got the numbers and made the call using the commandant's name and authority.

Chapter Ten

On the road – time to run!

The truck was rolling along at a steady speed. The speed and hum of the tires were sleep-inducing. Colonel Reeder was about to doze off when his phone ring. It was Dr. Bern's number. "Yes, Doctor, What can I do for you?"

"Vello, Colonel. Vere are you"?

"On the road to Kuwait, now."

"Ok, Gut. All is well?'

"So far sir."

"Ok, vatch for overhead surveillance." He related the commandant's call.

Reeder listened. He was uneasy knowing that the commandant was pursuing him so early and and that he had discovered the track of the Brinks truck. It wouldn't take much to put together the rest of the picture with time release analysis of those camera's. He would see the truck leaving. The commandant was not a stupid man.

He will put everybody on full alert.

"Also, I have talked to your Sheik Hamoud and Ve put everything together and ve discussed coordinated for his airstrip. The plane is being dispatched as ve speak. It will be there soon before you arrive. Communicate with the Sheik at his number. A good man. Colonel, Turns out he has money on deposit at our bank.

"He was pleased to corroborate in our adventure. Call him with your updates. Vie vill see you all, sometime tomorrow. Good luck. God speed. Oh! Ishmael's, his family and Dufay's citizenship papers were approved. I rushed them along. Now they are foreign nationals. Keep this in mind, they still have to sign off, though."

Yes sir, Doctor. Thank you for the head's up on Azaria. He is a bit of a hound dog. I'll watch out overhead."

***

The General was on the phone.

"Hello," Azaria said.

"Ok, Commandant. One drone, tasked for three hours. Southwest area toward Kuwait. Best I could do for you. I will call you if your image turns up," and he hung up.

***

Colonel Reeder decided to call his client and friend, the Sheik. He first used his cell phone. The Sheik knew exactly where they were. The lead truck was in FM radio contact with his office. He was expecting Dr. Bern's Jet in about five hours. *A- OK! Just relax and enjoy the ride*, he thought. Problem was, this was going too smooth. He was used to crisis mode. That's what made him good at what he did.

"Kruger."

"Sir?"

"You had your travel pack on in the minivan, didn't you?"

"Yes sir, always bring it." Kruger said.

"Do you still carry that portable, tactical tadar unit in it, the one that folds out with the expandable dish?"

"Yes."

"What kind of power does it require? "

"It'll work on 12 volts, sir"

"Ok, we have those auxiliary jacks in the camper. Put it up on the rear deck of the flatbed. I am looking for any possible air vehicle. Hilo, drone, plane, anything. No surprises."

"Yes sir Do my best, sir, but we already have a radar unit under all that Visqueen, mounted on the roof of the camper/trailer."

"That's right Kruger. Good thinking. That's more for weather but see if you can get up on that rear ladder mounted behind the trailer. Go to the roof and cut a hole in the wrap. See if you can splice into the power source. I believe your portable is better suited for aerial surveillance. We will use the camper unit for linear, ground-level info. I'll watch it from inside"

"Also mount and man those .50 Cal's on the front and rear chair mounts on the truck."

"Roger that sir. I'll be on the rear mount with the radar close by. I will ask the trip master to get someone for the front gun seat." He got on the portable radio connected to the front cab.

It was a clear day. The sun was bright and the sky was clear and blue. *Good visibility*, he thought.

Chapter

Prop Jockey

Hasan, was at his post. A drone had been fueled and was being removed from the hanger. Soon it was taxiing down runway 30 It had been tasked by higher-up's to climb to 15,000 feet initially, and do camera surveillance. It was an observation drone. Unarmed.

Their sector was an area southwest of the city. He was to scan the desert en–route to Kuwait or even Iraq. He was looking for the footprint of a flatbed truck, carrying a travel trailer for delivery. *How strategic,* he thought. *What kind of a threat is this? Oh well, it's a job.*

Finally, he had rotate speed. Up went the nose. It would take some time to get to the assigned altitude. He would spiral up

The first thing he did was to climb to 10,000 feet. This way he could pick up the main highway leaving to the south west. He, remotely, moved the lens to 3x power. And glued his eyes to his monitor.

There was a small sports car going very fast. This was a two lane road so it would have to slow for traffic ahead soon.

He glanced back at the file he was given. It estimated that the truck could have left as early as 9:00 AM. It would be well on its way to the border by now. He, nostalgically remembered his youthful forays with pals into

Kuwait for a weekend. Back then it was known to be city where you could cut loose and have a good time. *A far cry from the restrictions of the Mullahs back in Tehran.* Those memories put a wide smile on his face. *That black eyed beauty with the petite little face, what a beautiful smile....*

Back to the monitor. He flew the drone down Route No. 37. This was the main highway for commerce, west to Kuwait and Iraq. He saw a truck or two, but they were covered trailers, presumably 18 wheelers.

He took his eyes (the lens) off the highway for a moment looking to the right of the main jighway. There! Just leaving the high roof protection of the weigh and tax station was a flatbed truck, hauling a rectangular payload, wrapped in Visqueen, with banners all around. That must be it!

He reached for the telephone. "Hello, Commandant Azaria, please."

"Yes? Azaria here."

"This is Hasan. Drone operator. I think I have found your truck, sir."

"Good news, Hasan! Where?"

"According to the GPS reckoning on my screen, they are just leaving a tax and weigh station along Route 37 about thirty miles southeast of Arak, Sir."

"Good job, Hasan."Azaria said."Arak? I have vehicles on standby at that depot. Stay on the line, I may need to patch you in."

"Yes sir." Hasan beamed with pride at his accomplishment.

The commandant dialed a number.

"Arak Depot, can I help you?"

"This is Commandant Azaria. I need to speak to the Dispatch sergeant."

"Sergeant Daran, here."

"Sergeant, this is Commandant Azaria. I called earlier. I believe you have some military Humvees on hold for me."

"Yes sir, I see it here on our manifest, sir."

"What is in your notes?" asked Azaria

"Looking, sir. Oh yes, a flatbed truck with a payload.... travel trailer, wrapped, sir."

"Good, Daran. We have located it. I am going to patch you through to the drone dispatcher for coordinates. I will need a two Humvee's, armed, detailed to chase and apprehend the truck. They are about thirty miles southeast of you on Route 37. Do you have a Hilo you can spare?"

"Don't know sir, will have to check."

"Ok, hustle, Sergeant. Huddla, Huddla! Call me back on this number when you have them in sight!"

Hasan lowered the drone down to 5,000 feet for a closer look. It tripped both radars on the camper trailer. Loud beeps were heard outside by Kruger and inside by Colonel Reeder.

"Whattya got, Kruger? Any visual?"

"Yes sir, think I see a drone. Small footprint, but I was trained to recognize them at Quantico, sir."

"If he gets any closer, get on your .50 Cal and neutralize it," said Reeder.

"Roger that, sir," replied Kruger. He put on his HERO-3 Go Pro camera on top of his helmet. He wanted to record this. Then he sat in the steel chair at the gun post. It also had a protection shield for the shooter. He called the truck cab for the front mount position to be manned. A man came from the cabin while they were moving and worked his way to the flatbed gun mount. *That was so smooth, he had done this before,* Kruger thought. They both locked and loaded and stared intently at the sky above. Kruger pointed out a quadrant for the helper.

***

Dr. Bern's Lear Jet 75 was on base turn and then right final, on his approach to the Sheik's company airfield. There was no control tower. He wanted radio silence. There was no visual air traffic to contend with. Soon the chirp of the tires on touchdown was heard. Then they saw an attendant with flags run out on the runway, far ahead. He was waving them over to the large fuel storage tanks off to the right of the runway. The pilot, Gorge, nodded. *Good idea. Let's get refueled right now.* As he turned down the taxiway to the fuel depot, he saw a familiar sight backed into a free-standing hangar. The unmistakable silhouette of an A-10 Warthog, with those two huge jet engines in the rear and that super gun protruding from the nose. He had a similar one on the Lear, installed at Andrews AFB, along with the afterburners. There were loaded rocket launchers on the wings. *What the hell?* he wondered.

Gorge had flown one of those planes when he was in the Air Force. He flew sorties over the desert in the "Desert Shield" action. They were an ideal platform for low flying attacks over the desert. They could neutralize a tank in seconds. He had about 2,000 hours logged in one of those.

Gorge planted the Lear where the flagman directed and shut it down. A fuel truck appeared. He pulled up close by the wing and pulled a long hose from the spool on the rear.

By now, the co-pilot was out the door, directing the fuel man to the wing tank outlets and the special outlet for the auxiliary tank installed on Dr. Bern's jet to accommodate the afterburners installed at Andrews, AFB in Virginia. Dr. Bern had arranged the modification as part of a U.S. defense treaty with Switzerland, several years ago. "Don't Ask" was painted in small letters, along with a cartoon of a small Leprechaun (finger on his lips) back by the afterburner and around the nose gun.

The, ever gregarious Sheik was in his Jeep and came to greet his guest. He surveyed the Lear with its additions, slowly walking around it, taking it all in. In short order, Gorge was out of the Lear, grinning and bowing, shaking hands.

"I am Sheik Hamoud. Nice Lear," he said.

"Nice A-10. Where did you get that?"

"U.S. is selling them as surplus."

"Loaded up like that?" asked Gorge.

"Your Colonel Reeder told me to ask for everything now while they are desperate. I made it part of the deal. It worked."

"Do you know the plane?" asked Sheik Hamoud.

"About 2,000 hours' worth, in combat sorties. Desert Shield," he added.

"Ah, you saved our asses here in Kuwait." said the sheik. Then added, "I have no one now to fly it. My nephew may come next month but I am not sure."

Gorge said, "If not, I am sure I can find you a pilot. What do you use it for?"

"There are bandits out in the desert. I have import/export business." Hamoud said.

"Well, that will sure clean 'em out!" Gorge said.

"Come, you and co-pilot. I have good lunch prepared over in main office center. These men will fuel your jet for return. Come."

***

Hasan dropped the drone down to 2,500 feet and made a ninety degree turn left to crossover the road path. He backed off the small motor to glide mode to make a silent pass.

Kruger called. "He is coming overhead and descending, sir. I can't tell if it's armed or not."

Reeder siad, "Roger that." Colonel Reeder alerted everyone inside the trailer to take some cover. Ruth barricaded herself and the children with a mattress. Ishmael helped her.

Reeder called the team master in the front escort cab. "We have a drone on our tails. Open your FM channel with Sheik Hamoud and keep him informed in real time. Next we could have a chopper with a drop team."

"Yes sir, right away sir."

"Kruger, light him up."

"Roger that, sir," said Kruger as he slumped in the gun chair. He pulled the chamber slide and he was hot. The man on the front gun followed Kruger's lead. Hundreds of incendiary rounds were unleashed toward the passing drone. It took about twenty seconds of unrelenting fire and the drone burst into a hundred pieces.

"Got him", yelled Kruger into the microphone.

Colonel Reeder knew there would be hell to pay now!

The sheik, Gorge and the co-pilot were just finishing their lunch when the call came through. It was over the radio so everyone could hear the conversation.

Then in the background, they could hear a ratt tat tat as Kruger lit up his .50 Cal. on the low passing drone.

"There are two army depots along that route. They will deploy on us. They have helped me before, said the Sheik, so I know they can act. Come with me. We will go in my jeep to the A-10. Are you sure you can fly it?"

"Oh, yes sir, you bet. Those are my guys out there. Got keys?"

***

Hasan's screen went blank. He could see that they were firing at him and he tried a few quick evasive maneuvers. It was safe to assume that they had been successful in eliminating the drone. He immediately called Commandant Azaria.

"They shot me down sir!" exclaimed the prop jockey.

"What! Are you sure?"

"I am off line, sir."

Chapter Eleven

The chase is on

The commandant called the barracks at Arak. "Sergeant Duran, please,This is Commandant Azaria."

"Duran."

"Commandant Azaria, here. Those guys in the flatbed moving southeast just shot down my surveillance drone. I will need you to mobilize those Humvees right away. They are maybe fifty miles from the border now. Can you catch them from where you are?"

"I think so, sir," said Duran. He hit the warning horn. "We will be in pursuit in 3 minutes, sir."

"Did you find me that chopper, Duran?"

"Not yet, sir. I will check again and send it along immediately if I can get authorization."

"If you need to, tell them to call me. This is a fire fight!"

"Yes sir. Let's use the FM band to communicate."

"Good, Duran."

***

The sheik and George were listening on FM. They had a scanner and knew what and who was coming. Gorge took the keys and he mounted the A-10. A small tractor pulled it out of the hangar. Georg lit it up and checked for fuel and armaments. He pulled the microphone up and waved it at the Sheik, signaling him to get on the radio. The sheik nodded affirmatively and moved toward his jeep to go back to the office, but he wanted to see his baby take off.

There was the old, rectangular red cap protecting against accidental unintentional arming of the defense/offence systems. George left it down for now. He went through the checklist in his mind as the engines warmed, spinning ever louder. *Boy! Is this ever nostalgic.* He taxied slowly out to the runway head. He applied the brakes and performed a short sun-up testing all the control surfaces. He glanced at the Hobbs meter and found that there was not a lot of time on this aircraft and that the name on the plane was Cobra. He tried the radio: "This is Cobra, do you copy?"

"We copy. This is base, Cobra."

"How do you read me, base?"

"We read good." It was the sheik himself.

"Do we have any orders yet?"

"I say get it up and on Route 37 while you have a visual capability. We heard that machine gun fire." Do some maneuvers and re-acquaint yourself

"Cobra, Roger that."

Gorge pushed the throttles forward. He was on the runway. He looked for any traffic overhead. This was a VFR flight. He reached rotate speed and pulled back on the yoke. Effortlessly, the A-10 lifted up. He climbed out at 300 feet.

"Roger that sir. Route 37. 300 feet/" Gorge said

There, lower right he saw Route 37. "Route 37 in sight, sir," he repeated into the microphone

Gorge lined up on Rt. 37 and lit the fires. The plane accelerated to 250 nautical miles per hour.

He could go a lot faster but didn't want to miss any-thing. He stayed at 500 feet.

***

The two Humvees sped toward the Flatbed at twice the speed limit. They were armed with a turret machine guns and there were rocket grenades on board each one as well as four personnel per unit.

Azaria's phone rang. "I can get you a chopper in twenty minutes sir. We have to arm it."

"Good, make it happen, sir," said the Commandant. "We have no coordinates without the drone. The Hilo will have to fly low along that route. It was Route 37 at max speed until you reach them. Stop them and repel your team." Azaria said "They have state property and docu-ments. They want to cross the border."

"Yes sir, I will relate those orders, sir."

The chopper was dispatched and soon caught up with the Humvees pursuing the same target. Together, they re-ally weren't but a few miles from the fleeting flatbed. The chopper flew ahead to try and pinpoint the truck.

Gaining altitude, they had a much longer view of the desert. They were in radio contact with the Humvees. They accelerated to a higher altitude and then to 180 knots level flight. They knew the truck was armed but they did not know with what. They were careful to stay out of range of small gun fire or rifle fire of up to a .30 Cal. Better to find out their capabilities. The target had already shot down a drone. High overhand they flew until through binoculars they could make out the truck, moving at a fairly high speed, east. Their orders were to appre-hend the items taken from the bank being careful not to destroy the items.

This meant a precision assault. Not a grenade launch.

"Chopper to Azaria."

"Azaria, here", came the reply.

"We have them in sight. Purpose to land 1 mile ahead and let them come to us. We will deploy the drop team and advance on foot to board vehicle."

"Roger that. Good. Bring me the package taken from the bank and Agent Bly. He is a traitor. The Pahlavi's and their security team are not of interest to me. They may go as they please unless they do not cooperate. And commit no more crimes against the state. Like shooting down our drone. If there is resistance, arrest them."

"I understand, Commandant."

***

Reeder and Kruger both saw the chopper. It was too high to fire on. The Colonel Knew it would settle in front of them. He called the cab in front.

"On my order, hard right this truck and make it per-pendicular to the road. Get ready to deploy your men with arms. There will be an assault team from the front. I want both of my .50 Cal' to have a line of sight ahead and be-hind." He could see a cloud of sand billowing up behind them and perceived the Pincer move. Land vehicles com-ing at a high rate of speed. *Probably armed Humvees left over from the war. Americans always do that.*

"Ok, everybody stay down. It;s goanna get dicey, folks. We are ready." Reeder announced, and went to the front .50

"When that chopper is in sight, say 150 yards, make your hard right, not fast. Line me up for the 50's front and back for a clear shot. We have an assault team following.

I will launch rocket grenades, front and rear, when each is close enough."

The chopper settled to the ground softly and left the engine at idle. A six man team deployed in full gear and ran proactively, offensively, and back in the direction of the truck.

We got 'em now. Front and rear! Where can they go now? thought the commandant and the chopper captain. *A successful mission! We've stopped them this time!* Their grins were wide, their anticipation complete. *Just a matter of time, now.*

The truck cab guys were down behind the fenders for cover with their AR15's. Kruger was on the rear 50 cal., Reeder on the front 50. He had run two grenade launchers back to Kruger.

"Make these count. Wait until they are close enough to stop them. These and mine up front are all we have." He told Kruger.

Dufay popped out the door and wanted to know what he could. He knew his life was over if he were apprehended.

"Just take care of everyone inside. Make sure they are secure. That's your job now."

"Yes sir," and he went back inside.

The team from the rear was getting closer now. Kruger was anxious. They were coming at a furious pace. Kruger readied his grenade launcher. *This will stop them in their tracks.*

Reeder was watching the six little black dots running toward their position from the front. *An assault team,* he mused. How often had he been a part of one in places like this one. He decided on a warning volley when they were close enough. He would rather turn them back than kill them. This was not a war. There were un-written rules. Unless they shot first, of course.

Like a vice closing on its object the pinching ends were getting ever closer. The Humvees were closing faster than the assault team on foot, in front.

The Humvees, getting closer were slowing cautiously. Kruger couldn't stand it any longer. He let loose a grenade from the launcher designed to land in front of the two vehicle assault Humvees. It would blow a considerable hole in the road and warn them.

Then he jumped on the .50. He laid a volley, *Boy, was that .50 loud!* directly into the grill of a Humvee literally splitting the engine block in half. Water and oil ran profusely from under the vehicle! The driver slid to a halt. The engine locked up tight. Kruger grinned. Nobody wanted to mess with that .50. These were cops, not regular army. Two men jumped out and ran to take cover behind the vehicle.

OK, Cat is out of the bag, thought Reeder in front. The assault team was close enough now to scare 'em off. He too let loose a grenade launch positioned to go off in front of them to scare them off. All could see that these launches were not designed to kill.

The men dropped to the sand.

Reeder fired a volley from the .50 cal over their heads. The sound left no doubt in police or military mind that it was a .50. A person didn't get wounded from those. The recipient got hambugered. As the Britt's would say, *Bloody Rare.*

The chopper was a sitting duck and as procedure would have it began a low lift off. There was a side-mounted gun and two rockets in its pods. It had to pick up the team, get out of range and make a wide turn back at the truck.

Colonel Reeder knew this move well. When the chopper had picked up the crew and was still low to the ground, lifted off and turned left, the pilot exposed the vulnerable tail section to fire. Colonel Reeder let out a volley of automatic fire designed to disable the rear rotor or cut the tail. It would go into a spin and drop to the ground, while it was low. Chances were nobody would get seriously hurt. The gun and the chair jerked violently as he unloaded. The chopper began to spin, slowly. Rounds were coming at them from the side-rail gun on the chopper as it spun, when there was a clear shot. Reeder knew when it landed those six guys were coming hot.

The-rear most Humvee was on the radio reporting to Duran and Commandant Azaria the events so far. Both were furious. "Fire to kill" was the order. Do not destroy the vehicle. It is believed it has bearer bonds aboard."

"Yes sir.".

The rear Humvee pulled out from behind with a man on the upper machine gun. He was firing, fully expecting a report from the .50 in return.

Kruger was not one to disappoint. He let loose about 60 rounds. It completely destroyed the little Humvee. The men escaped, running wildly away from the vehicle before it blew up.

Chapter Twelve

Sheik Hamoud to the rescue

Gorge witnessed this carnage as he approached in the A-10. He made a wide left turn left of the road to get maneuvering space. Then a hard right to pass over top of them at low altitude.

The radio burst forth with a loud "Hey, boys! Looks like you got a mess down there. Sit tight, don't fight. Everything will be alright! This is Gorge in Cobra One at your service.

George made a pass between the truck and the now downed chopper. He opened up with that awesome nose gun on the A-10. It could put a shell in every square inch of a football field. No wonder they called it a warthog! The assault team in the chopper ran the other way like fleeting Olympians. They didn't want any part of this devil from hell.

Gorge crossed the road and made a figure 8 to come back on the two Humvees, now burning and empty. He pulverized the two vehicles into scrap metal. The chopper was now empty so he made another 8 and passed over the road. He came back over the chopper and when on a line a quarter of a mile away, he pinged the metal hull and fired a wing rocket. It could not miss. It was electronically controlled. BAVOOM! And the chopper was a blaze of molten shrapnel. Those rockets were designed to take out tanks!

"Nice job, Gorge" Colonel Reeder said over the radio. "We can get out of here now. See you at the factory. Get the Lear ready to roll."

Reeder went to the trailer door. "Is everybody all right in there, Dufay?"

"Yes sir, so far. There were some shells that passed through."

"There won't be anymore. Twenty-six miles to go."

"Gorge, I know you're having fun. That's your old ride. Watch our six until we cross the border. The only thing they could catch us with now is a fighter jet on burners. Don't know what they'll do. We screwed them up pretty bad. Well, you did!

"Sorry sir, I just couldn't help myself. All that training, I guess, sir"

"Right, Gorge. We thank you." Watch your radar!

***

The truck moved back onto the highway and they built speed slowly.

Ruth and the kids with the aid of Ishmael and Dufay came out of there cramped hovels into the daylight. A blast of cold air came from the air conditioner, now alive again. Each one gave their private thanks. They wouldn't be out of the woods until they crossed the border.

***

Sheik Hamoud was already in his jeep heading for the border crossing. They knew him well. The Sheik thought they would heard from Iran by now and wanted to be there with influence and pay-off cash. He knew his countrymen well.

***

On the remaining part of the trip to the border, Colonel Reeder decided to call Dr. Bern and get him up to date. After listening carefully, the doctor exclaimed, "Magnificent job as usual, Colonel. I vill call my friends at the Embassy and stir up some protest with the Iranian government. They will be Swiss citizens as soon as they sign final papers. We won't tell the Iranians that, though. They fired on foreign nationals bringing assets to me to invest. I think some heads will roll. I'll let you know. At the very least, it should stop any further advances. I will call now and I will be very mad. Give it a half hour to sift back to them. I think Iran will call off any further pursuit."

"Great, Doctor." Reeder said. Thanks. We should be on our way to Geneva and the bank within an hour.

"I vile be ready for you all. Oh, and tell Gorge 'Good Job'. I owe him a bonus."

"Yes sir, he deserves one," Reeder said.

***

When they approached the tax and weigh station at the border, they were motioned over to the side. There was the Sheik Kibitzing with the personnel.

Ah! Welcome, my friends. I will get in the truck driver's seat and we will pass right through." He told the driver to bring his jeep back. They were all among friends now. The sheik took them across the border, waving to ail of his very familiar friends. He crossed, sometimes more than once a day. It was his habit to spread his cash lavishly and they all loved him.

Soon, they pulled onto the campus of the sheik's compound. As standard Middle Eastern hospitality protocol would have it, he wanted to be sure everyone was fed and refreshed—especially the children—before continuing on their journey. When he was introduced to Ishmael he announced, "I knew your uncle Reza back in the old days. We did business. I am honored to help you with your escape. Your uncle was a great man. He was railroaded, as they say. I am sorry to hear of his demise. He looks down smiling today."

He beckoned Ruth and the children inside. "You are welcome. My house is your house. Please come in. Ask for anything you require. My assistants will see to it. When do you all last eat?"

Ruth said, "We had the items you so kindly placed in the trailer. Thank you. What a help on a ten hour trip. And then, those last miles! What an adventure. I thought we were goners. Your jet plane certainly saved us. Thank you. We are thirsty." Except for 50 years they could be on a friendly merchant caravan, passing through.

"It was your Colonel Reeder that convinced me to buy it."

Ruth responded. "After that news gets around, and it will, no Bedouin or robber would dare attack you. A wise investment, Sheik."

He made sure they were refreshed and comfortable. He knew there was still a long trip ahead of them.

"I have been to the Chalet where you are going. Dr. Bern has an annual meeting for investors held there. It is a special place."

Ishmael was nodding affirmatively. "Ruth has not been there yet", he said.

"You will find it quite enjoyable. Dr. Bern's hospitality was well known."

***

The military guys hit the showers. They had exuded a fair amount of sweat, and were covered with sand, dirt and gunpowder residue from the attack. Ten hours in the close quarters of a Lear jet was a bit much to endure on such a long return trip. They borrowed some fresh fatigues from their host.

The Sheik received a call that he would not have answered except it was the Kuwaiti consulate.

"Yes. Yes this is he. Yes, they chased us down. Yes, they fired on my truck. Yes… and children were aboard. No, we did not attempt to kill anyone. Just nutralize, sir."

By now the whole room was silent and listening intently.

"Yes sir, I have a jet plane I bought at surplus. I got a radio distress call. We flew to rescue them. There were two trucks or Humvees, military issue, and one Hilo with a drop team. Well, sir, let's just we discouraged them from their task. I think they are still running. Yes sir, it was an A-10 Warthog. Thank you, sir. It did perform rather well. Swiss embassy? Yes sir. They have documents and securities for deposit with that bank. Yes sir, anytime. Thank you. Yes sir, consider it verified. I am in business 30 years now. Good bye, sir."

The sheik hung up and clapped his hands. "Dr. Bern has the Swiss Embassy on their butts. That call was to verify events. Ye – he! And he burst out laughing. "Heads will roll, I bet!

"I don't know where they get their information, probably an Embassy back office geek, but the BBC was all over this. Photos of the downed chopper and the scrap metal that used to be two Humvees was on the nightly news. It was particularly news worthy when tied to last month's fiasco with the first nephew's dramatic escape from Iran. International news again. A NSA satellite had picked up the firefight."

So much egg on face to go around the Regime, thought Ishmael. He knew enough about how they operated that it was a fair bet that Commandant Azaria and the other general would be mopping floors for a long while, after embarrassing the Regime so badly. He vowed he would send him a mop when he got settled. *A nice mop.* He chuckled.

***

It was aat that time Gorge and his co-pilot returned from the airfield. They entered the room to a resounding applause and endless thank you's. Certainly, they had been saved by his skillful maneuvers. Gorge raised his helmet in victory.

They were all jovial and happy. They could relax after a week of stringent observations and stress. They were unwinding and it showed.

Ismael's son said in a loud voice. "Where is Space Mountain, Dad?"

They all broke out in laughter.

"Not in this country, son. But I promise you we will get there. Almost as good, we are going to take a Jet plane ride next. Way up in the sky. Things on the ground will be so small you won't be able to tell what they are. We will be above the clouds. You will look down on them. Higher than any bird can fly."

His son's eyes were so big, they could fall out of their sockets. "Really, Dad? Really?" And he ran to his sister to tell her the news.

Chapter Thirteen

Let's take the booty and go home

Cornel Reeder stood up and tapped on a water glass with a spoon to get everyone's attention. When they quieted down, he said, "It's time to go if we want to see Geneva tonight, folks. Our gracious host, Sheik Hamoud has provided a limo for us to make the last mile of our journey from here over to Dr. Bern's Lear Jet. On it we will take the final leg of our trip. I would like to take this opportunity to thank Sheik Hamoud for a memorable assist to our mission. I am certain we will all remember it for a long time."

Everyone agreed with numerous comments all at once. Ruth had the children and they were herded to the loading dock outside the right hand side of the building. A long, white limousine was waiting to be loaded. They got in carefully. The Lear was already pulled from the hangar with its entry door opened. It ran at a slow idle, a low whine to keep the air conditioning going. The Lear could seat ten in a pinch. They were nine altogether. Ruth took the kids to the small seat in the back. There was a restroom there, also. She showed them how to operate it.

"This will be a fairly long flight, folks, "Reeder announced from the front. Get comfortable. I am pretty familiar with the plane, so if you need anything, just let me know."

"Yeah, where is the scotch!" yelled out Kruger, in jest.

"Just pull out the seat trays and you will find whatever you need."

It took about fifteen minutes before every one was settled. Gorge and the co-pilot were busy pre-flighting the plane. Now for the checklist and charts. They would head west and then turn north over Iraq. West-northwest. They decided to file their flight plan shortly after take-off. Flying over Iraq was still not a walk in the park. They needed to declare themselves, for the record.

The door was pulled tight and secured. The engine whine increased and a blast of cool air emanated from the inside air valves. "Wave to the Sheik on the left," came the announcement from the pilot. Everyone turned left to see him waving at them and they all responded accordingly.

The plane nudged ahead and maneuvered slowly to the runway. There was a run-up and control surface check.

"Here we go!" Gorge said.

The plane accelerated slowly at first and then came the powerful surge that moved them swiftly down the runway. Georg wanted to get some altitude quickly so soon after rotation he pointed the nose heavenward and kicked in the after burners that were custom-fitted to that airplane. At 35, 00 feet he cut them and preformed a slow level off to 43,000.

Ishmael's son was heard from the back to comment "Wow! Dad."

The white Lear was just a small spec in the sky. Barely noticeable.

The boy ran to a window to look down. Oh how remarkable this was!

Ishmael picked him up and went forward to the cockpit door way. There was no door. He wanted to peer in to the flight deck. Gorge saw them and invited them in. "Gee, Dad, look at all those clocks," he exclaimed. "What is that and what is that? What does that do?"

Ishmael knew the questions would not stop and thanked Gorge for his indulgence.

***

"This is Nancy 91710 to international control"

"Go ahead, N91710"

"I am filing a flight plan for North-northwest on vector 340. We will terminate in Geneva, Switzerland. Need wind speed and direction at FL 43."

"Roger that, 91710, Vector 340. Wind at 35 Knots, direction, directly east. Squawk 03688"

"03618, Roger"

"We got you, N91710. Have a good flight."

"Thank you and out."

***

All were sitting back and relaxed now that the tension had subsided, and the conversation turned to the day's events once again. Compliments given towards each one's participation at pivotal times, this became a congratulatory buffet, a litany of deeds, well done. Sincere thank you's for events that, even now, seemed far behind them. As indeed they were. It all helped in assuaging their anticipatory anxieties about events to come. This was a new life and a new world for Ismael's family. Ruth had heard so much about people and places she had not met, or been to. Cousin Bobby, Michael Charles, Dr. Bern and this fabulous Chalet, really a Chateau. Oh, the stories of its setting grandeur! A meeting place for world 'Makers and Shakers', world leaders, bankers and financial Guru's, symposiums and special honoree celebrations. Very exciting, indeed!

***

They were high over the Mediterranean Sea, one cradle of civilization.

"Ruth, come and see."

Ruth hadn't flown since her college days in England. Their daughter came forward with her. A teaching opportunity, Ruth began to point out the countries, so much in the news these days, all around the periphery of the Mediterranean Sea. These were also the cities and towns of the Bible. The children had been schooled in these studies but this was the first time from 43,000 feet. They were silent with wonderment. Ruth pointed out where St. Paul had traveled on trips to the various churches north of Jerusalem.

"Wow! So far he traveled," was daughter Naomi's comment.

"Yeah!" Chimed in Amyl, her brother. "This is how the birds see us!"

Although they were Muslim, Ruth had insisted they also understand the other major world religions, as well, before a prejudice could be taught or set in. They were at a very absorbent age.

The copilot came back to the small galley and opened the refrigerator withdrawing nine trays of finger sandwiches and began passing them down, along with peanuts, and canned drinks. These had been prepared before they left Geneva. They were received enthusiastically. "Coffee anyone?"

Dufay said "Oh yea!"

***

"This is Nancy 91710 calling Med control."Said Gorge.

"Med control, N91710"

"We need to declare a change in vector airway. We are turning right to Vector 15, more direct to Geneva, Switzerland. Please advise, N91710 to modify current flight plan."

"Roger that, N91710, Vector change to V 15."

***

Colonel Reeder got on his cell phone and called Dr. Bern in his office. "Hello, Dr. Bern, Reeder here."

"Oh yes, Colonel, how are you?"

"Sir, we are in-bound, clean and green with all hands. I am not sure of our exact location but we passed the Med a while ago."

"Good progress, Colonel," said Bern."

"Sir, we have some hungry people here. I promised them one of Steven's famous banquets when they arrive at the Chalet tonight."

Pilot Gorge noticed a glint in the sunlight off to their right. He immediately switched his radar intensity. Oh, there were two objects shadowing him. He looked left and right to re-confirm a visual on each object. He turned to his copilot and said, "Confirm a visual with your field glasses."

"Roger that, sir." He looked port and then starboard.

"Sir, they are F-18 Hornets. Israeli."

Pilot Gorge smiled to himself. "N91710 is a popular plane with them." He said "They are an escort. Probably picked us leaving Kuwait."

Gorge picked up the cabin mike and said "Everyone in a seat with a belt, please. Secure the children in 10,9,8,7 and so on." He knew what he was about to do would pin them in their seats.

He abruptly pulled back on his control yoke and went to after-burners nearly straight up in a ninety degree climb like a porpoise breaking water. At the same time he executed three snap rolls. It was a signoff and thank you to the Israelis for their guardianship. The Israelis each did a wing tip wave and snapped into an aerial slip down, several thousand feet and turned one hundred and eighty degrees in a wide birth, to say goodbye.

Gorge got back on the cabin radio and explained what had just happened and why.

***

Cruising now high over Western Europe, he had burned extra fuel and decided it would be good to set down in Berlin or thereabouts and top off the tanks. He had a commercial field in mind that they had used many times before. *Better advise Dr. Bern.* He made the call on his cell phone. He called air traffic control on his radio and began the long, gradual descent into the Berlin area.

Colonel Reeder's cell phone rang. He could see it was Dr. Bern at the bank.

"Hello, Sir," he said.

"Hello, Colonel, Ve got your message that you are refueling in Berlin. That's fine. Please assemble our guests and place me on speaker phone. I must speak to everyone."

"Roger that, sir, right away."

All gathered around to listen. They had heard him.

"You all probably don't know this but the newspaper, Al Jazeera has joined forces vith the Iranian cause and they have been airing photos of your escape, your A-10 attack etc. They are claiming that vhen Uncle Reza nationalized certain industries, it enabled him to appropriate millions of dollars from the people of Iran. They allege the USA vas complicit in this undertaking. I have received calls from their consulate and their ambassador. They are presenting our former episode three weeks ago that hit all the news media, internationally, and this incident in an attempt to focus sympathy in the Arab world. Again, you have become most notorious entities. You vill see when you turn on your TV's. As a cursory move the US has put you on a no-fly list for appeasement, vhich is a pointless move anyway. Now, the reason for my call. The US ambassador has communicated through the U.S. State Department that he vould like to debrief everyone at my Chalet, if we vould allow it. He needs to put his own spin on events. It has been used for international meetings before.

"They need the cover of eye vitness reports to contravene the AL Jazeera efforts before they gain momentum and they don't vant the BBC or other press to get to you first. This is certainly in your best interest, as I see it. I vill have my international law attorney present. There is nothing substantial in their claim. We vill establish unquestionable authority for your claim of ownership of these assets. They vant to bring two prominent press people for interviews. Vhat do you think?" I

n the airplane the parties looked at one another, and nodding heads in agreement, acquiesced. Colonel Reeder said, "All in agreement, sir. Glad to get ahead of the curve."

"Very gut", Ve vill see you in a few hours then." And he hung up.

"Nancy 91710 calling Berlin control."

"This is Berlin Control, N91710, Go ahead"

"N91710 requests descent and ILS approach to the executive side for fueling. We are currently at FL27 and descending."

N91710, request to ILS approach, Runway 15. Continue descending into TCA and wait for coupling to ILS. Squawk 2718."

"2718, Roger that."

"OK, we've got you." Maintain 270 knots.

George spoke on the cabin intercom: "We are descending into Berlin executive for re-fueling. You may go into the lounge to stretch and refresh. Do not talk to any press, if asked. And stick together. Eyes on the kids!

The decent was a little bumpy. Ruth had the children at the window as things became clear and recognizable. The kids were excited at what they saw.

Colonel Reeder went to the back of the plane. He asked Ishmael to come along. There was a rear bench seat which covered a safe. He pulled on the back of the seat dislodging it. There was the safe. He showed it to Ishmael and said, :Can you fit your case with the bonds and jewels in here?"

Ismael surveyed it and said, "I think so. I'll get them." He brought them back to the tail of the plane. His package fit nicely. They fitted both of the package inside the safe. Reeder then gave Ishmael the key and replaced the back of the seat. "I will leave a man in here while we are on the ground here."

"Yes sir, good." Ishmael said.

The Colonel went to Kruger and gave him orders to stay on the plane. "If anybody wants to come aboard to search or gets anywhere near the safe behind the rear seat, shoot 'em! Do you want anything? I will get it for you."

"No sir, I am good." Kruger said.

***

Several turns were required to line up with runway 15. After a while they were on the glide slope and on the glide path with the runway in sight. Soon crossing the threshold, throttles back and the chirp of the tires on the runway. They rolled down to taxi # 3 which led them to the staging area of the executive airport and lounge. Engines were winding down and they came to a stop. Colonel Reeder stood up at the cockpit door and made a few announcements.

"Please stick together inside, especially the children. I and my men will be watching from the periphery. Do not speak to any press if approached, Just a 'No comment' will do. Refresh yourselves, get a snack and a drink, if you like. Stretch your legs. Refueling will take about 20-30 minutes."

The door popped open and the Colonel descended the staircase first, to guide the others. They were only thirty feet, or so from the door.

They went insider into a very luxurious executive lounge. This was rare territory reserved for the captains of European industry. A nicely dressed gentleman walked over to introduce himself.

"Colonel Reeder, I presume?" as he offered his hand. "Dr. Bern called ahead and told us to take special care of you and your passengers. I am Bertrand. Dr. Bern and his jet are regular clients of ours. We will have you on your way in no time. We have his specs on file. Our lounge is just around the corner here. Our chef has made special finger sandwiches for the children."

"Ok, thank you."

Gorge went to the flight counter to file a flight plan for Geneva.

Ishmael, Ruth and the children were grouped together on the couch eating their finger sandwiches. The chef came out from behind the counter with a Styrofoam to-go box with food for the last leg of the trip and gave it to Ruth. "This is for the trip back."

"Oh how thoughtful, Thank you." Ruth exclaimed.

There was a news brief on the lounge TV from the BBC. And Whoa! There were satellite pictures of their firefight in the desert, with commentary, to include Uncle Bobby's (Buruse) adventure, last month.

"Oh boy!" Ishmael said.

"Look Daddy, is that us?" The kids said excitedly.

Agent Dufay was amazed at the coverage.

Colonel Reeder had walked into the room and was watching and listening. He decided to call Dr. Bern.

"Hello, Dr. Bern. Are you watching the news?"

"'Yes, I have seen it. Vhere are you now?"

"We are in Berlin for refueling. We are ready to leave now."

"Ve vill see you in a few hours' time. The chopper vile be ready in Geneva"

"Yes sir, see you then." And before hung he up, knowing that Dr. Bern would have any eventuality under control, said, "Please tell Buell and Connor to maintain a lookout in the Cupola. Taking off in 10."

The fuel attendant came in. He walked over to Gorge and announced that the refueling was completed.

All were seated and strapped in. They began to move out toward the taxi way. The takeoff roll was always a thrill in the Lear 75. They were at FL12 before long and then on higher to FL 25. They made a right, climbing turn. It wasn't long before the fords, seas and snowcapped mountains were visible on the horizon. The children had only known desert all of their lives. They were struck with curiosity when Ishmael told them that that's where they were going.

"Like in the cartoons, Daddy?" his daughter exclaimed.

"Yes, just like in the cartoons, but no monsters," he quickly added.

"Oh good, we are going to see snow!" the kids said.

"We will be descending into Geneva soon," came Gorge's announcement over the cabin intercom, "Please prepare yourselves."

The view from the air became increasingly clear. The view of this idyllic city was quite a contrast to anything in the Iran world. There were quaint villages and cobblestone streets. Steep roofs and steeples. The children were glued to the plane window with "Ooo's and Ah's"

Gorge locked in on the ILS and they were on their way down. N91710 was well known in the executive section of this airport. As the jet rolled into the staging area, Colonel Reeder stood up and announced, "I will lead you to the chopper. There will be a lot of press. 'No comment' is the word of the day. The trip to the Chalet is fairly short one." He turned to Ismael, almost forgetting, "We need to get the bonds from the safe".

"Oh yes," said Ishmael and he helped the Colonel take the seat apart. They retrieved the case from within the safe and placed it back into Ishmael's attaché case.

"Give that directly to Dr. Bern as soon as you see him."

"Yes sir."

***

The Hilo pad at the Chalet looked different this time. There were four additional pads emanating from under the main pad on long hydraulic arms, like a carnival ride, each arm had a landing pad attached to it. The port would now accommodate five Hilo's at one time. The center pad was still the largest.

The pilot called Dr. Bern. "This is neat."

Dr. Bern, recognizing his voice, said, "Oh Victor, I forgot to mention the Hilo pad modification. How do you like it?"

Looks grand to me sir." Victor replied.

"You vill be going back to Geneva anyway, to pick up Bobby and Michael but others are coming."

Yes sir, we will just set down on center, as usual."

"Bobby and Michael ought to be vaiting vhen you get back."

"Yes sir", I'll bring them right away,"

***

Ruth and the kids could see the size and scope of the Chalet now as the chopper began a decent to the Hilo pad. They were simply speechless and awestruck. Indeed it was more like a Chateau. So impressive! It was certainly a world class structure.

The security team was standing at the ready on the pad as they landed. Exit doors were opened and all parties were directed to the exit ramp which led to the rear of the Chalet. Ruth and the kids were wide eyed at the rear gold overlay on the back doors. Dr. Bern was greeting everyone as they came forward and through the door.

"Dr. Bern. May I present my lovely wife Ruth and my two children, Amyl, my son and Naomi, my daughter, said Ismael.

Dr. Bern gave them both a hug.

Stevern took them all upstairs to get comfortable.

Ishmael handed Dr. Bern his attaché and said, "Everything—bonds and jewels—are inside here, sir." And he surrendered the case to Dr. Bern.

"I vill go over the serial numbers and get back to you right away.

"Velcome all of you. Stevern will show you to your rooms upstairs and get you anything you require."

Ruth said, "I've, heard so much about you, sir."

"I am so pleased to meet you, Ruth. My house is yours. Make yourself comfortable."

All followed the Pahlavi family and soon the house was full of voices.

"Velcome back Mr. Dufay! You are now a citizen here!" The doctor exclaimed. "The chopper has been ordered back to Geneva to pick up Bobby King and Michael Charles, who are flying in from the U.S.

"Vie vill have many important guests this veekend, they vill be vorld leaders. Ve ville have a big conference, yes!" Dr. Bern announced.

Colonel Reeder pulled Dufay, Ishmael and Ruth aside. He said, "We will have NSA, CIA and U.S. State Department reps here. They will want to debrief you about what happened. Just tell them the truth. Anything above and beyond that about Iran is up to you."

***

There was a huge banquet table set-up in the dining room, Ice carving, steamship round and all. The Colonel ushered the two into the dining room. "Where are the children?" he said.

Ruth said, "Oh, upstairs with a video game, for now."

Chapter Fourteen

The Big Pow-Wow

Bobby King and Michael Charles exited their commercial flight and proceeded on to the gangplank to their gate inside the airport in Geneva. They traveled light, each with a single bag.

As soon as they were visible, they were recognized by the press and were approached all at once.

'No comment' was their instructions and that's how they played it. Part of Colonel Reeder's team was there to take control and usher them to the chopper pad. They were taken to a remote metal door in the bowels of the airport which, when opened, lead to a bright, sunlit tarmac on the General Aviation side of the airport and not far away was the Hilo pad.

There was the familiar chopper, rotors already spinning, and ready to go.

They approached the pad and got inside. Seatbelts buckled, there was a low, slow sweeping turn in the direction of the mountains and they were on their way.

"Hey, man, look what we started! We are supposed to have national security people and some state department geeks at our meeting!" Bobby said.

"Yeah, they need 'Cover' for the Iranian claims." Michael confirmed.

"I liked it better on the beaches of California." Said Bobby.

"I hear that, buddy!" Mike agreed. "And to think this all of this got started over my motorcycle accident." He rubbed the pain in his shoulder. "Think of it, it was only a little less than a month ago."

"Yeah, and what a month!" Bobby said. "It'll be good to see Ishmael again. And Ruth, this time."

"Oh yeah, a nice lady", said Bobby.

"Do you know what they plan to do?" Michael asked.

"Not really, but I would think Ishmael would get plenty of offers. He was involved in their nuclear program," Bobby said.

"Oh yeah, they'll be all over him," Mike said.

***

Soon the Chalet was in the far distant view as they approached the snow covered peaks. What a spectacle!

They could already see that the Hilo pad had been modified to accommodate more traffic. There were fivepPads now, all emanating from the one center pad. It brought to mind the old octopus ride at the carnival when Michael was young.

Each pad had a walkway to the center pad for accessing the back entrance of the Chalet. As they drew closer, they could see Buell waving them down to the center pad where strobe lights were flashing.

Carter was up in the cupola, for security.

Soon they were at the pad and gently touched down.

Buell opened their door and guided them out to the pad walkway and down to the rear entrance to the Chalet. He, enthusiastically, greeted these two old friends. "Welcome back," he said to Bobby and Michael.

Ismael was just inside the back door, waiting to greet them. After his desert experience he felt a certain kinship with these two. He embraced Bobby in a Middle Eastern hug and kiss on each cheek. "Hello, my brother, welcome, how are you?"

"No, how are you, Ismael? And your family? You went through the ordeal."

"We owe much to former agent Dufay. I will introduce you. We are all fine, Colonel Reeder was excellent with his plan. Here we are a half a world away and we are safe."

"Yes, brother, thank Allah for that. I think you will have a wonderful life from here on. Much better for your wife and children. There will be much opportunity for you. "

"Yes, Bobby; it's all so new to me now"

At the end of the hallway stood Dr. Bern shouting grand salutations. "Velcome, Velcome, all together and safe."

Colonel Reeder was at his side.

"Could the Colonel and I have a vord vith you two?"

"Of course, Dr." came the reply. They were ushered into Dr. Bern's office. When all were seated, Dr. Bern began. "Gentleman, there are some sensitive issues. Ve vill have representatives here today from various security agencies from the U.S. and around the world.

"You two," looking at Bobby and Michael, "may recognize some of them from a month ago, a group from the U.S. State Department. Please, no Hi's or recognition. Ve have guaranteed their individual anonymity because of the sensitive nature of their positions. Accordingly, names vill not be used, except I vill present you all, by name. Just tell your story and ansver any questions they have.

"Ishmael, they vill probably vant to know about. the extent of the Iranian nuclear program because of your former position and knowledge. You are free to divulge, or not, as you see fit, sir. I vile caution you, however, that a representative of the Iranian consulate here in Geneva may be present to hear your explanation of events. I vill point him out to you.

"Of course, everybody, no camera's vill be allowed."

Both Bobby and Michael were nodding their understanding of what was being said.

"Most of the choppers vill be here vithin thevnext two hours. Then ve vill begin."

"Yes sir, understood," said Michael.

***

"Wow, long trip, lets hit that buffet table. Stern always does a great job." said Michael. The three went to the dining room.

They could hear and feel the distinct sound of an approaching Hilo.

"Another arrival," said Ishmael. They walked over to the skylight and could see the chopper descending. It had Israeli markings.

"Oh, I need to thank those guys for their watch care," said Colonel Reeder, who had walked into the dining room. They all went down the hallway that led to the Hilo pad to greet them.

Of course, Dr. Bern was already there ahead of them. The Israeli delegation consisted of a well-dressed man and his assistant, along with two pilots from their Hilo. Each had been to the Chalet before and thus enjoyed Dr. Bern's famous hospitality and accordingly, had brought gifts of wine and delicacies from their country.

A very friendly crew indeed!

Michael, Bobby and Ishmael enthusiastically offered their sincere thanks for the Israeli Air Force's unsolicited support.

"It was truly a comfort knowing you were there."

One of the pilots commented that he also flew a jet and had witnessed Gorge's last maneuver on the way back home. "This is a special machine with its after-burners and vertical snap rolls!

"Oh! That was you out there?" said Ishmael

"Ya,Ya, it was me." Pretty fancy for a Lear Jet."

They all had a hearty laugh.

There was a large well-furnished living/ lounge room adjacent to the dining room and they all went there for further discussions.

Another Hilo was approaching. Colonel Reeder had stationed himself under the skylight. "Iran consulate in Geneva," he announced.

"Oh boy!", said Ishmael. "Let's get Dufay in here."

Colonel Reeder and Kruger appeared at the door with Dr. Bern. They already had their orders. Just in case. The delegation's Hilo settled onto the pad and the three men went out to meet and greet them.

Ishmael, formally known in Iran as Dr. Pahlavi, Bobby, Dufay and Michael settled into the large lounge where everyone would refresh themselves with a beverage and initially meet, before entering the conference room.

Michael could not help but observe that this was rather like mixing a pot of nitroglycerin. Here were the delegations of Israel, Iran, the Pahlavi's, defector and traitor, Dufay, soon all in the same room.

"Gee I hope they have metal detectors at the door," said Bobby.

"Yeah, and suicide bomb detectors", said Michael.

Stevern was serving Dom Perignon champagne and interjected, quietly, "Nothing gets by Colonel Reeder"! That's why Dr. Bern called the Colonel and Kruger to the door."

Carter was on the roof and Buell, suddenly appeared at another door coming into the room. He stood at attention like a sentry.

***

The conversation in the lounge among all was friendly and jovial. These ex-Iranians had reason to be beholden to theIsraelis. And also, the other way around.

Ishmael, reflecting, had a sense of relief. He chuckled to himself, thinking, his family was safe and here he was in Switzerland, rich and untouchable. He had beaten the Regime. They, his family, would enjoy a life of opportunity and prosperity. *Oh yeah, Disney world, don't forget.* Or... was it the Dom Perignon. ? He chuckled again. *Pinch me!.*

Remembering that these Iranians were from the consulate in Geneva was of some comfort. These officials would not be the ones he had encountered back in Iran. *Perhaps they are more Europeanized and refined,* he thought to himself.

There was one, well-dressed man, the Ambassador and his, rather attractive, female assistant. They entered the room with cordiality, and broad smiles. They took a seat and accepted a glass of champagne from Stevern.

Ismael couldn't escape the feeling that he had seen the young lady with the Ambassador before. She seemed familiar. It was a long time ago, though. Maybe at Oxford. *Let's see if she recognizes me,* he thought. Also, Uncle Reza had insisted that they all travel the hostels throughout Europe, in the summers. He thought it would serve their characters well. Meeting different classes of people would round them out. After all, these were future rulers of his Kingdom at that time. Maybe in these travels, he had met her. It just wouldn't come to him. He finally dismissed it.

***

Kruger walked over to where Colonel Reeder and Dr. Bern were standing. "Yes, Kruger?" the Colonel Said.

"I just wanted you to know that I often wear my HERO-3 Go Pro camera on my helmet. I have the whole battle on video if you should need it down in the movie room. It will show how aggressive their pursuit was. It will show the drone, the Humvees and the chopper. Also, our A-10 intervention."

"Excellent!""said Colonel Reeder.

"That's marvelous," said Dr. Bern "Can ve go and preview it now, before everyone gets here?"

"I'll get Carter off the roof to watch this room while we are gone," said the Colonel

"Oh good," added Dr. Bern. "Give us a few minutes and we vill meet you down in the movie room. Stevern vill show you how everything works down there. Stevern!" He yelled.

When Stevern appeared, Bern just said "Go vith Mr. Kruger, please."

Kruger said, "I must retrieve my camera from my room. I will meet you down in the Movie room in 5 minutes.'

"Yes sir." Stevern said.

***

When they were assembled, it didn't take long to set up the Go Pro to the 60 inch, high definition screen. They sat back and began to screen the footage. It pretty much, showed everything that took place, from the Drone approach, the Humvees and the chopper firing on the convoy. Also included was the A-10 Warthog clean-up of the hostilities.

"This is excellent, Mr. Kruger," said Dr. Bern. "Good thinking!"

"Good move, Kruger." The Colonel added. "This will no doubt come in handy today."

"Vhy don't ve start the meeting vith the showing of this footage vhen everybody arrives?" said Dr. Bern

"Good idea," replied Colonel Reeder.

Kruger was smiling now, happy that he had thought to film it.

***

When they went back upstairs, Colonel Reeder told Ishmael and Dufay that they had the whole episode on video and that they would start with a synopsis of their mission and would follow up with the film.

"Wow," said Ishmael."

***

The American contingent arrived with a man from the NSA, the CIA, the FBI, and a deputy secretary of State. The chopper barely fit on the pad. The room was getting crowded. Stevern had an assistant and they were very busy, serving. "There is a buffet in the adjacent dining room if you are hungry, gentlemen and ladies." Stevern announced to the group.

***

International attorney Rizzo, drove to the Chalet with a paralegal. Although based in Palm Beach, FL he also had a shingle hung out in Geneva.

***

"Stevern, ve vill need extra seating downstairs," said Dr. Bern.

"Already on it sir," replied Stevern

"Gutt man, said the Doctor."

Chapter Fifteen

The Interview

Dr. Bern walked to the center of the room. It was obvious to everyone that he was going to make an announcement. They became quiet and attentive.

"Velcome, everybody. I am Dr. Wilhelm Bern. I am a banker and I velcome you to my Chalet today for this fact finding coalition.

"I know some of your identities are to be protected and so I vill only introduce the active parties to our inquiry." With a wave of his arm he pronounced, "Here, in order, are Dr. Ishmael Pahlavi—he is a nuclear physicist—Burse Bakka, nephew of the ex-Shah of Iran, and these are the inheritors. Next, we have former agent Absalom Dufay and then, our Colonel Reeder and Sergeant Kruger, Mr. Buell and Mr. Carter of my bank security team.

"If you need refreshment, the buffet is in the next room as Stevern has told you. Ve vill adjourn downstairs to the movie room in twenty minutes vhere ve vill begin our presentation to open our session today. Again, thank you all for coming."

Several arose and went to the dining room.

Everyone understood that civility among this dispirit group was to be the hallmark of the meeting and behaved accordingly.

***

There was a buzz of conversation in at the buffet, mostly remarking at the abundance and variety of the presentation.

Truly, Stevern had out done himself again.

***

Down in the movie room representatives were straggling in by the two's. They all had met at the buffet table. The seating was a raised stadium style arrangement, ascending with a podium at the center bottom. There was a still picture on the screen with a welcome message.

Dr. Bern took a position before the podium. He waited another few minutes for the room to fill and everyone to be seated. Tchaikovsky played in the background. A stage light from the back finally focused on Dr. Bern.

It became quiet.

"Again, I vant to velcome you all to my Chalet and thank you for coming. Ve are here today on a fact finding mission in regard to the removal of certain assets from Iran. These assets are purportedly a lawful inheritance of two members of the Pahlavi family, the ex-Shah of Iran. I have engaged Dr. Rizzo, a noted international Attorney to speak to these issues.

"Several of the groups here today are here for clarification of the events following the removal of these assets from Iran. Others have a vested interest in the outcome. Our vorldwide press has had much to say, not always accurate though, I am sorry to say.

"These assets consist of German gold-backed Bearer Bonds issued by J.P. Morgan Bank and undervritten by them principally; and some precious jewels. These assets

are now held in trust at my bank in Geneva vhere a foren-
sic analysis is being conducted. They are over 50 years
old. Vhich may speak to the time of their acquisition. This
can be determined by the serial numbers on the bonds. Ve
have a film of Dr. Ishmael's journey from Tehran over the
desert and into Kuwait and the pursuit of his convey by
one Commandant Azaria of the Iranian national police. I
vill present this to you all. You are free to make your own
observations. This film is un-edited and has not been
modified in any way. But right now I vill turn the meeting
over to Dr. Rizzo. Oh, any of you are velcom to address
the group from this podium but ve will return to our meeting room upstairs for discussions. Dr. Rizzo."

"Good morning, distinguished guests. I am Anthony
Rizzo. I am licensed to practice law in Geneva and Florida in the U.S. I have analyzed the inheritance documents
for the protection of Dr. Bern's bank as to their authenticity. I can tell you that they are completely in order or
Dr. Bern could not accept them. Indeed these bearer
bonds have increased in monetary value over the past 50,
or more, years but also have a premium as art objects. The
issue here is, moreover, the source of the monies used to
purchase them, so long ago. There is much self-serving
conjecture on both sides but the origin of these specific
funds cannot be accurately known at this late date. We
have looked back at money transfers of the day when the
bonds were acquired and it is impossible to say. From our
analysis, these two nephews of Reza Pahlavi, the ex-Shah,
have legally inherited all of the assets in question. Now,
to the issue of their removal from Iran and a certain pursuit of them by a certain Commandant Azaria of the national police. It would seem that he acted, mostly on his
own in this pursuit. It was aggressive and potentially le-

thal to the Pahlavi's and their security team. You will see in this video that they engaged the services of a certain Sheik in Kuwait who is proficient in the import/export business in the region and affected their safe passage from Tehran, Iran, in convoy to Kuwait. There are two defections here. The Pahlavi family and agent Dufay. One a nuclear physicist, who worked in their development program and another, an agent of the Regime. The Regime, understandably, is not happy about this, nevertheless, it is the sovereign right of the parties to make such an election.

"Now, as to the pursuit by the Regime. Sergeant Kruger here," he pointed him out, "had among other equipment necessary for the convoy's protection, a certain HERO Go Pro camera mounted upon his helmet and was able to record the encounter on a video tape. This tape has not been released to the press, although they have promulgated some virtual, computer-generated, representations in their media coverage.

"Colonel Reeder will narrate these events for us, but first, let us hear from Dr. Pahlavi."

"Hello, ladies and gentlemen. I am Dr. Ishmael Pahlavi. I am trained in nuclear physics, formally attached to the Regime in Iran. I thank you all for coming here today to hear and see the facts surrounding my family's defection and flight to Kuwait. I did not defect specifically to trade proprietary information on the Iran nuclear program, but rather to seek a greater freedom for my family and to retrieve, in peace, the assets left to me by my uncle, the former Shah. I must say that the events of my cousin's Buruse Bakka's similar flight and success was an eye opening experience and provided encouragement for me. Although, if it were not for the help of our Israeli friends it is doubtful that he and his partnership team would have survived.

"I believe that my former countrymen are under the influence of a radical regime, engaged in a foolhardy and stated mission to 'Wipe Israel off the map'. Let me explain how this has worked out in the past. The Israelis have successfully attacked and destroyed the Iraq nuclear program.

"They have attacked and destroyed a secret nuclear plant in Syria.

"They shot down 700 planes in a single day in the 1967 war.

"In short, why stick your nose in a beehive? I believe this overall ideology is ill-founded and dangerously foolish. It can only lead to death and destruction. If reasonable minds had not prevailed to date, they could have wiped us off the face of the earth with their far superior nuclear arsenal. This is not a nation to aggravate.

"Moreover, the vast monies being spent to enter the nuclear age in weaponry has robbed our people of legitimate infrastructure vital to bring our people into the 21st century. Much needed infrastructure. Oh, they will tell you that this is their goal but they want to develop small nuclear devises to locate on the Dome of the Rock and with a 100 man guard and a real-time video feed, extort upon a 30-second destruction window, any outcomes desired both political and geographical. This is the mentality of a street-level bully who is insecure and overweight! We are all decedent from Father Abraham. Ask yourselves, is this what his God would want to see happen?

"Even as we speak, the Shite rebel forces are going after, that is killing, beheading thousands, in several cities and are now in Bagdad without opposition. Iran is supporting Syrian rebels and an American Aircraft carrier and a missile cruiser is in the harbor. Iraq is about to fall. Where will this lead? More war and I for one have had enough. I want out. It seems to me that we have significant conflicts here at home. What will happen if the wrong weapons fall into the wrong hands? Clearly, we are not able yet to manage the responsibility that comes with the development of nuclear weapons. Yes, we are one of the world's oldest civilizations, but we lag far behind in social and humanitarian development. Our infrastructure, needed to support our people is seriously deficient and yet we are in possession of abundant resources.

"I have not personally worked on the "Dome" project but I have many colleagues who have. I want my family out of there when and if this were to ignite. In my opinion, humankind was never meant to be controlled by religious fanatics.

"You will see this on film as they pursue me and my family, agent Dufay and others, with intent to maim or kill all of us. In all fairness, this was principally one man's mission. That of Commandant Azaria. Our goal was to shut him down without having to kill anybody. We disabled the effort without any casualties. I will leave the narration to Colonel Reeder but I would like to say, in closing, it is not an easy thing to leave the country of your youth. Then again, this is not the country of my youth."

There was an enthusiastic wave of applause.

"Colonel Reeder."

The Colonel came to the Dais. "Thank you. The film begins in the desert, southwest of Tehran, about 35 kilometers from the Kuwaiti border. The Sheik provided an escort vehicle and a flatbed truck, where a camper, containing all of us and two small children, were housed for the trip. It was intentionally disguised as a delivery of the camper to a retail outlet in Kuwait. It was through surveillance by their street-mounted cameras that Azaria was eventually able to posture that we were, in fact, aboard this little delivery convoy. Note, the Sheik's long time business is clearly marked with signage and advertising.

"The film begins at a point when an unmanned surveillance drone is sent out to investigate and makes a, threatening low altitude sweep of the convoy. Not knowing if it was armed, Sergeant Kruger shot it down. He was, necessarily, protecting his charges as a security agent.

"Now, please dim the lights and commence."

***

The film started with a view of the unmanned drone overhead, swooping down on the caravan. Colonel Reeder had a pointer and tapped the screen. "Sergeant Kruger felt that there was an imminent threat to his life and those of his charges. Knowing that the drone was un-manned he chose to attempt to eliminate the threat and proceeded to shoot it down with his rear-mounted gun. Let me say that we were armed, principally because of Bedouin tribes who attempt to rob convoys traveling in the desert. But the sergeant was not unaware of the attempt on the lives of Buruse and the team, almost a month before, with their F-16s.

"Now about 45 minutes have passed before we see the two military Humvees in pursuit. We saw that they were armed and dangerous.

"They fired a rocket-propelled grenade into our rear path, we presume as a warning. Of course, they wanted to retrieve the bonds and other assets, not destroy them.

"Now, you see, in return Sergeant Kruger returns fire with armor-piercing .50 caliber munition fired only into the grill of the Humvee in order to disable it by destroying the engine. It quickly came to a stop but not before they fired a few more rounds into our trailer. At that time none of the parties inside were Iran subjects. They had changed their citizenship, so they were foreign nationals. A few more rounds from Sergeant Kruger's .50 and they deserted their vehicle and began a retreat on foot. We let them go.

"Here you see they sent an armed military chopper. There were rocket pods mounted. Again, not wanting to destroy the assets aboard, they landed about half a kilometer ahead, directly in our path. A ten men assault team emerged in full armament and began running toward our lead truck. I personally launched two rocket-propelled grenades', directly in their path to dissuade their attack. It worked.

"I had advised Sheik Hamoud to purchase a surplus A-10 Warthog. A perfect desert weapon. I called ahead on our company radio to enlist its assistance. Gorge, our corporate pilot answered, 'We are airborne, our eta is three minutes'. It seems they had been listening on the front truck's radio.

"Now, you see the A-10 arrives from the west and makes two figure eight passes in front of the assaulting vehicles. Perceiving that they are sitting ducks, the assault team heads for their chopper to evac. As soon as they are all aboard they began their liftoff. If you have ever flown a chopper you know you are vulnerable at this point. If the tail section and the rear rotor are disabled, the chopper will just spin and lose directional control. So, accordingly, I shot the tail of with my front-mounted .50 Caliber. You can see here that it barely got off the ground. It settled back down to the ground and the assault team jumped out and ran like hell in the opposite direction. No one was hurt, as planned.

"It seemed that no one wanted to contest the lethal power of the A-10 warthog. They all ran far and fast.

"Here you see that we are crossing the border into Kuwait."

The lights were turned on.

"Are there any questions before we go back upstairs?"

"Yes," said the Iran consulate. "Would you write down this Commandant's name and the office he works out of?"

Dufay stood and said, "In a repressive regime, the people are made insecure and tend to extravagance to gain recognition. I am sure that the Commandant thought he was acting in the best interest of his country. I, personally, bear him no malice.

They adjourned among mummers and went upstairs to the conference lounge.

***

Once everyone was seated, Dr. Bern asked if there were any questions or comments.

The official from the Iran consulate stood and said. "Clearly, from the film it is amply clear that the convoy acted to defend themselves only. Sheik Hamoud has much commerce along that route. This was a personal attack. I am satisfied and I will report same."

All the parties nodded agreement.

A man from the U.S. contingent stood and said to Ishmael, "Are there any other cousins or inheritors in the wings?"

A round of laughter broke out.

Ismael answered. "I am not aware of any, sir."

The man from the U.S. said, "I think I speak for my contingent that the international press was and is wrong in their characterization of events. Clearly, we now have a more accurate picture."

A chopper was heard overhead.

"Vie are all here," said Dr. Bern and he went to the skylight. He observed a large Hilo with BBC News markings hovering around the Chalet.

"It's the Press," he exclaimed. "Did anybody leak news of our meeting?"

A round of "No's" followed.

"I vill call. I don"t vant this location to be compromised." He went into his office and ordered his assistant to get the BBC editorial desk on the phone.

When he came back, the discussion was lively about the close call and reserve of the defending parties. With the A-10, they had the advantage to wipe out their attackers and did not choose to do so.

The U.S. state department official stood and said. "Gentleman, with the level of hostilities in Baghdad this morning, I am sure we all have imminent matters that must be attended to back in our offices. We thank Dr. Bern for his very kind hospitality but we must begin our return home. It is a very long trip."

"Yes, of course," said Dr. Bern as he escorted them down the hall leading to the Hilo Pad.""Thank you for coming."

They made it into the dark green chopper and soon the whine of the two turban engines was heard warming up. The lift-off was uneventful and they headed toward Geneva.

The rest of the group was lined up at the door now. Shaking hands and thanking Dr. Bern personally for the meeting. One by one they boarded their Hilo's and dis-embarked.

Bobby, Michael, Dufay, Colonel Reeder and Dr. Bern were all standing inside the Hilo Pad door.

"Well, I thought that went well," said Ishmael.

"Yeah, thanks to Kruger's movie," said Colonel Reeder

"Ya", agreed Dr. Bern, "Give him a bonus, Colonel"

"Oh yes, sir," said Reeder.

"Now gentlemen. You are velcome to stay and formulate your plans for as long as you like. Make yourselves at home. I vill be working on your bonds, Ishmael, and vill let you know vhat vie can do."

Oh, Mike, can I talk to you for a minute?" Bobby asked.

"Sure."

They went into Dr. Bern's office. A quiet place.

Bobby began. We have both seen the film. Ishmael and his family went through a lot. I am beginning to feel funny about our 50% split negotiation with Ismael. I know we provided facilitation through Dr. Bern...

Michael held up his hand as if to say, 'Say no more'. "I agree, Bobby. I have enough money. How about dropping it to from fifty percent to twenty percent?".

Bobby said, "That is alright with me. Let's be sure and tell Dr. Bern right away."

"Done deal!" Mike offered his hand.

***

Dr. Bern was on the phone with the return call from the BBC. He insisted they not air the footage showing his Chalet. His bank advertised heavily in their paper, so he had some clout and knew the Editor.

"Ya, Ya, ok"

He hung up and turned to Bobby and Michael, who had walked in to a private area of his very large office. Michael pointed to Bobby, allowing him to present the new deal with Ishmael.

"Dr Bern, we have decided, in light of Kruger's video, to reduce our cut of Ishmael's proceeds from a 50% handling fee to 20%. We have not told him yet but since your firm will be doing the disbursements, we wanted to tell you, officially, and in person."

"Vell, ok and I must say, I agree vith you. Consider it done. I vill set up a separate account for your 20% at 10% each."

Mike and Bobby looked at each other and said, "That will be fine".

They went to find Ishmael. He was standing with Ruth.

Bobby asked that they all sit in the lounge.

When they were seated, he began. "Ishmael, Michael and I, after viewing your video adventure, have decided to reduce our original facilitation fee of 50% to 20%. Looks like you went through as much hell as we did. We feel greedy and you two deserve a larger share."

"Well, I don't know what to say."

"Nothing is necessary, said Bobby. "It's probably only a couple hundred million, anyway," and laughed.

Bobby added, "We have already informed Dr. Bern, just now, so it's all set.

"Well, that is most generous of you two." Said Ishmael.

"You deserve it." Said Michael.

Chapter Sixteen

We are going to Disney World

"Well, I am off to Disney World. I promised the kids." Said Ishmael

"The bank gets a deal on travel. Call Dr. Bern's agency to book a flight. He will have you choppered to the airport. Book first class, it's a long flight. Stay at the Colonial. It's on the property. Here is the agency's card, or tell his secretary. She will book it and arrange for billing to your account at the bank. Do you have any credit cards you can use here? She can get you an American Express Card billed to your account." Michael said. "Dr. Bern will advance you $500,000.00, on account until the bonds are facilitated."

Dr. Bern walked in, overhearing, said "Ya, Ya! Enjoy your trip to Disney."

"Dr. Bern," Ruth said.

"Yes, Ruth." He replied.

"I would to go shopping in Geneva while we are here. The children and I left quickly and they are need of....."

Dr. Bern held up his hand. "I vill send you on the Hilo whenever you like. I have a special lady at the bank who vill be happy to guide you. It's really her job for special visitors. Also, Just tell Helga when you want to leave and that you will need an American Express card."

"I'll get right on it." She said. Just give me the dates for arrival and departure."

"I'll confer with my wife and let you know right away. Thank you." Said Ishmael. "Are the children in the upstairs playroom?" he asked Ruth.

"Yes, let's go tell them," said Ruth and they went upstairs. "Well, children," Ishmael said with a drawn and serious face, "it's time to go to the house."

"But we like it here, Daddy, we don't want to go back there." They protested!

Ishmael broke out into a big warm smile and said, "I mean the House of the Mouse, Disney World!"

They jumped for joy! "When, Daddy? When can we go?"

"Arrangements are being made now. We are a long way from Florida." He said

They just couldn't contain themselves. They ran back into their room exclaiming, "We are going to pack."

Ruth had a big smile and said, "I better get in there."

***

At the airport, there was a guy in a dark suit. He looked familiar. *Oh yeah, he was at the Chalet with the American contingent. CIA, NSA, who knows.* He walked over and sat down next to Ishmael.

"Hello, Ishmael. Do you remember me?"

"I think so, but we were never introduced."

"Oh yeah, security, said the man. He handed Ishmael a business card. It was marked. National Security Agency (NSA) Steve Wilson.

"Are you guys following me?" Ishmael asked.

"Oh no", said Steve but I must admit, I was on the lookout for you. I called Dr. Bern and he said you were headed for Disney World., so I took my chances.

"Dr. Pahlavi, our government would very much appreciate a talk with you when you are in the States. We would like for you and your family to be our guests for a trip to Washington D.C. All expenses paid. We will provide excellent accommodations at our Willard Hotel, Dignitary suite. It will include a tour of our city, the Smithsonian buildings, very educational for the younger ones, and a personal tour of the White House. Whenever you are finished with your Disney adventure, just call me and I will make the arrangements. Make no mistake, world events are impinging as you yourself pointed out. This ISIS terror group is threatening all of us. They seem to be pure savages. We could use a little help trying to understand and formulate an effective policy. Can I count on you?"

"Well, how could I turn down such a kind offer? I will call you when we are finished with Disney. We will be at the Grand Floridian on the property, I am told."

Excellent. You all have a good time. And if you need anything while in the States, you just call me."

"Ok, I will, Mr. Wilson. Thank you."

Well, he couldn't go wrong with that and considering the hourly disintegration of events, he hoped he could be of some help.

***

"Hey Ruth, Guess what? We've been offered an all-expense paid trip to Washington, D.C. after Disney and a complete tour, including the White House."

Ruth looked somewhat askance from the corner of her eye.

Ishmael, understanding his wife, said, "Yes there is a quid pro quo attached but it will be very educational for the children. What an experience. That reminds me, we ought to look into some kind of tutor to keep them up to date in their studies. Emphasis on English. Don't want them to get behind. We should call the Iran consulate for information."

"Well, I guess it would be beneficial," said Ruth, finally

***

The call came over the P.A. system for their flight to begin boarding. Ruth gathered the children and, together they all walked forward to the gate entrance.

An Arab-looking man dressed in a turban approached Ishmael and gratuitously, commented, "Oh what a nice family. A big smile and then "What beautiful children. I think its Naomi and Amyl".

The kids said, "That's right," thinking it was a magic trick.

Ishmael became very serious, with a furrowed brow, he said, "Who are you?"

"Oh, just a friend," he replied. "And as a friend, I would caution you to be very careful what you say to the Great Satan," he said in a low voice that only Ishmael heard. He departed through the crowd quickly. Ishmael looked around looking for anybody friendly like his NSA contact. He decided to make the call as he was invited to do.

***

"Hello, Steve Wilson, here."

"This is Ishmael. I and the family are boarding a plane for Disney and I was approached by an Arab-dressed man, white turban. Geneva Gate 12.

"He knew my children's names and told me to be careful what I said to you people. A veiled threat. If you have an agent here you can still apprehend him. He is tall, white turban. Arab dress. And Steve? I don't mind a protection detail behind us. Say, Orlando, FL. My itinerary says it will arrive at Gate No 22. Swiss Air. The flight number is 1293. Arrival scheduled for 9:15 AM."

"No problem, Ishmael. Looks like I should ordered that already. Got it!" I'll get back to you." And the line went dead.

***

The kids couldn't believe that they walked down a well-lit tunnel and ended up on a huge airplane. It was a jumbo Jet. It was unbelievable to them. It seemed bigger than their house. The family had their own row of seats. "Daddy, does this plane really fly?" said his son, Amyl

"Oh yes. Even with 400 people on it."

"Man oh man!" was the comment, in disbelief.

Before long, they were moving down the runway.

"Dad, are we going to cross the Atlantic Ocean", the son Amyl, again. Naomi was quiet and wide-eyed, taking in everything.

Ruth had seen the exchange between Ishmael and the Arab man but decided to wait for Ishmael to tell her what it was all about. It would be un-seemly for her to ask him.

Ishmael thought he would wait until he heard from Steve Wilson before he mentioned it to Ruth.

The giant airplane lumbered down the runway. It seemed like forever. Then, when rotation speed was attained it gradually began to rise into the air. This was no Lear Jet! They lifted-off. The airport got smaller and smaller underneath them. Then the city and before too long, they were over water.

"Is this the Atlantic Ocean?" Amyl asked.

"No, son, this is probably the English Channel. We will see England and then Ireland and then will come the Atlantic Ocean. We will be up pretty high by then. It will probably just look dark below." Amyl sat at the window, transfixed on what was below.

"How does a plane fly, Daddy?"

"Well, I don't know everything son, but it is a thing called Bernoulli's principal. It has to do with the shape of the wing with thrust applied. The wing creates a difference in air pressure and therefore, lift. Let's get a book on it."

"OK," said Amyl. Soon, he drifted off to sleep.

***

Ishmael's phone rang. It said Steve Wilson on the caller I.D.

"Yes, Steve," he said.

"We found him and trailed him to the Iranian Embassy.

I am sure he just wanted to scare you. We asked about him through our channels and were told he works in their defense, think tank. They considered him to be harmless. A little too protective."

"Ok, thank you for getting back to me. Will we still see you in Orlando?"

"Yes sir, from now on."

"Thank you, sir. I take comfort in that, sir."

"You bet. Have a great time and don't worry," said Steve and hung up.

Now it was time to tell Ruth. He knew she had noticed the encounter and was trusting him to tell her about it. He asked his daughter to switch places with him so that he could be close to Ruth. The switch was made and just then the flight attendant came by serving refreshments. "Two sodas and two hot teas, please," said Ishmael.

"Would you like the finger sandwiches for the children and yourselves?" He looked to the kids who were nodding approval.

"Yes, please," said Ishmael. "hank you."

When everything arrived, they settled down. He turned to Ruth and said, "No alarm but the Arab man made a veiled threat to me about our kids and family,"

Ruth's eyes grew as big as saucers, her brow furrowed in anger. Her grip on the seat arm tightened. "No alarm!" she repeated in astonishment.

"I had Steve Wilson at the N.S.A. catch him, trail him and investigate. Also, we will have a protection detail from Orlando forward."

"That's a relief," said Ruth. "What did he want?"

"He told me to be careful what I said. He knew the children's names and commented on what a nice family I had.

"Don't worry, I think we are in good hands now. Steve apologized for not setting protection up earlier."

Ruth said, "Whew! Let me take this all in." She became silent, glancing over at the children. "We will always be a target. Private, secure, schools," she said out loud."

"Just the money alone would dictate that." Ishmael said.

"We should have a talk with Colonel Reeder about what systems and precautions we will need. Bobby and Michael did and Bobby doesn't have children. Michael does though. During their trouble, he sent them to Disney, spending cash only and with fictitious names."

"I feel like we are being catapulted into a new reality."'" said Ruth.

"We are, indeed. Let us be careful and circumspect." Ishmael said.Then he added. "Let's just have fun with the kids for the next few days. We will have a protection detail, so rest easy. The children will remember this adventure at Disney for the rest of their lives. We will try to make it all it can be for them."

"I am with you on that," said Ruth.""Let's make it a magical time for them," she added.

***

Ishmael's phone rang, it was Cousin Bobby.

"Hello, man," How are you-where are you?"

"Still back at the Chalet," said Bobby "How did it go for you?"

"We are approaching Orlando now. It's been smooth except for an incident at the Geneva gate"

"Oh," said Bobby

"Yeah a tall guy in a turban, looked Iranian, warned me to be careful what I said. He already knew the kids' names and kind of made a veiled threat about what a nice family I had. I've already reported it to Steve Wilson at the N.S.A. He traced it down and put a protection detail on us from now on. He apologized for not having done it from the start." Ishmael said.

"I'll relate this to Colonel Reeder for you but I am sure you're in good hands now. We can present you with several options for secure housing when we get back. Mike and I went through the same thing."

"Ok, good, we will be having a great time at Disney. I want it to be special for the kids. We will be at the Grand Floridian if you need me."

"Have a special time, Ishmael," said Bobby

"Will do that, we will be here a week at least. When do you plan to return?"

"A few days. We want to get in some skiing."

"Ok, I'll wait for your call."

Chapter Seventeen

Florida

Florida was a ways off. They had descended to about 25,000 feet, Ishmael thought. He pulled out the airplane magazine from the seat pocket. He was looking for a map of some kind. There was one! It was advertising showing the southeast coast and Florida.

He called for the kids' attention. "Look at this map." He pointed out the coast line and the state of Florida. "This is where we are going. Now, look out the window and you can see that peninsula in the far distance. That's Florida."

"Oh good, we are almost at Disney!" Clapping their hands.

"Well, we have to land first."

There were lots of billowing Cumulus clouds rising high in the atmosphere. It became a little bumpy on the decent. The seat belt sign flashed. Ishmael visually checked all belts.

Then it came! All at once, their stomachs were in their mouths. There was a cacophony of sound. Overhead doors opening. Items falling out! Screams, One guy, not belted hit the overhead panel with force. Items left on a tray table went flying into the air and then crashed to the floor. Drinks spilled everywhere. Ishmael reached for the children, instinctively, so did Ruth. Their eyes met as they re-affirmed their belts were secure.

The plane had hit a large air pocket in this turbulent air and must have dropped a thousand feet. The kids were scared hysterical. Ruth assured them it would be alright. The stewardess were attending the mess and the man who went flying.

"Seat belts, everybody!" she screamed. "The air is a little unstable."

The pilot came on over the speaker system. In a calm voice he said "I' am afraid we hit a rather large air pocket. We are through it now. Please observe the seat belt light. Attendants will help you."

Ishmael and Ruth took stock of their surroundings. *What a mess.*

Before long there were attendants there to pick up all the cups, glasses, plates, cartons, bags of snacks that had fallen to the floor.

"Oh, thank you," said Ruth. They dare not release their own belts.

The pilot came back on and said, "I think we are through the roughest part now but keep your seatbelts on, unless you have an emergency, please."

"Wow!" Ruth exclaimed, relieved.

"Amen," said Ishmael

"Are we going to be ok now, Daddy?" said his daughter Naomi.

"I think so but don't worry honey, we will be fine."

Still scared, she said, "I'll be glad when we get to that Florida place."

"It will be soon now," He replied.

Amyl and Naomi were glued to the window. It was a beautiful, sunny Florida morning. They were excited about landing. They were much lower now and every-thing could be seen.

"Look, there is Disney over there!" They yelled. They could see all the parks from the air.

"When we land we will have breakfast at the airport," said Ruth

"I want pancakes," said Amyl.

"We will see." Said Ruth

Twelve minutes later the plane made a wide turn to final at least five miles out from the landing threshold. It was a slow and smooth approach.

"Seat backs and trays should be returned to normal. Keep your seatbelt fastened until the plane comes to a complete stop at the gate" was the announcement." After the earlier disruption, the pilot wanted to see how gently he could set the Jumbo down. There was a marked in-crease in drag when the landing gear and the flaps were lowered.

Ishmael could see alarm in the children's eyes and body language. It startled them. "This is normal," he said quickly. "The flaps and landing gear help slow the plane down for landing."

They seemed satisfied with his assurances. Soon, the airport building was speeding by through the side win-dows. A huge complex, even a monorail. Ishmael's itiner-ary said "pick-up" by Grand Floridian limo. So there would be transportation to the Hotel.

The giant machine came to a halt and began a return down the taxi way back to the gate. They pulled up to it and before long the engines wound down. "Let's just wait for most of the passengers to leave. I don't want to be in a crowd." Said Ishmael. "Sit tight until I say."

He wanted to make it easy for the N.S.A. agent to pick him out.

"Ok, this is the back of the line, let's go."

Out of the long gate tunnel and into the bright, colorful airside. *Wow! What a sight!* He wasn't three steps out on the concourse floor when Steve Wilson, himself touched him on the shoulder.

Wilson said, gently, "We've got you from here, Ishmael. These are the children and your wife Ruth?"

Ishmael presented them.

"Amyl and Naomi. Hello, you two. Boy, are you going to have fun here."

"Steve is our friend while we are here."

"We will be close to your room. You're covered. Just don't worry and have a great time. "Do you see this pin on my collar? When you see it, bright green, red and white background, it's one of my crew. Just act like we aren't even here.

"Ok," said Ishmael, and Ruth nodded.

"Your limo van to the Disney Complex and your hotel is outside at the luggage curb. We will load it for you. You all are the only ones being transported. The Colonial is fabulous. Get settled. There are five great restaurants and shops for whatever you may need. Luggage is that way. See you at the curb outside." And he walked away and soon disappeared into the crowd.

They moved on, following the signs to the luggage pick-up.

"He seems like a nice man, I like him," said Ruth.

"Me too," said Ishmael.

The van was parked at the curb. It was marked The Grand Floridian. Steve Wilson was supervising two porters who were loading their luggage. There wasn't much of it. They would have to do some shopping. He waved a metal detector or some kind of a detector over the luggage in case something was added in transit. "Can't be too careful," he said and smiled at Ishmael. They boarded the van. There were windows all around.

Soon they were at the entrance to Disney World. All along the long parkway entrance were sculptured shrubs of Disney characters and animals. Amyl and Naomi were transfixed, watching agape every new discovery. They arrived at a station. A monorail station!

"Look at those Monorails. Are we going on one of those?" they shouted.

There was a large, long entry ramp ascending to the boarding level. There were hundreds of people walking up the ramp. The children grew silent with wonder as they reached the top of the boarding level. The monorails were painted in lively colors. Yellow, green, red, aqua. There were at least seven monorails marked with different desti-nations. *This was such another world,* they all thought.

"Let's take the one marked Magic Kingdom for now," said Ishmael. He was as excited as the children.

"No, first the Grand Floridian. Let's get settled." Said Ruth.

"You are right, dear. That makes sense." Said Ishmael.

Then, slowly they began to accelerate out of the station.

All of a sudden, all of the center of the park was in view from the elevated monorail. They could see the center lake with at least five different kinds of boats to ride. In this vast expanse, they could see the Contemporary Hotel building and the monorails going right through the middle of it. They were heading in that direction. Beyond "look at this and look at that," the kids were speechless. It was just too much! It overwhelmed their senses.

And then when they entered the Grand Flordian Hotel, halfway up the building, the scene that unfolded beneath them of the lobby and the restaurants, so huge an expanse! Oh what a different world than the one they grew up in. There was a tapestry, beautiful in all colors and textures, hanging maybe ten stories of the building, in the center.

Then, they were moving again toward the hole at the other end of the building. They passed through it and out to the lave vista. They were heading toward the Polynesian Resort. It seemed like every foot of the journey on the monorail there was a new visual experience. And, there were a hundred thousand people. Then they stopped at Main Street and the Magic Kingdom. They were treated to the sights of Main Street. The buildings. Horse-drawn carriages and street cars

"Oh Daddy, I want to ride in a carriage!" said Naomi.

Also, there were all the Disney characters, walking and life-sized.

"We will get to all of it, my dear. We will be here at least a week." After more embarking and debarking, the monorail began to move again. "Hey, Dad, see the train moving over there?"

"Yes son, it's a ride. We will go on it."

"Did you see Space Mountain? It's that big white, mountain."

"Wow, yeah!"

Now, after a long ride around almost half the park they arrived at the beautiful white Grand Floridian. Of course all destinations were announced beforehand. This heightened their excitement and anticipation. *Oh, if Uncle could see what pleasure we are having,* Ishmael thought back through the years.

This Grand Floridian was vast. The lobby was cavernous. Rooms with inner balconies went many stories up. A shopping mall could be seen on the third floor. Ismael went to the check-in counter. It wrapped around the room. The van driver was right behind them with their luggage. He had a porter and cart with him, ready to check their baggage into their suite. When Ishmael was issued a key he gave it to the porter and asked him to put the bags inside the door and to hang the clothes bag in the front closet. "We are going over there for breakfast."

"I have a master key card, I will turn it back in to the front desk when I return from your room. You keep yours, you will need it to gain access to your room."

Ishmael gave him a generous tip. He said, "You're Pakistani, aren't you?"

"Yes sir", he said.

"Iran here," he said.

"I will take good care of you. Ask for me if you need anything while you are here. I am Ravi."

"Ok, I will, Ravi." He said. And he gave him a large tip.

"Victors can afford to be generous" he thought. Then it was "Ok, Pancakes, Disney style. Are we ready?"

"Yeah!" said the kids and followed him over to the restaurant entrance.

They sat down and grabbed a menu. "Look, they have them with cherries, strawberries, blueberries, whipped cream. Sure looks good in these pictures!"

The kids consulted and Amyl said "We want the cherries pancakes."

"Ok, cherries it shall be! Also juice and milk." He said to the waitress. "Ruth, order what you like. It all looks good to me. I feel like steak and scrambled eggs with hash browns. Coffee and tomato juice."

Ruth said, "I want a Western Omelet. A little hot sauce on the side and orange juice, please."

It seemed like all the service personnel were well trained. *Very efficient and professional. Good looking, too.*

"Oh, look! Here comes Mickey and Minnie Mouse. And Pluto!" said Ruth. They had seen them on their TV at home. These were the life-sized versions in costume. Very colorful. They came over to the children and acted their routine. They did not speak. They just hugged, and mimed. They moved on to another table of guests.

"Wow!" Said Naomi, "That was neat."

"Honey, said Ruth, let's go up to that mall I see. I will need to get the kids some things. I saw a beautiful, big swimming pool outside and I need to get them bathing suits."

"Good idea, Ruth." Ishmael said. "After we check out our room."

"Oh yes, of course." Said Ruth.

The drinks came out first. "Pancake are on their way, kids.' Said the waitress.

Here came Peter Pan and Tinker Bell, followed by Captain Hook, trying to catch them with his hook-hand. Big, tall, Pluto came back over and blocked Captain Hook, allowing Peter and Tinker time to get away.

"Run, Peter!" Said Amyl.

Captain Hook was groaning in protest, trying to get around Pluto, who was gesticulating wildly to block him.

The Pahlavi's all laughed.

Here came the Breakfast! After such a long flight and the Disney excitement, they were each very hungry.

A tall lady dressed in a dark blue suit walked up to the table. She asked if everything was acceptable. Ishmael naturally assumed she was a hostess.

"Oh yes, very satisfactory," he said. Then he noticed the small lapel pin on her suit coat. It was the same one that Steve Wilson had introduced him to.

"Just checking," she said and moved on.

"She was N.S.A," said Ishmael to Ruth

"How do you know," answered Ruth.

"Her lapel pin. Steve Wilson told me to look out for it."

"Wow!" said Ruth. "Very subtle."

"And comforting." Said Ishmael

They finished breakfast and paid with the Disney account card they were issued.

"Now, let's go check out our room and then we will go to the mall up there. He pointed to the third floor."

"I want a yellow sundress," said Naomi

"Can I get goggles for the pool," asked Amyl.

"I think so," Ruth assured them.

They got off the elevator on the third floor and followed the wall signs to room no. 317. The hall way carpet was brightly colored and well lit.

When they arrived at 317, they were surprised to find the door wide open and several people inside. One of them was Steve Wilson, their N.S.A. contact.

"Oh, glad you're here. We got a "Door Open" message down at the front desk. I gave orders that any such message on your door be reported back to me. I sent my agent Millicent to your table to see if you were still having breakfast and when you were, we deployed to your room. I am sorry to say that we walked in on two men rifling through your things. They are in lock-up now awaiting my interrogation. Please come in and look over you things and tell me if anything is missing.

"Children, please go into that adjoining room and have a seat." Ishmael directed.

"Well, I see I still have my 35mm camera. Our clothes and hang bags are intact. I see my briefcase is open and papers are everywhere. Really, nothing sensitive in there anyway."

"They don't appear to be common hotel thieves," said Steve Wilson. "They seem to have left valuables behind. My guess is that they were looking for papers; i.e., secret papers of some kind."

"There aren't any," said Ishmael.

"The front dust has made you a new card key. Here it is. Give me your old one. It's no good anymore."

"Of course," and he gave his old key card over. "Ruth do you have your key?" Ishmael called to her. She was with the children.

She brought it to him and he gave her one of the two, new key cards Steve Wilson had given him. "Is this related to the incident at the airport in Geneva?" Ruth said.

"Perhaps. We are running down that possibility now." Steve said. "It appears they were after any incriminating paperwork Ishmael might be carrying. No harm otherwise. I am sorry. Now go have fun. I will get back to you with what we find out. I don't think you were in any danger from these guys."

"How did they know which room? Do we need to move?"

"If you would be more comfortable?" said Steve Wilson

"Yes, I think we, particularly the children, would feel safer."

"Yes, of course. I'll see to it and send someone to find you at the mall upstairs with your new keys and room number. I will supervise the moving of your things."

"It looks to me like front desk security has been compromised." Said Ishmael

"Steve raised his eyebrows, showing agreement. "We are looking into that."

"Ok, we will be on our way then. I'll leave it in you capable hands sir."

He called for Ruth and the kids. "Let's go shopping!"

They appeared almost instantly.

"What happened, Dad?"Amyl asked.

"Oh, nothing to worry about," and they headed out the door. They were already on the third floor so they followed the wall signs marked mall on the other side of the hotel.

The window dressings were beguiling! Outfits and toys, trinkets galore. "Ok, kids take your time and choose carefully."

"Let's start at the bathing suits," said Ruth. They shopped aggressively. It somehow eased their tension.

Before long, that same lady they met at breakfast came up to Ishmael with two new card keys in her hand. "These are the new ones."

She turned to the children with their bags already full and said, I see you two are having a great time," with an engaging smile.

"Sir, do you need anything else?"

"No, and thanks for bringing the new card keys." He looked down and they read room number 210.

"210 it is," he said quietly, with a generous smile.

Ishmael turned to the others and said, "I think the room is moved by now. When you're finished shopping, we can go back to our new room and drop off your purchases and go to the Magic Kingdom and check it out."

"We got you a bathing suit, Daddy," said Naomi as she held it up before him.

"Oh that's pretty, I needed one. Love the dolphins. Oh, it's a Guy Hardy model." He instinctively looked inside the waistband to see what size they had chosen." Ok, 36." That would do. "I like it." After a few more purchases, they were ready to return to the room.

Room 210 was even better than 307. It was bigger. So was the adjoining room for the kids. "Wow! This is neat," said Amyl.

"Why not just put your bags on the bed and we can put them away after we get back," said Ruth.

Ishmael said, "Ok, down to the monorail!"

Chapter Eighteen

I.S.I.S. Hostilities spill over into Iran.
Must get Uncle Brahmin out of the country

Before they could leave the 12:00 news came on the TV. Naomi had turned it on to see the wide flat screen. *Must be a 60 incher,* Ishmael thought. The caption was 'War spills into Iran'. It detailed how the I.S.I.S. terrorists had made some forays into Iran. Mainly around the outskirts of Tehran. As the camera panned the landscape, it showed some bombed out residential areas.

"Oh my God!" exclaimed Ruth. "That's our house! Right there," She touched the screen. She recognized a toy they had left in the driveway when they left so abruptably. It had been reduced to a burned-out shell. Still smoldering. She ran to Ishmael and hugged him for solace.

"Looks like we got out just in time. Surely we would have been killed."

Both children were crying. Lamenting, "Our house!"

"We won't need it anymore. We were never going back."

And then it hit him like a freight train. *Uncle Brahmin! Is he alive?* If so, he knew he had a responsibility, a duty to rescue him. He must get Uncle out of the country! He would bring him to stay with them. He was the last relative of their family. *My God Allah.*

Who could he turn to? Colonel Reeder or his NSA contact, Steve Wilson. If they wanted information on the nuke program, he was now ready to trade it for Uncle Brahman's rescue. Yeah, that's what he would do.

"We have to get Uncle Brahmin out!" He exclaimed to Ruth."

"Do you have a number for the house?"

"Yes, I do" She checked her phone.

"OK, you call him and I will get Wilson on the line."

Steve Wilson answered, "Hello Ishmael."

Ishmael cut him short. "Have you seen the 12:00 news?"

"Not yet," said Steve.

"The insurgency in Iraq has spilled over into Iran. My old house is destroyed. Bombed out! But look, I am not going back there. OK, how about quid pro quo." Said Ishmael

"Excuse me?" said Steve

"I will tell you all I know about the Nuke program in Iran, without reservation, but you have to help me get my uncle Brahmin out of the country and back here with us."

Ruth was nodding affirmatively, indicating that she had reached Uncle Brahmin. "Excuse me, for a moment, he said to Steve and grabbed the phone Ruth was holding.

"Uncle, this is Ishmael. Are you all right?"

:Yes, my son, but they are getting closer."

"I must get you out of there. You can come with us."

"How will you do this?" Uncle said

"Hold on, a minute," said Ishmael

He went back to Steve, who had heard the whole conversation.

"Do we have a deal?" he said

"I am sure I can clear it. We have a small facility just outside of Tehran. We park an Osprey V-22 there. Can Uncle get there? I have directions. Or should we go get him? I can sent a team and pick him up."

"Good. Ruth will give you the address. How long Steve? Time is of the essence?"

"Two hours."

"Great," said Ishmael

"I'll let you know when he is safe with us."

He gave the phone to Ruth for the address.

He took Ruth's phone, still connected to Uncle and said, "Can you be ready within two hours, Uncle?"

"I don't need much. Yes, I can."

"Ok, these will be N.S.A. operatives. They will take good care of you. They will keep me informed. We will see you in sunny Disney World!"

"OK, my son, Thank you, my nephew. May Allah be praised."

"Ok, Ishmael, let me get on this. I will keep you informed." Steve hung up.

Ishmael paused in silence for a moment. The children had stopped crying. He said "So far, so good. Good thing you turned that TV on, Honey," he said to Naomi. "Every minute counts. We would have been gone for hours."

"Are we going to save Uncle?" The three asked. They had grown close to the old man when they sought refuge in his house. He was very kind.

"I think so. We are sure trying. They are sending a team after him now."

***

Steve Wilson went to the secure communications room in his building. He accessed the satellite phone.

"This is agent Wilson at command. Can I speak with Cell Chief Ryan?"

"This is Jim Ryan."

Steve identified himself.

"Steve, how are you? What can I do for you, sir?"

"I need an immediate extraction."

"It's crazy around here. Where?"

"Just outside Tehran." Do you still have the Osprey?" And do you have a chopper?"

An old Viet Nam era, Huey Gunship. We keep it operational and armed though.

"Ok, the man's name is Hamoud Brahmin. He is an old man but related to the Pahlavi family. I have an address you can turn into GPS coordinates. This is important, Jim. Here is the phone number. Coordinate with him. He will be ready to go.

"From your base, take the Osprey up over the Caspian Sea and then west to our military base in Azerbaijan. We will recover him from there. How soon can you move on this?"

"Give me 10 minutes, Steve." They had served together in Iraq.

"Good, call me when you have Mr. Brahmin."

"Will do, sir." He secured the GPS coordinates and assembled a crew. There were two gunners for the side guns, and the pilot controlled nose guns on the Huey.

"We are going to extract a V.I.P. Top priority. We will use the Huey and then the Osprey. Let's get him back here first."

He made a call to the phone number. "Mr. Brahmin?"

"Yes, this is Hamoud Brahmin," he said.

"This is Agent Ryan, N.S.A. sir. We have orders to pick you up and get you out of the country. When will you be ready?"

"I am ready now, sir."

"Good. We have a Huey Hilo. Can we land close by?"

"I live on a farm, sir. My front yard is at least four acres."

"Excellent, Mr. Brahmin. Look for us in about thirty minutes."

"Ok but hurry. There is activity around here. Be careful!"

"We will be ready for that," said agent Ryan. "Hang in there, we are on our way."

The Huey was already pulled out to a staging area on its dolly. The crew boarded and took their positions.

"Make sure the Osprey is fueled and prepped. We will be leaving immediately when we get back." He said to the ground crew.

"Yes sir," was the reply.

"Ok, let's go."

They lifted off and turned toward the coordinates. The Huey was a little slow but fast enough. They took some fire while crossing a country road from insurgents below. The chopper gunners gladly raked the little convoy with the side-mounted 50' Cal's. "Looks like we are just in time," said Ryan. "This can't be far away from the farm."

"Roger that sir. Looks like about eight miles from the farmhouse." Returned the pilot.

"Ok. Set down and get out quick. Number three team, your go inside and get the old man."

When they approached, Brahmin was already outside, waving. They hovered very low to the ground. Brahmin ran up with one bag in hand and they literally pulled him inside. They performed a rapid ascent away from the road. When they attained some altitude they could see the insurgent convoy heading straight for the farmhouse.

Brahmin saw this and breathed a noticeable sigh of relief. He put his thumb up to the man in charge. *Ryan.* He could see his name tag. "Many thanks, sir," he said.

"They were heading right towards you. They already shot at us." He pointed to a hole in the fuselage.

***

Twenty seven minutes later, they were setting down at their base. The Osprey was warming up. The engines were in the vertical position. Ryan had called ahead.

The whole team piled into the Osprey. The V22 held 22 asses. He gave the pilot a thumbs up when the access door was locked. The engines were winding up to a fierce level.

They lifted off and slowly moved to a level flight configuration.

They headed toward the Caspian Sea and then Azerbaijan.

Ryan called Steve Wilson on his secure satellite phone.

He said "Steve. Ryan here. We got him! And just in the nick of time. Actually took fire from an insurgent convoy headed directly for his farm."

"Oh great, Good work, Ryan. I owe ya!"

"I'll let you know when we get to our base in Azerbaijan. We are probably two hours out. This bird isn't all that fast."

"I will set up a transfer there." said Steve. Then he called Ishmael and repeated what Ryan had told him.

"Oh, wonderful, Steve. I am so relieved Thank you for the quick, decisive action. I will look forward to talking to you."

"I don't know the exact path or time schedule yet but we will get him to Orlando. You can ride in the hotel limo van to meet him. We will arrange all that. We will probably have to fly him in on a military transport of some kind. I will keep you posted. We will take good care of him. I am sure it will be tomorrow at the earliest."

"Ok, Steve. I will wait to hear from you. And thanks again."

His Middle Eastern poise was being tested. He turned to Ruth and said, "All is well. They have him. Just as he about to be killed."

Ruth opened her mouth wide and covered it with her hand. She gasped. "Oh my God." She had to sit on a nearby bench outside the hotel door in case she would faint.

Up came the monorail to the transportation stop for the Disney attration.

"Are you all right," Ishmael said. We can wait for another if you like."

"Oh no, I will go now." Said Ruth.

Chapter Nineteen

Disney World

The Magic Kingdom monorail was huge. They all walked down the ramps and into the main Street staging area. There were beautiful buildings all around them. There were the horse-drawn trolleys and carriages. The buildings were large inside and offered many souvenirs. Ishmael saw a Kiosk marked 'Tours'. "This place is so overwhelming. We ought to take a tour first to see what is available. The girl said it would include a hands on tour of all the parks."

Ismael turned to the others and said, "We are going to take a tour to get oriented to what is available and where. A sampler so we know what and where for our week or so here."

"Ruth said, "I think that is an excellent idea."

"Yeah," said Ishmael. "It includes everything! We have to get organized. This place is so big." He signed up for the excursion. They would be leaving in ten minutes.

The guide walked them out into the large square and began her presentation. She pointed out the immediately surrounding buildings and described their purpose. Then she moved on to Main Street. They all began to walk with her. Main Street was replete with fudge shops, candy shops, Ice cream and every confection you could imagine. They proceeded up to a center garden circle. Several streets connected there. She pulled out her tour map and presented Ishmael and Ruth with flyers describing the parks and their locations. She also had an overall map for them and one each for each of the children. Then she began, "Now to my left are rides and amusements, also a concert hall.

"Wow, look at those airplanes," said Amyl.

The guide continued. "Eventually you will come to Space Mountain. See, the large white volcano like building in the distance?"

"Can we go to the big castle?" Naomi asked. It was right in front of them. She pointed to it.

"Yes, in just a minute," said the guide.

"To my left is Frontier Land. There is a Mississippi River paddle boat you can take a tour on. Above that is the Famous Haunted House, a special ride. Also, Country Bears. All these streets interconnect, so you can't get lost." She started moving around the circle towards the Castle. Everything was landscaped beautifully. There were abundant and colorful flowers, lining the streets. There was a bridge leading to the Castle. It was a huge castle. Maybe 200 feet tall! The kids were awestruck by its immensity.

"Can we go inside?" said Naomi

"Just briefly. We will come back another time." Said Ruth.

The first floor was, in reality, a giant gift shop. There was an overhead Tram from which to view the Magic Kingdom from on high.

"Now, around this way you will find several ride exhibits. 'Pirates of the Caribbean' and 'Small World.' There are a host of smaller rides for small children in the area. Many shops and places to eat."

"Let's get on the train over here," the guide said. "We will see some animals from Africa!" She told the children.

"Ok!" They said excitedly.

They boarded the train at the depot and chugged away. It was a large, circumferential route around a great deal of the park. It came to an open, grassy area with giraffes, lions and other beasts found in Africa. The train went on through the wooded area and then around to the Main Street Station where they had entered.

"End of the line," the guide said. "Back to where we started. Do you have any questions, Sir?"

"Yes," said Ishmael. "Where are the waterparks?"

"Oh, I am sorry, they are here on your overall map. And here are individual flyers on them. The Monorail will take you. It'll be marked "Water Parks.""

"Well, that's easy enough. Thank you for your orientation tour. We have a much better idea of what here now."

"Stop back anytime if you have any additional questions or issues. We are here to help." She said.

"We will be here at least a week, perhaps I will." Ishmael said.

***

"Ok, let's go back up Main Street to those rides and the Castle, shall we? Does anybody want an ice cream cone?"

"Yeah, Yeah! They said in unison. There was an Ice cream emporium up the street on the right. Then back out on the street and they all moved forward to the large circle beneath the Castle.

"Oh, wait a minute," said Ruth. "Here to the left is the Haunted House, Country Bears and the Mississippi River boat." She was looking at her orientation map. "We know what's inside the Castle and we will go but let's not pass up these exhibitions."

"Good idea," said Ishmael and they turned in that direction. They came to the Country Bears first. *What an example of robotics!* thought Ishmael when it was over. The kids had loved it.

Next was the Haunted Jouse. There was a significant line for this one. Once inside, they found out why. Ghosts, faces in glass balls, ghosts wafting all through the room cadavers in coffins and there was a ride to boot. There were some 'pop-outs' that surprised the kids. Shouts of fear were heard!

Once out, they saw The Hall of Presidents. *A good opportunity for a history lesson,* thought Ruth. After a superb presentation, they headed over to the riverfront for a ride on the Mississippi paddle boat. Oh, it was so colorful! They went down to the dock and boarded the twin-stack Mississippi Queen. Every sight was a new adventure. There were several decks. Inside rooms authentic to the time period. Poker tables and a casino. Music by fiddlers. Soon, they cast away from the dock. The steam horn was blasting. They went around the bend, the big paddle propelling them along.

Amyl wanted to see the paddle close up. They went to the stern. The boat used steam like a locomotive made inside by a fire oven.

"See, this is like a train wheel but it's turning the paddle. Often there were fires on board these boats. Not this one, it's made different." He said when he saw a furrowed brow of concern on Amyl's face.

There were adventure scenes on the shore around every turn. Frontiersmen and Indians. Campsites and Grizzly bears. There were foxes and even tiny squirrels. All of the characters and animals were automated. "They call them animatronics." Said Ishmael. "It's amazing what they can do and how real looking they are. They use a form of these in some medical procedures, these days, they are so precise."

"Wow!" said Amyl.

"There is a Japanese Robot on the market, made by Honda. His name is *ASIMO.*"

"Yeah, I've seen him on TV," said Amyl.

When they docked, they debarked and went from Frontier Land around to where there were mistral shows on front porches and live dancing shows. An example of the American west. This was very engaging to all of them.

There was a large fast food restaurant on the right.

"How about some lunch?" said Ruth. "Are you all hungry yet?"

Here is an opportunity to sit and rest for a while, thought Ruth.

The kids were discussing what they liked best from what they had seen so far. They were very excited.

"Hey Dad, can we go up past the castle where those other rides were?" Naomi was the spokesperson.

"Yeah sure," said Ishmael. "When you are finished with your lunch. We have plenty of time to see everything you like. You two need not be anxious."

A Mickey/Minnie parade was passing just outside. They were in an open air restaurant and they could see it, close up. It was full of Disney characters from various movies. The kids were delighted.

"Oh look! It's so and so." And they would point out a character from a Disney movie they had seen.

"Finish your burgers and we will follow the parade around to where you wanted to go earlier." Said Ishmael as he traced the connecting route. That moved them along fast. They were up in no time.

"Wrappers in the trash can over there. "Said Ruth They cleaned the table off, ran to the trash can and fell in behind the parade with their parents.

The parade cycled around the promenaded to the Castle campus and was heading down Main Street where they had come from. Ishmael pulled the kids aside and pointed to Pirates of the Caribbean. A popular exhibition and they all went in. It looked like the waiting columns would hold a thousand people. It just never ended. Thank goodness the park was not too full at this time of the day. Soon, they could see the actual ride itself. It was water born.

Ishmael couldn't help but to reflect on the logistics of managing all the visitors in an orderly manner. It was impressive, he thought. It probably took 10 minutes of walking in line to get to a boat to mount, to enter the actual entrance of the exhibition. They all climbed into the ride boat and off they went. The boat moved along steadily, slowly and then unexpectedly, without warning, it dove down a ramp about forty feet into a pool where all the pirate scenes and characters were engaged in various activities of pirate lore.

It was cavernous! Everywhere you looked there was another scene. The detail was phenomenal! The children were transfixed. Their senses were overwhelmed.

When the ride had ended, all the parents heard was, "That was really cool!"

They moved on to 'It's a Small World'. Another water-born ride inside a huge, subterranean cavern. It was musical and very uplifting.

"Let's go on that gondola ride way up there," said Naomi It was probably sixty feet up and traveled over a significant area of the park.

"Ok, let's get a bird's eye view of everything," said Ishmael and they all boarded the gondola seat. Soon, they were high in the air, viewing the park from on high. They could see more rides outside below. "Look at all of those rides!" Exclaimed Amyl, wanting to ride every one.

When they got off the "Sky Lift", they spent time on the large campus stretching from the Castle and rode all those smaller rides. Most were for smaller, younger, children.

Ishmael and Ruth were beginning to feel the effects of all the walking and rides. They were getting tired.

"Now kids, there is a laser show and fireworks after dark. If you want to see them we will have to go back to the room and rest and have dinner before we go. See that giant ball?" He pointed. "That is Epcot center. That is where we will be going to watch. Epcot is a little more educational than The Magic Kingdom. So let's make our way back to the monorail and ride to our hotel."

"Ok, Dad." They responded. "Did you bring the camera?"

"Yeah, right here," he pulled it out.

"Can we get a picture of all of us in front of the Castle?"

"Sure. I am sure we can get someone to snap one for us."

When they were poised and ready, a gentleman walked up to them and said "I'll be glad to help you with a picture, sir." Ishmael noticed that he had one of those NSA lapel pins on his collar. He said "Oh yes, thank you sir. And they got several shots in.

They went into the castle briefly and bought a few souvenirs and then proceeded down Main Street to the Monorail depot.

Wow, this was a lot of walking, thought Ishmael. He was looking forward to a nap. Soon, they were speeding towards the Grand Floridian Hotel. There was a message at the desk for him.

"Uncle arrives in the morning. 9:30 AM at Orlando International. Go to military desk for Flight No. 201, a military transport. They will give you a gate number. Take the limo from the hotel to the airport and back. All been arranged. We got him a room at the Floridian close to yours." It was signed, *Steve Wilson.*

Ishmael turned to the others and with genuine excitement, declared, "Uncle will be here tomorrow! We are picking him up from the airport tomorrow morning."

The kids jumped up and down with glee. They loved their Uncle Brahmin.

***

After a rest and darkness was approaching, the family ventured to Epcot Center to enjoy the laser light show and the fireworks. For them, it was spectacular beyond words. Especially the Laser Light show. They had never seen such a thing in Iran.

On the way back they stopped into the 360 degree cinema and were stimulated into an extra ordinary perspective of a theater moving all around them.

"One could lose their balance," said Ruth.

Ishmael said, "Now here at Epcot, many countries are represented. Their customs. Their foods and their dress."

"Ok, it's dark and getting late. Back to the hotel. Water Park tomorrow!

They had become quite used to the monorail as the overall form of Park transportation by now. Of course, everything looked different at night. A new adventure. The Castle was completely shrouded in lights. Main Street was spectacular! When they got to the Grand Floridian there was yet another eye treat. Multi colored lights were all around the landscaping and swimming pool. Just fabulous!

"OK, we have to get up early to go get Uncle tomorrow morning. The limo leaves at seven o'clock for Orlando." Said Ishmael. :Let's get to bed." He left a wakeup call request.

***

The morning was busy and bustling. Breakfast downstairs and out the door. Everyone was excited about seeing, Uncle. He would be a part of their family now, wherever they ended up.

"Will Uncle live with us, Dad?" asked Amyl.

"You betcha," said Ishmael.

True to his word, Steve Wilson had provided the limo. It was waiting for them outside. They all climbed in with expectant anticipation. Off they went to Orlando, International. They arrived in about 45 minutes. They walked in and asked at the information desk where the military desk could be found. It wasn't far away.

To their complete surprise, who was walking down the Airside but Uncle Brahmin and Steve Wilson. Uncle had a large smile pasted on his face. The children yelled, "Uncle!"

Uncle was kind of advanced in years and was gratified to see these rascals. He knew he had been snatched
from certain death, just minutes away and now, here was
the last of his family. He was sure brother Reza was smiling down on him. There were tears in his eyes.

Ruth ran up and gave him a huge hug. They had
spent those tense days together, waiting for Ishmael, back
in Tehran, not long ago.

Ishmael also embraced him enthusiastically. "What a
relief to see you in the flesh!" Ishmael said. "We will
have many more years together, now!"

"Yeah, yeah," said Uncle as he squeezed Ishmael and
hugged the children.

"Uncle, wait till you see Disney World!" they exclaimed. "It's really cool!"

Ishmael turned to Steve Wilson and said, "I can't
thank you enough, Steve. You have accomplished a great
thing here," as he pumped his hand.

"Are you hungry? Do you need the restroom? It is a
little drive back to the Hotel." Qualified Ishmael, to all
parties, but mostly to Uncle. He knew it had been a long
journey.

These necessities consummated, they went out to the
waiting limo. They got comfortable for the long trip. The
kid's vied for seating abreast of Uncle. They started tell-
ing him about the wonders of Disney World. "Wait till
you see, Uncle," was heard often.

Uncle was advanced in years. He had been through
the revolution and survived it. He had been used to royal
treatment all of his life. His cousin was, after all, the
Shah. He spent a career in the administration. He was
weary of conflict. He was about enjoying whatever life he
had left. Being grey of beard and white of hair he was a

very distinguished-looking character. Of course, all of the Pahlavi decedents and related family were good looking.

He was looking forward to being around Ishmael, Ruth and the children he counted it as a blessing. And, so far, the U.S. was a great adventure.

They were approaching the long road into Disney World. The children were pointing out every character shaped shrub, identifying it, and moving to the next one. A barrage of input for old Uncle, who could only nod and say, "Beautiful."

Before long, they were at the monorail station. Uncle said in his broken English, "Wow, what a sight! I feel like I am in a science fiction book."

The children each grabbed his one of his hands and led him aboard. Ishmael and Ruth sat directly behind them. Off they went, the long way around where the best overall view was available. They went around the center lake. They didn't stop at the Magic Kingdom, but Uncle could see the Castle at the end of Main Street. "Ooh!" said uncle as he pointed to it. They went on through to the Contemporary Hotel. It was an impressive sight from the monorail. Uncle was bug-eyed and could only say as they entered the third floor portal, "This is science fiction." There was the immense lobby, far below them. "Do we stay here?" He said.

"No," said Ishmael. "We are in the Grand Floridian. We will be there soon.

They continued around, past the Polynesian Resort. A good view of the center lake and all the boats were in view. The train was also moving in the immense and panoramic view. "It really is a Magic Kingdom," Uncle said.

"Next stop, the Grand Floridian, came the announcement inside the monorail. A few minutes later, they arrived at the hotel entrance and they exited the monorail. Ishmael grabbed Uncle's bag. He said, "You are traveling lightly. There is a shopping mall inside."

"Oh." Said Uncle with a raised eyebrow.

"Yes, we will go shopping for a bathing suit and new shorts and casual wear as soon as we get settled. We promised the kids a water park today. It's hot outside. Better off in shorts and a light shirt."

Uncle responded, "Yes, Yes."

"Let's find your room," and they went to the front desk. There was that mysterious NSA lady again. She came forth and said, "Mr. Brahmin's room?" She handed over a key, saying, "Just two doors down from yours, on the third floor."

"Oh, good." Said Ishmael.

"Do you need a porter?"

"Oh no, I've got this." He held up the single bag.

"Have a great stay," she said.

"Would you like some lunch? Ishmael asked every-one. "There is a restaurant on this floor, right over here."

They hadn't really eaten at the airport and were hun-gry. Ishmael led the way. They settled into a large booth.

"Eat hardy everybody. We have a long afternoon coming up." Said Ruth.

Up came the waitress. It was a big order. Philadelphia steak & cheese, fries and sodas. When they were finished, Ishmael said, "Let's walk across the lobby and get on the elevator over there to the mall. We will get Uncle some fresh things and then walk around to our rooms."

***

A few minutes later…….. "Ok, finish up everybody, our day is half gone."

"Ok, Dad, we are ready," said the kids. They all got up and headed for the elevator on the other side of the lobby.

Ishmael came alongside Uncle and asked him, "How do you do with walking, Uncle, there is a lot of walking here at Disney?"

"Oh, I am good, Ishmael. My legs are strong."

"Are your shoes comfortable for walking?" He looked down at a semi- worn old leather shoe. "We need to get you a pair of Nike's for walking. They are light and have good support. You will love them and at the end of the day your feet will feel much better."

They arrived at the door to the mini-mall upstairs. A sales person walked up to Ishmael. He and Ruth were recognized from their visit yesterday.

"Hello, what can we do for you today?"

"We need to get our uncle outfitted, today. We need sport clothes. Shorts, light airy shirts and a pair of walking shoes. Perhaps some undershorts and sox. Oh, and a nice cap for his head. We will have your best brands, for comfort," said Ishmael.

"Ok, let's get started," said the representative.

The rep led them over to the men's sport section. They picked out some red, yellow and green shorts. There was a stretchable waist band. She showed them shirts to go with each pair of shorts. *Very colorful coordinations.* Ishmael looked at the waist size and gathered five underwear packs. Nice, white sox would do.

"How about some 'wife beaters'?" Ishmael looked up to see that she was reaching for some tank-top undershirts, and smiled. This gal was very efficient and knew her way around the store very well. Uncle was loving all the choices.

"Now let's go over here to the shoe section. Here is a light weight casual walker by Nike and another by Sperry. We should try them on and walk over here on the carpet." First they put on the Nike's.

Uncle walked and said "These feel good. Very light"

"Guests here love them," said the sales person. They moved toward the checkout. "Is there anything else?" said the girl.

At that point, Uncle said to Ishmael,

"You know, I am not broke. There is money in my bank and I have a credit card. You have done enough already and I am thankful."

"Now, Uncle, let me get this. You helped shelter my family at a crucial time and I am thankful." And so, the girl took Ishmael's Hotel charge card.

Another $400.00 today! She was thrilled. "I can have these delivered to your room in just a few minutes," she said.

Ishmael said "Ok." There were lots of bags. "We will be leaving soon for the theme park, so right away, ok?"

"Yes sir, right behind you."

He gave her the room number.

They started around the periphery balcony to the other side where their rooms were, stopping only at the fudge shop along the way. They couldn't resist. They all got several pieces. Uncle wanted to treat them so Ishmael let him, for his pride.

They came around to Uncle's room. "See, we are just two doors down," said Amyl

They opened the door to reveal a beautiful, luxurious accommodation for Uncle. "Oh, this is beautiful!" He exclaimed.

There was a little sink and a wet bar. A huge bathroom. A king-size bed. "Very nice," Uncle repeated.

Soon came the new purchases. "Now you're ready", said Ishmael

"I will take a quick shower and be ready in a few minutes," exclaimed Uncle as he was picking out a colorful outfit.

"Ok," said Ishmael. We will go to our room and see you in about fifteen minutes. Take your time, and don't forget your bathing suit." And they all four moved out and down the hallway toward their room.

The kids donned their new bathing suits along with new outfits to cover them up, for the trip to the water park.

In fifteen minutes they all met and went down to the monorail. It was a long ride to the water park but worth it, as the children soon found out.

There was a wave machine, and a river ride, spray nozzles and a huge water slide! Several tubes, tunnels, water rides and a four-story structure with water sprays everywhere! There were rock cliffs to dive from into a large swimming pool. Wow, what an adventure on a hot day. There wasn't the like of this in all of Iran.

They lay out in the sun and became dry. After three hours, it was time to say goodbye. Poor Uncle was thoroughly beat and fell asleep on the chaise lounge. Ishmael went to the hot dog cart, nearby, and got five large dogs to satisfy.

It was time to mount the monorail and go back to the hotel. They needed a rest before the laser/fireworks show they wanted to show Uncle. "Wait till you see!" they shouted. "And the 360 degree theater!"

"Ok. I can't wait!" He said to further excite them.

They began the long trek back to the monorail. Everyone felt quite spent. The panoramic panoply was again laid out before them as the monorail took the circumferential route to the Grand Floridian.

Uncle said, "Wow, we should just live here!"

The kids said "yeah, yeah!"

Ishmael said, "That might be a little expensive. But if we live nearby in Florida, we can get season passes. But, ya know what? If you could come here all the time you would get tired of it."

They arrived at the hotel. They went inside and all were ready for a nap and shower before dinner and Epcot Center where they would see the laser show and fireworks later.

Ishmael took a moment to relax with a scotch from the room bar. *You know, I should check in with the guy's.* He made a call to Bobby and hooked in to a three-way call with Colonel Reeder, all still back at the Chalet in Switzerland.

"Hello, Bobby. Ishmael here. Can you bring Colonel Reeder into the call as a three-way?"

"Sure," he said. "Hold on a second."

"Colonel Reeder, hello"

"Gentlemen, this is Ishmael. I am still at Disney World. I wanted you to know, if you don't already, that Uncle Brahmin is here with me, thanks to the extraordinary efforts of Steve Wilson with the N.S.A. They extracted him moments before he would been killed or apprehended. They actually took fire from this ISIS group over there five miles from his farm. They were on their way. Mr. Wilson acted swiftly and decisively to get him out with a chopper and an Osprey V22 into Azerbaijan. We are having a great time here. My house was destroyed. I happened to see it on the news. I don't know what happened to his farm. I agreed to trade information for his recovery, and I will do so in Washington D.C. when we leave here. We will be at the Willard Hotel, expense paid. I just wanted you all to know how helpful the N.S.A. has been. They have us under protection. There were some minor incidents at the airport in Geneva and the hotel here at Disney."

Bobby and the Colonel both said "Good" and "Wonderful."

"I have worked with Steve before," said Reeder. "Good guy, for sure!"

Ishmael went on, "I will call Dr. Bern for an update on my bonds in a few days. We are having a truly great time. Uncle and the kids are beside themselves. What an adventure. We will be going to Washington from here. We are getting ready for the laser light show and the fireworks at EPCOT tonight. I'll keep you posted. Let me know when you arrive back in the U.S."

"Ok, we will. Has everything been smooth for all of you?" said Bobby.

"Oh, yeah, doing fine. Incidentally, how is our good friend Agent Dufay? Is he still there with you?"

"Oh yes. Dr. Bern is helping him get relocated."

"Oh good. Better go now. See ya when you get here," and he hung up.

He went for the shower and to bed for a brief nap. *This Disney activity can wear you out!*

***

Ruth came in to their room and gently shook Ishmael. "Time to wake up, honey. We must go to dinner and then make it to EPCOT before the show starts."

Some bones and joints still ached from all the activity in the water park. And the sun exposure had a way of wasting a person. "Yes, yes," said Ishmael." Give me a minute," as he sat up on the side of the bed. He put on a fresh shirt and said "Ok, I am ready!" he announced. He walked out into the main room and everyone was waiting, ready to go.

"Sorry, people. Guess I needed some rest. Getting old, I guess. Shall we go down to dinner?"

The kids were up and led the way to open the door.

Chapter Twenty

Uncle at Disney World

They all went down to the lobby restaurant. Each ordered to their taste. Lobster, steak, grouper and fried chicken. Each with trimmings. NSA Agent Millicent, walked by and smiled just to make her presence known. Ishmael gave a small wave of recognition and said, "You didn't tell me my bones would ache!"

She laughed and said, "The cost of having a good time, sir"!

Ismael chuckled in return.

Each was satisfied with their meal and stuffed. *Biscuits and banana bread were the culprits,* judged Ruth.

Ishmael paid the check and they adjourned to the monorail station, just outside the Hotel door.

"Well, it's off to EPCOT," announced Ishmael. And they boarded the first car when it came in. Before long they could see the giant silver ball in the distance. All of Disney World looked so magnificent with its night lighting. Main Street shown out like an oasis in the distance.

When they arrived and disembarked, they went directly to the 360° theater. The children were excited to have Uncle experience the show. It did, at times, overwhelm the senses. The world moved around the audience. Viewers weren't sure if they were standing, moving or floating, in place. Everybody held fast to the railings provided. In reality they didn't move an inch from the spot where they stood. Uncle was quiet and when the lights came on, could only say "WOW! That was specular! What a physical experience!"

There was also a 'Tunnel Theater' ride where the entire tube was a screen. It defied all the senses. At times, they thought they were moving much faster but they were actually moving very slowly on the ride.

When they left the EPCOT silver ball, Ishmael pointed out to Uncle that EPCOT represented many countries; their foods, dress and cultures. Well lighted at night, it was something to see.

Next came the loud speaker and music just before the first laser light beam. Then there was a fusillade of coordinated laser lights. All colors and different intensities, were everywhere. The viewer's own identity was diminished to nothing in the face of such an overwhelming, giant display. Oh yes, the theme was beautiful and the full orchestra of musical delight was stimulating, so much so that it made the viewer feel like an ant. When it was over the viewers were able to regain composure that allowed minimal function. It must have taken ten minutes to be aware once again.

Mickey's parade had Main Street lit up in the distance. Ishmael thought better of it and said, "Tomorrow we will take Uncle back over the rides we went on in the Magic Kingdom, yesterday. Pirates, Presidents, Small World, Haunted House and the Mississippi River Boat. So we will need a good night's sleep. Let's go back to our rooms."

"Ah, Dad," was heard.

He quickly added, "An ice cream sundae before bed!"

It worked.

Back at the Grand Floridian, they stopped at the lobby restaurant for their promised deserts. Then it was upstairs to the rooms. Everyone was really tried. They just didn't know how tired yet.

***

Ishmael was beginning to feel the pressure of his obligation to Steve Wilson, soon to be upon him and he wanted to do right by the agent.

He recalled a study they had done in Iran based on two Congressional reports about the risks and outcomes of an EMP (Electro, Magnetic, Pulse) and pulled out his laptop to review them before bed. He wanted to organize his thoughts for a presentation.

There they were! He buried himself in these lengthy analyses. Soon, he had drifted off to sleep.

***

Ruth came in. She shut down his laptop, put it aside, took off his shoes and covered him lightly with a sheet. They had a very busy two weeks, from Iran to here. *What a whirlwind!* She knew Ishmael was doing his best to entertain the children and understood his fatigue. Also the upcoming meeting in Washington D.C. She was sure that they would be leaving for there in the next few days and understood his research. He was under pressure to perform.

Ruth walked out into the main room and said "Ok, kids. Big day tomorrow. Let's get to bed now."

***

They all woke up early and hungry. Belgian Waffles and Cheese Blinis' were on everybody's mind. Ismael attributed this to the colorful menu cover downstairs.

"OK", said Ismael, "Ruth, would you call Uncle and make sure he is up, please. We should leave for breakfast in about fifteen minutes. I am going to the shower."

***

Uncle had just gotten out of the shower. He said he would be ready in 15 min. It was good to get an early start at Disney World.

***

Soon, they were all downstairs in the restaurant. Those waffles and cheese blinis sure went down easy and quickly.

"Ok, kids, let's show Uncle those rides!"

Out to the Monorail they went. It was a beautiful sunny Florida morning and the park was not too busy yet. The Magic Kingdom, Main Street and a horse-drawn carriage took them to the base of the Castle. It was on foot from there.

Amyl said he would lead the way. Up to the left was The Haunted House. Country Bears. Pirates and the Hall of Presidents. Amyl knew exactly where to find them. One by one they were all seen for the second time. Of course, this was Uncle's first time. He thoroughly enjoyed each presentation.

"Now, Dad, we have to go down to the River Boat," Amyl said.

"Lead the way, son." Ishmael said, sweeping his arm forward.

Uncle came along side Ishmael. He said, "I am very impressed with everything. Thank you for this memory, it has been spectacular. I only wish Aunt Anna could have experienced it."

"Uncle, in a day or two we will all go on to Washington, D.C. We will tour the city and I have some business there. Then we will focus on settling down. We want you to be with us. Don't hesitate to give me your input as we search for a permanent place. It can be anywhere in the world. The Netherlands are nice. I want us to be out of the line of fire, if you know what I mean.

They were now down to the river's edge and the loading ramp to the Mississippi Queen. The horn was blowing and the smoke stacks belching black smoke. "Come aboard!" The first mate cried.

Then the big wheel at the stern began to slowly turn. Ropes were cast off. The dock got smaller and then disappeared. They were rounding a blind bend and into the woodsman scenes and survival scenarios. Amyl was narrating for Uncle, enthusiastically, and with sweeping gesticulations. Naomi could only add, "Yeah, wait till you see!" Uncle was genuinely impressed and gave the Ooo's and Ah's required. There was Tom and Huck, painting the fence.

Another and simpler era, thought Ishmael. *Now rather than some scud on the fence there could be a Scud in the sky! That would take more than whitewash to cover.*

***

Back to Port. They walked the plank to Terra Firma and went around the bend to Frontier and all the live entertainment. Singers and dancers.

"I wanna work here when I grow up," said Naomi.

"Anything is possible," said Ruth, to assuage the youngster. She had higher expectations for her daughter.

They came to the same restaurant they ate at the first time they made this trip.

"Let's grab a bite before we go on." Ruth said. "Even after those waffles this morning the kids would be hungry again. Maybe they would see the parade another time."

As they sat, Ishmael mused, *This is a special place, indeed. Insulated from the warring peoples and races, ethnic groups and pedantic, ideologues, competing in the outside world. Indeed, this is a Magic place. Then again, it is a fantasy land.*

***

They finished lunch and moved upward of the Castle Court. Uncle was curious about the inside of the Castle. Naomi was only too happy to show him everything.

Next they turned to the sky lift to give Uncle the bird's eye view of the park. He was impressed.

Amyl said, "Hey Dad, we haven' been over there to Space Mountain and those rocket ships yet."

"Well then, we should go now," said Ishmael and they went to mid-court and left to the other area.

Space Mountain was a roller coaster inside and featured in complete darkness, with lighted stations along the way. You couldn't see the dips coming. Wow, Scary! Everybody screamed out loud! One trip was enough!

They exited and went to the rocket ships 40 feet in the air. That looked docile enough, by comparison. Blast off!

***

Everybody was emotionally spent and it was a long walk back down Main Street to the monorail station. "Let's get going, Ice cream cones along the way!"

Here came the Mickey Parade down Main Street. Ismael realized it was a daily event. It delayed them a short time but they took shelter in the ice cream parlor.

The adults had had about enough Disney World by now. It was time for a nap at the hotel and an exit plan to another 'Fantasy Land': Washington, D.C.

***

Ishmael put in a call to Steve Wilson at N.S.A. headquarters.

"Hi Steve, I am ready. Day after tomorrow," he relayed to Steve on the other end of the phone. "I am afraid I will grow the Mouse Ears!"

"Ha!" said Steve, "I know what you mean. Ok, that's Thursday. We will fly you and family into Andrews Air Force Base in Maryland for security reasons. Go back to the military counter at Orlando International like you did for your Uncle. I'll leave instructions for you there. Say Thursday at 12:00 PM?"

"Ok, Steve, we will be there. The family is looking forward to seeing that great city."

"I will meet you at Andrews then. About 2:30 PM."

"Roger that Steve, 2:30 PM"

Now to tell the kids we are leaving the 'House of the Mouse'.

***

On the monorail heading back to the Hotel, Ishmael sat the children one on each side of him, and told them that tomorrow would be their last day at Disney World but that they were going on another adventure together.

They each frowned but were listening. "Where, Daddy?"

"We are going to Washington D.C., the Capitol of the United States. We will see the White House and the Capitol Building. We will see all the museums, Natural History and the Air /Space Museum exhibit along with many other interesting things. Daddy has some business to complete while we are there. You will love it. You will learn a lot. So tomorrow, we will relax by the hotel pool and reflect on our time here. And I promise you, we will come back here for vacations for years while you are still young. I urge you two to keep an open mind and you will learn many things in Washington."

"Ok Daddy, we will." They both said.

He looked at Ruth for her approval of his mission statement and she gave him a brief nod of approval.

"Let's go to dinner back at the Special Restaurant at the hotel. We haven't been there yet."

There was a special longing in their eyes, reflected in the monorail windows. A trip made maybe for the last time at night, as they made the monorail trip around the park to the hotel. Ishmael noticed.

"Are we going to the fireworks tonight, Dad?"

"I don't think so, kids. Dad has a lot of work to do to prepare for the Washington trip."

Once they arrived at the hotel, they proceeded to the main dining room, the 'King Fisher Dining Room'. It was appointed beautifully. An Ice carving in the middle of the room – a breaching Marlin Fish with blue accents. Well done, indeed.

***

They were seated and each ordered appetizers. "We will have the Chateau Briand for five," Ishmael said to the waiter dressed in his semi-tux.

"Yes sir, a good choice. And would you care for a red wine to go with that?" he said. "I am Peter," he introduced himself.

"Yes, you choose, sir."

"Yes sir, of course." And he spun around and left the table.

There was a violinist playing over in the corner. A calm, peaceful, piece, suited for a pleasant dining experience. Conversation tones were low. Clearly, this was the flagship hotel restaurant.

"Are we going to meet the President of the United States, Daddy?"

"Oh, I doubt that, Naomi," said Ishmael. "He may not even be in town. But we will see the inside of the White House, I am told."

"Also, this is a pretty time of the year," added Ruth. "I think the famous cherry blossoms are in bloom at the end of the national mall. They were a gift from the Japanese people."

The appetizers and the wine came.

"Can we have some wine daddy?" Amyl wanted to know. Ishmael looked over at Ruth who was hold her fingers slightly apart indicating just a little taste. "Well, you are too young, legally."

"Well, ok, just a little." He looked at the waiter for acknowledgement. The waiter poured out a small taste in the children's glasses, with a smile. And filled the adult glasses. This is a red wine I think you will like. It usually goes well with your menu choice," he said

"Thank you, Peter," said Ishmael, acknowledging Peter's good will in letting the kids have a taste, illegally. *Of course,* he surmised, *this will enhance his tip.*

Salads came. They were abundant and delicious. Various types of breads were served. The main course was served. A carver came with the Chateau Briand to piece it up and serve it to each person. It was simply delicious. A memorable experience, indeed. Each person relished the magnitude of this meal. They realized it was their farewell to Disney World.

"Peter, could we have some Cherries Jubilee for desert?" Said Ishmael. "Oh, and for the adults, a Baileys, please."

"Oh yes sir, right away. An excellent choice, sir"

***

As they walked back to the room after dinner, Uncle was interacting with the children as Ishmael and Ruth walked in front. Ishmael turned to Ruth and said, "Can you take Uncle and the children down to the pool tomorrow mid-morning so I can prepare my talk to Steve Wilson? I have a lot of material to review. I need quiet to concentrate."

Ruth said, "Certainly, dear. We will leave you undisturbed."

"I may get a head start tonight. I have to proceed from memory because most of the sensitive material is never allowed out of the office. You know, funny thing, most of what I can tell them they already have in two of their own Congressional reports that were compiled a while ago. I have to print them out and work from their own material. Ironic, isn't it? I'll bet the hotel has a computing and printing service room somewhere. Most hotels do these days. I'll ask at the desk. I may do this tonight while nobody is around in such a facility." Thinking out loud, he said "I better check and see if that Millicent or another agent is around to stand guard at the door."

"Yes, better to be safe than sorry," said Ruth."

His plan was taking shape in his mind.

***

When they came to the room he said to the kids, "Ok, see if you can find a movie to watch in your room tonight. After your baths, of course. Daddy will be pretty busy tonight and tomorrow. Your mother will take you to the hotel pool after breakfast in the morning."

They came abreast of the front desk. Ishmael asked for Mrs. Millicent. It was about 9 PM. "I think she went home for the day," answered the desk clerk.

"Is there a replacement for her?" Ishmael expected the clerk to know his meaning.

The clerk looked back at her computer and said, "Oh yes, I'll call the person on duty."

"Thank you," said Ishmael. Now is there a computing facility area in the hotel? I will need a printer also."

"Yes sir. Room 127 on the first floor. Down this hall and to the left. Let me make sure it is unlocked." She called a porter over and gave him the keys.

"I won't need it for about twenty minutes. Need to get the kids to bed first. If you could send Mrs. Millicent's replacement down to that area about that time minutes, I will meet him or her there."

"That will be fine, said the desk clerk, and repeated, "Twenty minutes."

***

Ishmael and the family returned to the room. Ruth took over supervising the children's baths, while Ishmael packed up his computer in to its leather carry case to take downstairs to the computer room. No sooner had he settled in near the computer then a tall, robust man in a Seersucker suit came in.

"Are you Ishmael?"

"Yes sir," said Ishmael. He noticed the N.S.A. identification pin in his lapel.

"My name is Jason Higgins. I was asked to come here for your protection. What can I do for you?"

"Well Jason, Pleased to meet you," They shook hands. "I am working on a report for Mr. Steve Wilson. It contains sensitive information for your national defense. I would just like to have you on hand. I have been threatened before regarding this information."

"Of course Mr. Pahlavi, if you need anything, I will be right here outside this door."

Ismael looked around and saw that there was a printer in the room.

"I will be here for a few hours tonight and also tomorrow from say 10:00 on. I will erase my document but you may want to scrub the hard drive when I am finished."

"Yes sir. I understand perfectly. Again, I will be right outside the door, sir."

"Thank you, Mr. Higgins," said Ishmael and he sat down to the table where he had set his computer. He pulled up the two United States Congressional reports he had given a cursory review and printed them out. Then he took his yellow highlighter and began to highlight the salient points. Of course, he was not privy to top secret information but he suspected that the U.S. had reacted to the potential disaster laid out before him. He was wrong.

Actually, a very prominent Senator, the honorable John Rascain, who had brought this to light, and introduced legislation to address it was ridiculed, and laughed out of the Senate chamber! Little did they realize that this was one of the possible scenarios the Iranians had envisioned.

On he went with his yellow marker. There were details of the delivery system for the missile that they had not decreed in the report. He made a point of noting the congressman's name. He was still in office. Perhaps he should be invited to the meeting with the N.S.A. – Steve Wilson, et al. He made a note to call Steve about that.

He wrote a narrative background on his own first-hand knowledge, such as it was, about the status of the nuclear program and the amount of fissionable material that had been refined into weapons grade plutonium. Of course no body working on the project had accurate knowledge of that amount; just an educated guess. The Regime still claimed energy development as their sole goal for the program but it was a multi-faceted research and development endeavor. The military contingent involved was shrouded in secrecy. He included the Congressional reports as 'Appendix A' to his work.

Appendix: A – Volume 1, Executive Report
Report of the Commission to Assess the Threat to the United States from Electromagnetic Pulse (EMP) Attack

The report was extensive and covered every aspect of potential damage to the U.S. Banking and Finance. Fuel and Energy, Trucking and auto, Maritime Shipping, Commercial Avaition, Food and Infrastructure, Water Supply, even Space Systems and Satellites. Ninety percent of the population would likely die within a prescribed period.

These were catastrophic outcomes. Ishmael was certain they had been addressed. Nevertheless, because they agreed with what he had heard and gleaned in his job as a Physics with the Regime they represented the core of his report.

***

Well, that is enough for tonight. He would take this up again tomorrow. He deleted the files he had worked on from memory. Of course a pro could probably access them. Accordingly, he called Jason Higgins back into the room.

"I deleted these files on the hotel equipment but I wanted you to know they could be vulnerable to a pro. I have removed my hard drive." He handed it to Mr. Higgins. "On the side of caution, please put it in the hotel safe also."

"Yes sir, I talked to Mr. Wilson at headquarters and he told me to put the printer in the hotel safe until you are finished working and then to scrub or replace it. I will do the same with your hard drive. Please call me the front desk tomorrow when you are ready to continue working on the file. If I am not here, I will have left secure instructions at the desk for handling the issue." Mr. Higgins said.

"Oh, very good, sir," said Ishmael, "I will call you after breakfast."

Ishmael went back upstairs to his room. Everyone was asleep. He paused to take in a snifter of Brandy and went to bed.

***

Morning came quickly with the bustle and noise of the children making ready for their last full day at Disney World. Ishmael showered, got dressed and went into the front room of the suite. They were all ready for breakfast. They had a big one.

Ishmael said, "Now I want you children to go to the hotel pool with Mom and Uncle while I work on my project today. Behave and be safe. I will finish up and join you later." He placed a call to Jason Higgins.

"Higgins here," came the reply.

"Oh good, you are still here," said Ishmael. "I will be ready for the printer and my hard drive in half an hour in the computer room."

"Yes sir, I will have it ready for you."

He went upstairs to his room to retrieve his computer.

***

IT WAS GONE! The room was slightly ransacked. He immediately called Higgins. Maybe he could still catch the thief. Perhaps their surveillance could provide some clues. If not he would have to find the same model and insert his old hard drive in it.

A knock at the door. It was Higgins.

"Well, they didn't get anything. You have the hard drive in your safe. But I am still worried about my family's vulnerability. Whoever they are, they are going to be suspicious and pissed when they discover the missing hard drive. Do you have anyone in mind, staying in the Hotel?

"I have two agents looking now." Said Higgins. "Because of those innuendo threats at the airport, I have your family completely covered at this time. They are completely surrounded by agents in the pool and pool area, right now. Of course, they are not aware of it.

"That is very reassuring, thank you, agent Higgins."

My computer was a DELL lap top. It had 8 Megs of RAM and a Terabyte of storage. Of course we still have that in the safe. Intel Core I-5. 1.6 hertz if the hotel wants to replace it."

"I got it, I know the manager. I will speak to him. These could be local perps, working the hotel. We are checking it out now."

***

Ishmael's phone rang thirty minutes later. It was Higgins.

"We've checked the hotel surveillance cameras. They are well hidden in the hallways. Looks like it was a hus-band and wife team working the hotel. I doubt they were after your computer specifically. We tracked them down to another room. They are being interrogated downstairs now. I think we can retrieve your computer. I will call you back in a few minutes."

***

The phone rang again. "We have it! The wife was on the house keeping staff here. I told them you would not prosecute, nor would the hotel, if they returned the com-puter immediately, along with a lot of other stuff taken from other rooms."

"Very good, said Ishmael. I will be pleased to get it back. Can I meet you in the computer room when you have it in your possession?"

"Yes sir." Said Higgins. "About ten minutes."

"See you then," said Ishmael.

***

Ishmael met Higgins and after re-installing his hard drive, resumed working where he had left off.

"Again, I will be right outside the door, sir." Said Agent Higgins, before he left the room.

Ishmael continued with his outline scenario. The speculated outcomes in these Congressional reports were scary, even for him. A survivor would need a farm. Acreage, for planting. A hen house. Free range chickens running everywhere. Farm animals. Wagons. A buck board. Horse stalls. A tack room. The list went on.

Israel was fighting Hamas. I.S.I.S. was in Iraq. Russia in the Crimea. Civil airliners were being shot down with ground to air missiles, albeit, by mistake, The U.S. was being overrun by refuges/illegals from Central and South America, Asia and Mexico. It seemed like the world was on fire. There were too many nukes existent. Some were 'Lost'. Scary!

***

Where was a neutral, safe spot for his family? He would have to be thinking about that. The Netherlands? A reasonable government. Low taxes. High living standard. Close to Dr. Bern and his money. He made a mental note.

He knew steps could be taken to insulate against a completely devastating EMP attack and outcome. That should be the focus. 6he immediate goal of the U.S. defensive/scientific community. He did not know what their (U.S.) status and level of readiness was, but that would be his emphasis.

He knew there were economic sanctions against the Regime which had been imposed by the international community and at the behest of the United States. They were taking a toll. He had always urged restraint asking, "What about retaliation by the U.S. or other nuclear powers, i.e. Israel, The United Kingdom, France and others if they were to follow such a course of action?" He was sure it would amount to suicide for Iran. Better to ally themselves and trade oil for aid to build their infrastructure. Indeed a more reasonable posture for a Nation who would be a responsible member of Nations. Not pursuing ancient religious mandates, ultimately leading to wars and destruction.

There had been much genius in his people, dating as far back as the Persian Empire. Why act like an angry, mad man with tunnel vision, pawing the dirt like an enraged bull who would run, head long into the hidden, death, sword of a superior opponent? Religious ideologues were at the helm of their government. Old men from another era.

Ishmael paused and shook his head at his thoughts. He had been a member of their scientific community. Most of his former colleagues felt as he did. There was the potential to make great contributions and advance their culture. This should be a new age, a renaissance, a peaceful time of real achievement. *Couldn't the 'Old Men' see this?*

Religion had served the purpose of motivating and controlling the appetites of the species, with goals of mutual respect among dispirit tribes. A tribal economy of survival was tamed. Cooperation led to advances. The dross of discarded behaviors remaining must/ needs be skimmed off and discarded. How difficult was a paradigm change in the mind of mankind. Many were just incapable of it.

There should be a 'collective' effect to this 'new learning' of disciplined cooperation, leading to the mutual advancement of civilized peoples, he reflected.

Chapter Twenty

The United States of America

From what he had read in the way of reviews, he thought about calling Steve Wilson to try and enhance the impact and effect of his presentation. In Ishmael's mind, certain people should be present, if possible.

He placed a call to Steve Wilson.

"Hello, Steve. Got a minute?"

"Sure, Ishmael. What's on your mind?"

"First of all, can I send you a secure E mail?"

"Sure," and he gave him the secure, E mail to his office.

"Ok, I'll send you a laundry list, but briefly, as I prepare this presentation, it becomes apparent to me that time is of the essence and I know how slow bureaucracies work, sometimes.

I think it may be important to get a jump on some preventative action. It seems to me that the world is coming apart right now. Some forces may deem this an opportunity to implement strategies ahead of 'possible' schedules and act against the United States in a way that would allow them to simply walk ashore and take over with very little resistance.

"Your leader, at this time is weak and inexperienced. He seems to be strong-willed and has a 'murky' agenda. Who has influence over him?

"I believe there are certain people that should be present at our meeting, hopefully as a jump start to the actions, I recommend. At least I will have tried.

"I know I will find agreement and support from certain of your scientist, military and politicians already. It will serve you well to have a catalytic component, a spearhead, if you will, to overcome the inevitable inertia we may encounter."

"Wow," said Steve. "I think I understand you well, Ishmael, and I will do my best to a accommodate you. Send me your E mail."

"Yes sir, you will have it later today. As planned, I will see you at this Andrews AFB at about 2:00 PM, tomorrow."

***

Ishmael began to prepare the E mail. Essentially, he wanted these parties and materials present at their meeting:

Associative, preliminary reading material.
"A nation Forsaken" – Michael Maloof - Jan 2013
"One Second After" - William R. Forstchen
If possible: I would like to have present:
The Honorable Senator Rascain
Secretary of Defense
Nuclear Regulatory Commission; Atomic Energy Scientist.
Michael Maloof and or; W.R. Forstchen
O.M.B. budget people.
White House – Chief of Staff
This list may be a bit ambitious but each party here would have an essential role to play. I can postpone our meeting until the parties can be assembled, once in Washington.

Ishmael sent the E Mail to Steve Wilson.

A few minutes later, Agent Higgins came in and said, "I have been reassigned."

"Oh, sorry to hear that," said Ishmael.

Higgins held up a finger and said, "I am to accompany you, at your side, from now until we reach Andrews AFB. tomorrow. This is a diplomatic pouch. I will lock it to my wrist when we travel. Please insert your report, when you have finished writing it."

"Yes sir," said Ishmael, somewhat bewildered, but thankful.

Ismael went on with his work, placing extreme emphasis on 'Action'.

Chapter Twenty-one

TRIP TO WASHINGTON, D.C.

Higgins sat across the aisle in the airplane. The attaché was manacled to his wrist. Ismael had worked diligently to complete with a description of one case scenario he had heard in a think tank session he had learned of at work. He surprised himself with the lack of guilt he felt in disclosing this intelligence. He knew he was doing the right thing. No good could come from the execution of these tentative plans, either for Iran or the U.S.

The kids and Ruth had spent a wonderful day at the hotel pool. At dinner and breakfast each had re-counted all of the fun times on the trip to Disney. It was a bitter sweet departure. Ishmael had pantomimed a famous action hero when they left the hotel and boarded the monorail for the last time. In a heavy German accent he declared, "Ve vill be back," much to the children's pleasure. They were all ready for this new chapter in their adventure. They were looking forward to exploring the City of Washington D.C.

The airplane's approach included a bird's eye view of the Capital, the Mall, the Washington monument, The Jefferson and Lincoln Memorials. They came down the Potomac River before turning east to Andrews AFB. The children were glued to the windows of the military transport.

They approached and greased down the runway at Andrews, toward the terminal. This was a different experience for the children. Everyone was in a military uniform. There was no tunnel conveyance to the inside of the airport. Just an outside stairway, pushed up to the plane. At the bottom, waiting was, good to his word, Steve Wilson.

A big smile of greeting and a hardy handshake were exchanged. Ishmael turned to Uncle and said, "This is the man who acted quickly to get you out of Iran."

Uncle shook his hand and said, "Thank you sir. Not a moment to spare. Your immediate action probably saved my life. At the very least, I would have spent the rest of my time in prison. Again, I thank you. So glad to meet you sir."

A van pulled up and they all got in. *This is a nice van,* Ishmael noted. *Leather seats and spacious.* They fit comfortably inside.

"OK, let's head to the Willard and get you settled." Steve said. He leaned over to Ishmael and said, "I have contacted all of the people on your list. Not all have gotten back to me yet, but most were very enthusiastic about participating. The two authors were chomping at the bit."

***

It was completely across town to the Willard Hotel. They got a good look at the streets and monuments.

"I've scheduled a professional tour of the attractions here in our fair city. Only way to really see it. Lunch is planned at Duke Ziebrets where dignitaries hold forth. You will have a great time. The kids will never forget it. Steve commented. "This is the best part of my job."

"Wow, that sounds great," said Ishmael.

They pulled up to the long driveway of the old Willard Hotel. Inside, there were grand crystal chandeliers, flowered carpet, and brass appointments. It reeked of class and antiquity. The concierge was dressed in white tails. Everything was impeccable.

"Oh, how nice," said Ishmael.

Ruth, who had a minor degree in art at Oxford, was focused on the wall paintings surrounding the lobby. *So many famous people had been through here,* she mused. She imagined their comings and goings. *What an awesome experience,* she thought.

Ishmael was calling. It broke her daydream.

"We need to go to our suite, Ruth. Time to check-in."

How surreal, the day's events, so far, Ruth thought. They passed by the Grand dining room on the way and they all realized how hungry they were.

The suite had Queen Anne high-back chairs, a beautiful Tudor desk, brass headboards and a wine and fruit basket waiting. It was eloquent. The windows looked out on to Pennsylvania Avenue.

"The President of the United States lives right up the street," Ruth said to the kids.

"Can we go see him?" they replied.

"It's just a little more complicated than that," she laughed.

Uncle had an adjoining room next door. He looked tired. He said he wanted a nap. "The traveling takes a lot out of me."

"Take a load off. Relax. Get settled. I will be back in about an hour to pick you up. We are all going to Duke Ziebrets for lunch." Steve said.

"I will be right down the hall," said Higgins. "In room. 205, at all times, while you're here."

Ishmael nodded. "Thank you, John."

***

True his word, Steve Wilson was ringing the room phone from the front desk.

"Are you hungry?" he opened. "I got us a table at Duke Ziebrets for lunch. Not easy to do at lunch in this town!" he added.

"Oh hi, Steve. We will be right down," said Ishmael. He turned to Ruth and said, "Steve is waiting downstairs. Can you get Uncle and the children ready to go in a few minutes?"

Ruth went about her chore quickly.

Before long, the whole crew was getting off the ornately decorated elevator. Lots of polished metal and brass. Even though they were Middle Eastern in appearance, they were careful to dress in their Western clothes. They did not want to attract undue attention.

Steve met them in the lobby and greeted them. Walking out the front doors revealed a long, black stretch limousine. The doorman was holding the door open for them. Wow! This was impressive! The kids were enamored of the long lengthwise leather seats. Also the TV monitors hung towards the front. There was a recording of a tour highlights running. Right now it was describing the Capital building in detail.

"Cool," was heard from Amyl. He was glued to the screen.

They turned and headed toward 'L' Street, two blocks west of Connecticut Avenue.

"I hope you won't be offended," said Steve, "but this is the best Jewish food and restaurant in Washington. This is where Power Lunches are held. I wonder who may be here today."

"Some of my best friends!" \Ishmael said. "Ya know those Jewish pilots saved my cousin Buruse, or Bobby, as you know him, from certain death, when they were fleeing Iran. We make it a point Not to teach these ancient prejudices to our children. We don't want it in their 'World View'. It's such an inhibitor to their intellect. I am looking forward to the Hot Pastrami on Rye."

Steve laughed. "Good. I wasn't sure."

"We are all Semitics, descended from Abraham," Ishmael added.

Steve said, :See the difference an Oxford education makes." He elbowed Ishmael in the side, laughing. "Life is so much better without a prejudicial ideology, or even a concept of it, in life. My burden is light."

So true, thought Ishmael. *Shun the Baggage!* He continued to learn the accuracy of these precepts.

Steve Wilson turned to Ishmael and said, "Looks like I will be able to get everybody you requested assembled for our meeting day after tomorrow. Tomorrow, I have arranged a tour of the city. I know you will all enjoy it. Beginning at say 10:00 AM?"

"Sounds good to me," said Ishmael. He glanced at Ruth and said, "Maybe 10:30 would be better. Gott'a get the rascals ready."

"Of course, said Steve, "I understand, 10:30 it is."

They arrived at Duke Ziebrets. A busy place. "I hope everybody is hungry," said Steve Wilson as they followed the doorman's instructions, moving inside. They choose a booth on the right.

When the waitress came over, it was four hot pastra-mi's on rye for the adults and super "Super Sabrett Hot Dog" plates for the children.

They sat back and scanned the room for notables. They thought they recognized a couple of news people they had seen on TV. One gentleman was surely a con-gressman with a staff member, who was taking notes furi-ously as he held forth. *A working lunch,* thought Ishmael.

"So, you've heard from everybody, already," said Ishmael to Steve Wilson.

"Oh yes," Steve replied. "They are quite anxious to hear what you have to say."

"I don't mean to impose, Steve, but I have a request which I think will benefit all of us." Ishmael said.

"Yes, of course." said Steve

"I am in a strange town. I wouldn't know exactly where to go, but I would like to have ten copies of the Congressional Reports of '04 and '06 on the 'Effects of an EMP and CME'. 10 copies of Michael Maloof, former senior analyst for the Department of the Secretary of De-fense's book; 'A Nation Forsaken'; Also, 10 copies of William R. Forstchen's book, 'One Second After', and 10 copies of my report as collateral reading for those pre-sent."

"I believe that can be arranged," said Steve "Excel-lent idea. Something to take home with them. And these people go home a lot," Steve chuckled.

"That is wonderful. I only hope there will be a max-imum impact and action will be taken immediately. As far as we know, unless there is some top secret solution that has been implemented by your government, you are vul-nerable to a devastating attack from areas where no warn-ing system exists for the launch of a missile from a domestic location. I am thinking, the Gulf of Mexico. There are many cargo barges on shipping routes east."

"It is a location on a long list of possible launch sites on our strategic analysis study. As far as we know, there is no defensive coverage in that area." Steve said.

"This could be fixed for an amount of money that your government, literally throws away annually in the form of foreign aid, and that to governments which are hostile towards your own." Said Ishmael. "This oversight is untenable. Your people are un-protected. You would need horse and buggies again." He said in supposed exaggeration.

"Well, let's hope you will be able to bring a critical awareness to this exposure and be a catalyst for corrective action." Steve said.

"Also, we are at the end of an eleven-year, Solar Flair Cycle. You don't know what could be on its way. If you have the technology, it is criminal not to employ it.

"A CME (Coronal Mass Ejection) would have the same effect as an EMP, launched by an aggressor." Ishmael added. "You had one in 1859. It was called The Carrington Event. Railroad tracks became so hot they burned the ties they were mounted to. Telegraph lines were destroyed.

"You would not be able to function, as a world power, without this protection. In a CME, many nations would be affected. Economies would stall and then stop until the electric grid could be restored. If they are protected, they would soar to the top of the economic ladder immediately."

***

Well, here came their lunch order.

"Oh, this looks good!" Said Steve. "Don't you just love those kosher pickles and the hot mustard?"

A man came over to their table who knew Steve. Steve stood up and greeted him, obviously happy at seeing him. "Thank you for coming over, Senator," he said. He turned to Ishmael and said, "Ishmael, this is Senator Rascain. He is the Senator you invited to our meeting. He worked hard on your cause and is responsible for much of those Congressional Reports you cited.

"So glad to meet you, Dr. Pahlavi." The Senator was pumping his hand. "I sincerely hope you can bring some urgency to this cause."

"I will do my best," "Ishmael said. "Peace is the end goal. I am glad to meet you sir. Won't you join us? Ruth this is Senator Rascain. Senator, my wife Ruth."

Ruth stood for the Senator. "Very pleased to meet you, Senator," she said. "These are our children Amyl and Naomi."

They could only grin up at the Senator.

"Hello," Senator Rascain said. "How old are you?"

They each called out their age.

"I have grandchildren just your age. I'd love to sit but I must get back to the Hill. Dr. Pahlavi, I will see you at our meeting. I am looking forward to it, sir. Let's shake 'em up! Good to meet all of you." He looked at Ruth and the children, with a broad smile.

Chapter Twenty-two

The Meeting

"Thank you all for coming. I am gratified that we had the opportunity to get to know each other, casually, before this formal part of our meeting." Ishmael said. "Mr. Wilson was very helpful to me in providing the collateral reading materials in front of you, consisting of; a certain Congressional Report on an EMP attack scenario; two books, one from each one of our distinguished authors, present here. Mr. Maloof and Mr. Forstchen." He held them up for all to see. "I hope you will take the time to read them carefully. I find them to be absolutely on point for this very critical issue.

"I have prepared a power point presentation to illustrate my findings. Please pardon the amateurish nature of my drawings. There was no opportunity to have it professionally illustrated." He nodded at Steve Wilson, a signal to turn down the lights.

"Let me begin by saying that there is nothing hard and fast about my conjectures. Nothing has been set in motion. This is information which I have gleaned from my colleagues, sometimes at lunch, from different departments of our defense apparatus. There are many dispirit departments, which don't always agree on what should be done. More like your "Think Tanks" over here.

"However, I offer these findings in good faith, as indeed you are unprotected against these possible events.

"Also, we are at the end of an eleven-year, Solar Flair Cycle. You don't know what could be on its way here If you have the technology, to protect your grid, it is criminal not to employ it.

Ishmael repeated what he had told Steve Wilson previously. "A CME (Coronal Mass Ejection) would have the same effect as an EMP, launched by an aggressor." Ishmael added. You had one in 1859. It was called The Carrington Event. Rail Road tracks became so hot they burned the ties they were mounted to. Telegraph lines were destroyed. In the CME event, the whole world could be affected. Any nation protected would be able to soar to economic supremacy, while others would be looking for horses and Conestoga wagons for shipping goods. All labor would be manual. All forms of banking would revert to paper transactions. How long it would take to come back into an electronic and then a digital world?

"Now, more to the specific point of my visit. You should all know that I and my entire family have defected to Geneva, Switzerland. We are here on a visa kindly provided by your government. My reason for this action is because I and many of my fellow scientists are just not in agreement with the philosophy and direction of our political leaders. They seem to have disabused themselves of the concept of a retaliation by nuclear-powered allays of the United States—and there are many—who were not affected by their EMP attack. Muslim nuggets, anybody?"

Everyone laughed.

"The following is an attack scenario, I have heard, in passing. Again a caveat: This is not an imminent action. It may never come to fruition. Reasonable minds may and should prevail. However ill conceived, it could still work.

"Here is how it goes:

"A cargo shipping barge is towed out of Shreveport. Louisiana by an ocean-going tug boat. The barge has a motor but it is reserved to power a generator needed to power the launch. It has been well insulated against the effects of the EMP. The barge moves out of the shipping lane and turns northeast to this area." He pointed to the Apalachicola nook. "About fifty miles offshore it stops and drops anchor. Cargo containers are on board. One located in middle is fitted with a hydraulic top. It opens and revels a Scud missile—Scuds are easy to come by—and a launch ramp. The ramp, hydraulically raises to eighty-nine degrees. Four ballast balloons similar to airliner emergency door slides are deployed and inflated, two on each side of the barge as outriggers, out into the surrounding water, for ballast.

"The missile is fired. The warhead is set to explode two hundred miles above the Earth's atmosphere. You will not hear it detonate. It is in a vacuum. Your electric grid crashes. No banking. No transportation. No food and potable water. No sewer filtration. Anything computer operated ceases to operate. Six weeks out, millions have died. Cannibalism is not ruled out as a food source.

"You're back to the 1800's. If you have a farm and livestock, you may have a fighting chance. People dependent on services in the cities are doomed.

"The launcher retracts back down into the container. If need be, by the manual release of the hydraulic valves. Ballast ramps are cut loose, and sunk. If the insulation fails on the barge power, a 90 foot mast and sail is manually hoisted and locked in place. A lifeboat is deployed, big enough for all hands. The barge is scuttled. The preps row and sail ashore. There is a safe house located in Citrus County, Florida. They will be picked up later with working machinery from outside the affected area."

Ishmael nodded again to Steve Wilson who turned the lights back up.

"Please feel free to ask questions and do not neglect our expert authors who are eminently more researched than I am on this subject.

Chapter Twenty-three

Call to Action

"You can remedy this inexcusable Achilles' Heel to your defense readiness and the protection of your citizens against an EMP attack or a CME from that which has happened before and will happen again for a sum that is almost pocket change compared to what you give to other countries who may be hostile to you. About a billion dollars. One quarter of what your current executive leader is asking for to house the uneducated hordes crossing your southern border right now.

"A history lesson would be instructive here. When another great democracy or republic opened their gates and let in the hordes, it precipitated their decline and eventual failure. Rome. Will you burden your economy in this way? You may not survive it."

"And I am now faced with finding a place to settle. A place where my family will be safe and prosper, I am sorry to say it will not be America, not at this time, not for this immigrant.

"There are ominous clouds on your horizon. Don't you see them? What has happened to your great country and the leadership role it has played for most of this century? I did not come here today to scold you. I apologize. But, I believe you need a wake-up call."

"Do we have any questions or comments from or for anybody in the room?"

"Yes sir?" he pointed to Senator Rascain.

"Is it really possible to insulate ourselves against the catastrophic events such as you have described?"

"Well, the electronic failures, yes. It would take some time but you could insulate your grid, beginning with the high-power transmission lines. In my opinion and some others here, that should be the first priority. Most of your major electric companies are interlinked in some way.

"If they want to continue to sell electricity, they should put their considerable support, financial and labor, into it through their state legislatures. This is indeed shovel-ready for jobs."

"Dr. Pahlavi, if I could speak?" Said author Michael Aloof, ('A nation Forsaken')

"Oh, I insist, sir, welcome to the discussion"

OMB people were busy with projections of where to find and how to prioritize the funds necessary for labor and equipment costs to begin, if authorized.

Mr. Aloof moved to the dais and began. "We are grateful to Dr. Pahlavi for his salient and informative presentation. His points are spot on. I could only emphasize and endorse, as could my colleague, William Forstchen, his findings and predictions. I know Senator Rascain has worked hard to introduce legislation to commence this critical effort. The danger is everything Dr. Pahlavi says and more. I would be glad to consult with any of you, individually. My phone and office is open. We must begin immediately to rectify this dangerous omission to our defense system.

The Secretary of Defense was nodding affirmatively.

The Secretary stood and said, "The CIA has a hidden budget. We could begin there and avoid the "Harry" obstruction in our hose."

They all laughed.

"How difficult is it to produce these insulation devices?"

William Forstchen ('One Second After') stood and said, "Our ally Japan could have a few container loads of materials on their way inside a month. We already have enough to get started now. I've done the research."

The Senator stood and said, "I can work with the power companies."

"How about the job issue angle?" someone shouted.

"Let's get a national advertising campaign going on TV to enlist public support," said another from the State Department. "Politicians should respond to that."

Enthusiasm was building to a crescendo. The well-known patriot, Senator Rascain—who never met a microphone he couldn't use—stepped forward. Mr. Maloof moved aside to accommodate him.

The Senator said "My office is open to all of you. I have been working for this outcome for some time and have a great deal of information on navigating this through the labyrinth that is Congress. Yes, get public support mobilized first.

"Here's your campaign slogan, *'If the facts mean anything...'* I have friends at Fox Network. We should advertise there and they will very likely do a news item. A special human interest story for us," the Senator went on.

They adjourned after many, mutual congratulations were exchanged.

***

During the next few weeks, as the campaign spread, every congressional office was deluged with communications from constituents, demanding action, right away. Mothers were motivated to protect their children and no one wants to encounter mad mothers!

Fox news took up the campaign and one of the most prominent advertising agencies was hired and slogans abounded. The old *"Don't tread on Me"* symbol was resurrected and used in the advertising. This widespread call to action had not been seen since the beginning of World War II, when women were enlisted into the industrial work force.

America was Back!

~*~*~

Meet our author
Michael Plunkett

Born in 1946, second in a family of six children, in the then sleepy Southern town of Washington, D.C., where secretaries wore white gloves and hats when going to lunch. This, just before the migration of workers from the south expanded government offices. Michael's father's business would take him as a helper into many government buildings, agencies and international Embassy's where, as a curious adolescent, he would glean all he could from the desks of Ed Murrow, U.S.I.A. Radio Free Europe propaganda, many embassy's and the private homes of George Will, Walter Lipmann, Ray Chalk and others. This early exposure to the workings of government led him to Liberal Arts and the study of Political Science at Montgomery College in Rockville, Maryland and on to a Pre-Law curriculum.

Psychology and religious studies became hobbies with copious reading in both disciplines. Descendent from the Rommal's on his mother's side—Irwin, the Desert

Fox, and Bishop Oliver, now Saint, on his father's side, there were conflicted spirits in his closet.

Ever the adventurous one whether flying planes or riding super motorcycles at excessive speeds, he had to have the hair on fire and ride in the wind to feel at home.

In his books he incorporates his adventures and knowledge of people through thousands of intimate interviews in his business career where he had become a National sales director and executive vice-president of a prominent marketing company with tens of millions of dollars in sales productions each year. This is where he met the Shah's nephew and many other unique characters.